the LOSING ROLE

a novel

Steve Anderson

www.stephenfanderson.com

Also by Steve Anderson

Lost Kin: A Novel (Kaspar Brothers #3)

Liberated: A Novel of Germany, 1945 (Kaspar Brothers #2)

Under False Flags: A Novel

The Other Oregon: A Thriller

Double-Edged Sword (Kindle Single)

Sitting Ducks (Kindle Single)

For René,
of course

One

October 1944

Max lay flat on his back, in the mud. The mud was cold and seeping through his wool corporal's uniform. Why were his arms above his head? Someone must have been dragging him. Was he hit? He moved his legs. They worked, thank God —he'd still dance again one day. Fingers? All there. He could still play the piano. He felt at his stomach and chest, fingering the tin buttons, dry leather straps and coarse worn tunic, and found no blood. Lucky man.

The night sky burst with whites and oranges. In flashes he saw the men of his unit rushing by, their mouths wide open screaming.

He found his feet and yelled at them but couldn't hear himself and his heart swelled with panic. Every actor needed good ears—to hear his cues, for timing, to sing any song at all. He slapped at his ears. They popped and his hearing returned to the tumult of a thousand cracks and thumps. He remembered—his unit was being bombarded for the third time that day. The show must go on here on the Eastern Front, and the Red Army was pulling out all the stops.

Max ran. "Run, boys, run," he yelled as the others pushed him along. He'd been lying in the middle of the road, a road exposed in all directions by vast fields. The salvos kept coming. One had a whistle to it, a real screecher. It burst at Max's back and he kept going, the cold wind smacking his cheeks. Soon the bombs were landing behind them and Max glanced back to take it all in—the craters, the bodies and the heap of metal that had been their last working truck. Its tires burned, spitting flames. Nearby lay the tangled lumps of their last two horses. Their last screams were ringing in his ears now, and he wondered if maybe it wasn't better not to hear. If only he could make this stop. If only he could wear silk pajamas and sip a warm cognac. If only. Napoleon's winter retreat from Russia was a parade march compared to this. The whole German Wehrmacht was a right wreck in this sector, and his unit was only one shred of it.

After the bombing the air had a gritty, metallic reek. Max's thirty or so worn-out comrades trudged on with equal pace as if sharing one mind. They passed through a wood and entered a darkened town. One of the sergeants was waving them onto the main street, where the signs were a mix of German and Polish—*Fleischer, Piekarnia, Einbahnstrasse*. Rubble and debris clogged the side streets. The town square was too dark, too wide open, so they turned a corner and the sergeant led them into what looked like a modest church or a city hall. It was hard to tell, since its front was blackened from fire. Fatigue setting in, they staggered through the double front doors and hit the floor in the dark, toppling onto each other. The floor was soft, luckily—they had actual carpet under them. Moonlight shone through holes in the ceiling, giving them some light.

As the men tossed their gear into piles, the women appeared from wherever they'd been hiding, their farm girl headscarves making triangle shapes in the shadows. Whispering, they found their men and curled up to them.

Anka came to Max, her cheekbones shining blue in the moonlight. She pressed against him and squeezed his hands in hers, her grip as strong as ever (from all that milking, he guessed). These seven or so women were their only stroke of luck. They were *Volksdeutsche*—Eastern ethnic Germans, who simply could not and would not be left behind to the

Red Army. Anka had great legs under that peasant skirt of hers. Max pulled her closer.

She brushed dirt from his forehead. "The bombs, they knocked you down and out," she said in her antiquated German. "Drag you along is what I tried to do."

"That's my girl," Max said. He might be pushing thirty-three years, but Anka was young and strong enough to pull him through the mud.

As the group settled in, they lit cigarettes and passed them around while others slept, some snoring, some with eyes wide open from the exhaustion and constant terror. Someone wept. Anka pecked Max on the cheek.

"Say, Maxi. Our horses back there—what if there's any meat left on 'em?"

Always thinking, his girl. What a delight. Max stroked her straw hair. "Darling," he whispered "the Russians could be anywhere. Lying in wait."

Anka grunted. "Does not matter. It's October. So we must hoard now."

She was right, of course. This first real cold was harsh enough yet the truly grim conditions loomed. When Max lived in America, this time of year held so much promise. October brought the Halloween holiday, that strangely pagan dress-up *Fest* in a land of prudish Christians. It was his favorite holiday there. Everything seemed to remind him of America these days. The further he was taken from her, the more he wanted her. Anka, with her scrapping wiles, reminded him of New York City—and of Lucy Cage.

Anka sat up. Her face hovered over him in shadow and the glints of her eyes darted back and forth. "You hear me? Do the bombs make you deaf? It's good horsemeat, that."

"Well, I could lend you my knife," Max said, smiling.

"No. You go and starve if you want." Anka shoved at his chest and stood. She lifted her skirt and scurried past the intertwined bodies for the front doors.

What could he do? The knife line was meant to be a joke. He sat up and lit a harsh Polish cigarette.

Others were sitting up, hunched silhouettes facing each other. "Where are we?" someone asked. "Who can tell?" replied another, and they huddled around and rubbed their hands together.

"Maps are no good," added a sergeant. "Could be into Poland. Prussia maybe?"

Someone spat and said, "Screw Prussia." Screw Hitler, this really meant.

"Soon Old Prussia will be no more, I can tell you that much."

They were lost and doomed. If they didn't die first, they'd freeze in a Soviet POW camp. Max had heard it all before. He even half believed it. Yet something told him he was going to make it, something he'd learned from his time in America. In show biz alone the Americans had a thousand proverbs about survival. "It's not how you get knocked down," went one, "it's how you get up again." Or, "Rock bottom is a PhD." They tossed their slogans about like their penny candies, and he'd judged them silly at the time. But now? What else could he believe in?

Max woke with a nasty kink in his neck and a whopping headache. He must have gotten a concussion in the bombardment. In the carpeted room, the light had turned a faint purple. Morning was coming, and his Anka hadn't returned. The sad truth of it helped kill his aching hunger pangs.

Then, as his eyes adjusted, he saw a second set of double doors across the room. They were cracked open—through them he could make out, shining within shafts of morning light, the tops of rows of seats. This sight was all too familiar.

He crawled over to the doors. Farther down, beyond the seat rows, he saw the contours of a stage.

They were in a theater. They'd been hiding in the lobby of it. How fitting, he thought—a bomb-damaged drama house for a banished actor.

He nudged at the sergeant sleeping next to him, but the sergeant only snorted and rolled the other way. He clambered over to another sergeant and suggested they move the group into the main hall where it was safer. The sergeant agreed and Max led them in. The holes in the ceiling had showered the hall with dust and plaster chunks, yet its gilded decor still shined. Golden harlequin monkeys served as wall sconces. A red carpet ran down the center aisle. Max strode the gradually inclining lane and gazed at the plush seats, the balcony up above, the orchestra pit before the stage. The place was damp like a barn and smelled like an outhouse, but no matter. Again he thought of New York—there they knew a stage when they saw one. The group straggled in, rubbing their eyes, and Max showed them a little bow. A private smiled, a farm girl curtsied back and Max, grinning, produced one of his last German cigarettes that he had placed in his silver holder (which he kept safe in his boot). "A fine spot we got here," he said in American English, lighting up. "Just swellegant."

The Russians never came so they holed up. The sun beamed down through the punctured ceiling and lit up the gilding, and they kept the doors open so the breeze would kill the damp reek. In the afternoon, Max took the stage and sang for them. He did folk songs and they danced. He did schmaltzy songs. He took requests. He did his best at "Lili Marleen" and nailed "The Ballad of Mack the Knife." Meanwhile, the sergeants and privates went out on forays and scored sawdusty bread, turnips, and even a stray chicken. As evening came more soldiers wandered in, having heard about the good thing they had going at the theater hall. They brought wine and a potato schnapps that wasn't too bad. Max told them about New York City, about how much he missed the hustle, the color and the fair chances they gave you. All you needed was luck. He told them:

"If I can confide in you? I will return there, I can tell you that."

No one had seen Anka. They found candles and used them as footlights. Max did Rodgers and Hart, the corniest he knew—"I Wish I Were in Love Again," from *Babes in Arms*. No one got the English, but no one was complaining. To keep things lively, he trotted out his impersonation of their Commander-In-Chief, Hitler. Chaplin's was far better, he knew, but who here had seen the great Charlie? Of course, he was taking a chance. What motif could be more taboo? Yet he gave it everything he had, and soon most of his comrades were laughing and clapping, even the Austrians and the ones who slept with their machine guns. He pranced around and shook his fists and played up the Austrian dialect. He spat and stomped.

A private bounded in through the open double doors. "Stop, stop," the kid yelled waving hands.

Max halted center stage. All turned, listened. They heard vehicles. A sergeant barked at the private who pulled the doors shut. Outside, brakes screeched and engines revved. These sounded like German makes, but who could be sure? The women headed backstage while the men drew their guns and held positions behind rows of seats. Max blew out the candles, and the hall went dark. He crouched down at the rear of the stage.

A rap on the front doors. A shout: "Open up, please, open up."

No one answered it. The voice sounded German, but that meant little—the Russians played impostors all the time.

The fool kid private had not locked the double doors. The lever turned, the doors opened wide, and soldiers—German soldiers—charged in wearing shoulder flashlights that shot white beams through the darkness. Roughly twenty in number, they took up places along the walls, their machine guns aimed.

"You can come out. You're in good hands," shouted an officer from the doorway. The accent was educated High German—Hanover, most likely.

"With those guns trained on us?" Max said, chuckling. "My good fellow, show us some civility." A flashlight hit him in the eyes, but he didn't flinch. He'd had worse lighting.

"Very well." The officer waved for his men to lower their guns.

The farm girls came out first, clasping their hands together in thanks. Max relit candles for a better look at the soldiers. They were Waffen-SS—the standard combat SS, but this was no frontline unit. At least they weren't those Special Police bastards, or the Gestapo. Still, they had brand-new gear like those bastards. They shot smiles at the farm girls. Max pulled back, out of the light.

"What's the special occasion?" one of Max's sergeants said.

The officer who'd called them out was a captain. He strode down the aisle wearing a tailored, shiny leather overcoat. Max hadn't seen such fine costume in a long time. The captain had a passable henchman's look, but his jowls were flabby and his eyes too soft. He stopped halfway down, putting himself in the middle of the scene, and studied the worn, tired faces. He pulled his gloves off and slapped them in an open palm. Now that was better, Max thought.

"So. Who's in charge?" the captain said.

"Maybe you could tell us?" one of Max's other sergeants said. "Sir."

The captain wagged a finger. "Don't you worry. We'll get you right back to your regiment so you can keep up the fight." He shook a fist and showed his teeth. "That's right, *Kameraden*, we'll push those Bolshevik bastards all the way to the Orient!"

Such poor material—it was straight from propaganda section. Heads were down now. "'The Orient,' he says," someone grunted.

"First things first." The captain pulled a file from his map case and read. He cleared his throat and said in a monotone, as if doing a casting call, "I am looking for a man, and his name would be . . . Kaspar, or perhaps 'von' Kaspar?"

The word 'von' meant a noble background. The soldiers and farm girls gaped at each other. Max had never told this group his old stage name. Some were chuckling now.

The captain eyed Max. "First name, Maximilian?"

The group gathered nearer the stage, perhaps to protect Max, perhaps to get a closer look. The whole room was looking to him. He had sat back down, on the edge of the stage. His head felt heavy and he let it hang. This performance was over, show closed.

"This fine fellow right here is none other than Corporal Max Kaspar." It was one of the farm girls talking, practically shouting in her Eastern German. "Oh, you don't recognize him now, not like this—some sorry, worn-out, aging footslogger, aye, but he was a grand performer once. The toast of New York City he was."

"Well, not exactly," Max muttered, "maybe I was laying it on a little thick."

The captain held up a promo still from 1940 Berlin—Max in tuxedo and top hat, flanked by dancing girls.

"That's him! And our leaders are such good judges of talent, they went and made this man a corporal in the infantry," added a third sergeant (using one of Max's own favorite lines).

"He dances! Sings! Impersonates!" It was the first sergeant, sounding like Max's press agent. "You want it, our Kaspar has it, from opera to cabaret, drama to comedy . . ."

The captain held up a hand. He looked to Max. "Your name is Kaspar. In New York you called yourself Maximilian von Kaspar."

Max let out a sigh. "True story. Too true."

"I must say, you've been harder to find than toilet paper out here."

"Nothing is so hard," Max said. "So. Where are you taking me?"

"Why, we're taking you back where you belong. Where else?"

They had little time to say goodbye. Max squared his shoulders, set his chin high, and strode up the aisle as the old gang lined his way. "It's a special call from above," said one. "Look, it could be your great comeback," said another. They said it slowly, mechanically, the way you tell a child the trip to the dentist will be fun. They shook his hands. They hugged him. The women kissed him. One gave him the tongue. What a wench. He loved that about wenches.

At the top of the aisle, he pivoted to face them. "It was an honor to play for you," he said and gave a long and slow bow, one arm outstretched. No need to be too grim. After all, they were the ones who had to stay. It was the way the world worked. One day you're down, and the next? "Breaking a leg," as the Americans said. If he had any luck left at all.

Outside, the captain escorted Max to the rear of a late-model Horch command car. The seats were leather and almost warm. Feeling cheeky, Max asked for a blanket, and to his surprise they gave him one. He draped it over his shoulders like a cloak. Before they sped away, rain started to fall, tapping at the fabric roof. The driver handed him a cigarette. It was a rare French Gauloises, made it all the way to the Eastern Front, rich and full of life.

Max smoked and sat back and thought of lovely Anka. He looked out the window—and saw her. She had returned to the group, who were gathering in the doorway of the theater. She was with one of the sergeants now, inserting herself inside his overcoat, rubbing at his ribs, and laughing. It made sense, Max thought. His Anka had probably run into that SS captain and pointed him in the right direction. She could have made a play for Max, told them she just had to be with him, but she'd placed her bets on a warm sergeant and a shot at more horsemeat. Smart girl, Max thought. Sensible. Can't teach what she's got. The sad fact was, comebacks were a lost art these days, and his needy Anka knew it. Then again, he thought, chuckling, she should have seen him do that Rodgers and Hart number.

Two

The SS captain had orders to put Max on a train for Bavaria. The problem was finding the right train, since it was high season for full retreat on the Eastern Front. For a night and a day Max's SS escorts traveled the countryside in search of rail lines, crossings, stations. In better times it might have made a fine motoring tour. The low green hills shimmered in the late fall sun. A rocky stream rushed alongside the road, foaming white. Max kept his blanket draped over his lap. The captain's men brought him hot food and schnapps and played cards with him. And Max vowed to keep this damn good thing going as long as he could.

In the middle of the night, they stopped at an abandoned mansion. The usual scavengers—passing troops and forced laborers on the lam—had cleaned out the food and liquor; but in an antique armoire Max discovered riding boots, jodhpurs, a corduroy blazer, a lambswool sweater, and a floppy upper-class hiker's hat. He put all this on. In the mirror he saw a cultured German impersonating an English gentleman, the very look he'd given himself before the army. He would wear his finery the rest of the way. He even took an ivory-handled cane with him. The captain had no objections and let Max keep his worn field gray-green uniform in a rucksack. The men played along by calling him "*Mein Herr*," as if they were seeing off a rich and eccentric uncle for an adventurous trip abroad from which he'd have many interesting stories. They lent him a leather overcoat like the captain's. And Max played it up all the more. He had a shave with warm water and left a pencil thin mustache like the one he had in America. As they toured on, he told himself he was over his farm girl Anka. Had she really almost talked him into deserting? Wait out the war in a refugee camp and then score a little farm? Nonsense. Crazy girls put crazy ideas in your head. The war put crazy ideas in your head. Her new sergeant was probably dead already.

They ended up at another mansion. At dawn the captain invited Max out on the veranda where they draped their fine overcoats over their shoulders, drank coffee, and smoked as if this place was the captain's country villa and a real war was his future hope and not a daily nightmare far out of control. The captain told Max his name was Pielau— Adalbert von Pielau.

"I am a real 'von,' *Herr* 'von' Kaspar," the captain said and sighed. "These days, I mostly leave the 'von' off. Some see the noble background as a weakness. I never imagined it possible."

"They're just envious," Max said. "We all want what we don't have, isn't that so?" The coffee was perking him up. He tapped his cane on the veranda slate, two pops. "Now, good von Pielau, if I may, how about you telling me what they're to do with me."

Pielau smiled. Max had asked the captain's men this many times. They'd only shrugged. They were on a top-secret job, they said.

"When the SS comes looking for you," Max said, "it can mean a tight spot."

"Or, something great, something honorable. Don't forget that."

"It has to do with performing?" Max said. "I mean, what else am I good for? Maybe it's the Troops Entertainment Section, give our boys a good show. That's the only way you'll see me back at the front, I can tell you—in stage makeup." This last bit was pushing it, despite the sugar coating. He had to gauge Pielau's SS principles.

The captain's flabby jowls had stiffened. He moved to the edge of the veranda and glanced around to make sure no one was listening. He whispered, "Here's the thing, Kaspar. If I knew more myself, I think I could confide in you. Believe me, I want to survive as much as you."

Max took the captain's disclosure for one of those tricks of implied meaning. The playwrights called it subtext, but regular Germans had perfected the art in the last ten years. It required a response of equal measure.

Max walked to the edge of the veranda. "If I were in your boots," he whispered, "I'd get as far from the Russians as you can. Get to the Western Front. You're a nobleman, right? With contacts? Get nearer to the Americans. And for devil's sake, when the end comes don't be wearing that uniform with an SS death skull on the collar. The Americans will take it literally."

When the end comes, Max had said—when the war was lost, was his subtext. Did Pielau get it? Or was Max merely projecting his own hopes?

Pielau's face had lost color. "Let's not talk rashly. There are many ways to survive. Victory is the best way."

"Of course, yes," Max blurted and let out a nervous chuckle. "Who's talking rash, my good man?" He patted Pielau on the back. Pielau chuckled and offered Max another of his Gauloises.

That afternoon they crossed from what used to be Poland into Germany. In a town called Görlitz, Pielau found Max a passenger train west. On the platform, the locomotive pumped steam as people pushed their children and elderly into the packed cars. Pielau issued Max his papers. He saluted Max first, though Max was only a corporal. "With any luck, we'll meet again," he told Max.

Still in his fine clothes, Max climbed into a passenger car and muscled his way through to a cramped spot in the passageway. He sat on his rucksack, his head pressed up against the cold window. At least he had a window for the night. For long dark hours he slept sitting up, nodding off and jerking awake, as the car rocked and the tracks clicked, and the train stopped for problems he did not want to know. In the morning, he barely recognized Germany. Along the horizon, towers and spires he'd known had vanished. Barrels of black smoke spiraled up into the sky, and the air was peppery with soot.

Traveling into Nuremberg was like passing through a rock quarry. Once splendid medieval streets were rubble piles of gray and black. Seeing this, the elderly couple next to Max cried. The main train station was such a ruin that the armed forces check-in post was a tent outside. Max reported here. A teenage clerk issued him pea soup from the field kitchen and a truck ride to Grafenwöhr.

Grafenwöhr. Any German with the slightest military *Bildung* knew this massive training complex between Nuremberg and the Czech border. At least it wasn't a concentration camp, Max thought. His truck was packed with fifteen or more soldiers from all branches of service. They straightened for Max when he climbed in wearing his fine getup. They probably think I'm a producer, he thought. In no time he'd be telling them he was only an army corporal, and he hoped they could see the sad irony in that.

During the bumpy ride the men sounded upbeat, if not thankful, and it kept Max's confidence high. Most in the truck had volunteered, he learned—they were responding to an urgent armed forces-wide request for English-speaking personnel, and that was all they knew. Hearing this, Max let himself feel somewhat honored that the powers-at-be had come looking for him. And they all had so much in common in the truck! There were other actors, a dancer, musicians, a chef, headwaiters, a playwright, and even a screenwriter. A few had been merchant sailors before the war. Two of the sailors smoked large curved pipes.

Like Max, most all these men had been to America.

They rolled into Grafenwöhr at dusk, passing rows of army barracks shaded purple from the sun going down. The compound had perimeter fences as if for POWs. "That's for secrecy," someone chanted. "Right. It's for our safety," another said, and they nodded in agreement. At the front gate they poked their heads out and joked with the guards, but the guards only stared back as if deaf or zombies (straight from *The Cabinet of Dr. Caligari*, Max thought).

The trucks left them on a parade ground lit up with bright spotlights, and even Max had to shield his eyes from the light. Another truckload had already arrived. The men huddled in groups, mostly according to branch of service, and sat on crates that seemed to have been set out for them, the beams of white light illuminating their steamy breath. A group of Luftwaffe noncoms played Skat. A circle of medics passed around music magazines. An army private was juggling turnips, alone. He managed four, then five, and then added his knife into the mix. Around his neck he wore an orange scarf that was a little too bright and long. His hair flopped over his ears, longer than many women's. A real seedy cabaret type, this one. What sort of production was this to be? Max wondered. Could it be vaudeville? Not so bad there. He would be returning to his roots. Still, that didn't explain the sailors and chefs.

A group of sappers was doing some black market trading. Max strode over and let them jeer at his exclusive attire. He loved it. The sappers loved it. One offered a *Jägerwurst* and three potatoes for Max's cane, and Max commenced negotiations, "That's all good and well, but what a gentleman really needs, boys, is a nice country egg—"

"What the devil are you? Mister dandy pansy?" Someone was yelling. It came from the office at the edge of the ground, some thirty feet away. An SS lieutenant was standing on the office steps, his hands on his hips. Max assumed the lieutenant was yelling at the juggler, but the juggler had stopped. He'd tucked his longish scarf into his tunic. The lieutenant continued, "That's right, I'm talking to you! Speak up you!"

"Surely that little tyrant's talking to someone else," Max said to his group.

The SS lieutenant marched across the ground, the steam pulsing out his mouth. The sappers parted and stepped back. Max's uniform was packed in the rucksack on his shoulder. He lowered the rucksack to his feet. The lieutenant came straight for him.

"Excuse me, gents," Max said and turned to the lieutenant

—

Who screamed and spat spittle: "Why aren't you in uniform? Speak, you. Name and rank and unit."

Max smelled *Bockbier* and liver dumpling. What a bore, he thought. He stood at attention and saluted, and only then did he notice he still had on the white gloves he'd traded for on the train. "Before I tire you with the whole story, sir," he began, "I should clarify that I'm a lowly army corporal, in the infantry, just arrived from the Eastern Front and, well, my uniform was so worn from the hard fighting, I did not want to offend anyone."

"Another goddamned thespian, that it? Now strip and get your kit on." The lieutenant kicked Max's rucksack for emphasis and marched off with his arms folded behind his back like a drill instructor.

Men joked with Max as he stripped in the biting cold and switched into his itchy old uniform. The sapper returned, frowning, and gave Max one egg for his sore luck.

Across the ground, the SS lieutenant had stopped at the juggler. He screamed something in the juggler's face and the juggler, tottering, reached in his tunic and pulled out the length of his tucked-in orange scarf. It flopped at his belt buckle. The lieutenant grabbed at the stretch of scarf, pulled the juggler to his chest, drew his service knife and hacked the scarf off close to the juggler's neck. This got few laughs. The lieutenant laughed anyway and sauntered back to his office, his arms swinging.

Their training was so secret the enlisted men could not send mail or have outside contact. Max got a bottom bunk in a barrack and a standup locker slapped together with cheap pinewood. That first night he set his fine clothing in a neat pile in his locker and dropped into his bunk, worried. He was little more than a recruit again, it seemed. Then he lay back, his head snug in his new pillow, and decided worrying was pointless. Almost anything was better than where he came from.

The lone juggler got the bunk above him, and Max suspected the SS lieutenant put them together so he could keep an eye on them. The juggler's name was Menning, Felix Menning. As they stowed their gear, Max tried to chat him up, get his mind off that asshole lieutenant, but Felix Menning gave him little. He too had been in America, he said —for over two years, and he'd been in the circus to boot. Then he clammed up and climbed into his bunk.

Soon after lights out, Max heard what first sounded like sniffles. It was sobbing, but muffled as if into a pillow. It was Felix Menning up above him. Max nudged the upper bunk with a knee. "Buck up, *Kamerad*," he whispered. "Change is good, don't you see? Even in war. One door closes, another opens."

"Amen," someone said a couple bunks down. "He's right, circus boy," said another.

Felix Menning said nothing. Soon he was snoring.

Next morning at reveille, Max and Felix were the last two out the barrack door. Max was groggy and slow getting his uniform on, while Felix took his time. At the doorway, Felix waited for him.

Felix put a flat hand to Max's chest. "Listen, Kaspar, you leave that shithead lieutenant to me. I know how to handle the likes of him." He said this with emphasis, but not anger, as if he were counting out change.

"You can have him." Max fought a smile. "Such the blackguard, aren't you? I forget, you were in the circus—"

"And Berlin. Parts you don't even want to know about. So I know my way around a lug like him." Menning's stare had become a smile. He patted Max's chest. "We'll get on better that way. Trust me."

Max never got to the quartermaster first thing. That morning the interviews began, and Max was one of the first to be called in. Two of the strangely mute guards escorted him to a wooden bungalow that looked like a larger version of the standard German garden hut. They left Max inside, alone. A chair stood in the middle of the room before a desk. Max sat in it. The interior was little more refined than the exterior. As in the barracks, everything here was unpainted wood—floor, walls, ceiling, desk—all made of pinewood planks and so raw it was furry in the light. One could catch a sliver on any of it, he thought. Frightful. Four metal chairs and two file cabinets completed the dreadful decor. Only the iron wood stove in the corner helped warm this up.

The door swung open. Four officers entered—two horse-faced SS lieutenants who looked like young doctors, the shithead SS lieutenant who Felix Menning said he could handle, and to Max's great delight, Captain Adalbert von Pielau.

Max wanted to shout out the good man's name. He stood and gave his best salute.

Pielau did the Hitler salute, as did the others, and they sat, Pielau at the desk facing Max's chair and the other three behind Max. Pielau introduced the horse-faced lieutenants. Shithead introduced himself. His name was Rattner.

Pielau tried a curt smile. "So, we meet again, Corporal Kaspar—or is it von Kaspar?"

Max got the picture. This Pielau had to play it straight. "My army paybook says Kaspar, sir," Max said.

"So it does, yes." Pielau pulled folders from his map case and slapped them on the desktop. He stared at some papers as if reading, but his eyeballs weren't moving. Behind Max, one of the officers was trying to clear his throat, and the phlegmy screech combined with the greasy smell of the wood stove fire made Max's stomach clench up and his throat constrict.

"You lived in America," Pielau said. "Eight years. Your family had emigrated there and got themselves to New Hampshire. You end up in New York City. Why?"

"I'm an actor," Max said. "We like a new challenge." Pielau stared, expecting more. "And a shot at success, of course," Max added.

Pielau pursed his lips and moved them around, as if he had meat stuck between teeth. "Other Germans went too. They made films. Hollywood embraced them. That traitor bitch Marlene Dietrich. That little rat Lorre."

"Hollywood still embraces them."

"Lucky for them. You dabbled in American forms."

"Forms, sir?"

One of the officers behind Max said, "Musicals—with the Negro's jazz." It was Lieutenant Rattner. "And all the while you work with Jews," he added.

"I'm not Jewish," Max said. "My race certificate is in order and on file."

Pielau was glaring at Rattner. "No one's doubting your racial purity, Corporal. So, why return to Germany? Why return in '39?"

"I'm a German. By '39 I knew my place was here." Max too could play it straight. He wasn't lying so much as interpreting. He'd really believed something like this back then.

"You never joined the party," one of them said.

"You never joined the SS," another said.

"You were lucky not to land in prison, the schemes you've been up to," Rattner said. "Refusing good German roles. Exploiting the black market. We should have thrown your type back to America."

If they insisted on pecking, why sit behind him? Max turned and glared at the three lieutenants. He wanted to say what was really on his mind, but a modern German had to pick his battles. His refusals had been about art, at first. The roles he declined were melodramatic junk that not even Hollywood was doing. As far as the black market went, Max was only one of many. These sheltered SS clowns had no idea. Max simply had the poor fortune to be one of many minor scapegoats. The three met Max's glare with dead stares, their eyes dark. Max said, "No, instead you put me in an army uniform. Let me fight. And for that I am grateful. Sirs."

Rattner spat.

"Corporal, please, turn back around," Pielau said. "Thank you. Back in Germany, there was also a woman."

"Liselotte. Yes."

"Not just any woman, I should add. Frau Auermann was an inspiration to us all."

They had no idea of inspiration, Max thought, simmering. Inspiration took imagination.

"She died, in an air raid," Pielau said.

"In Hamburg. It was an American air raid, to be exact."

Silence behind him. They'd all lost someone close. Max turned to them and could tell from Rattner's looser stare that Rattner had lost more than one. He faced Pielau again, and they shared a knowing glance.

"Perhaps we leave loved ones out of it," Pielau said.

"In New York you changed your name, called yourself a noble," Rattner said to Max.

"My agent's idea," Max said. The name change was Max's doing. His agent thought it too corny yet hokum only seemed to help in America, Max had argued.

"And you let him," Rattner said. "*Amis* say jump you say how high, is that it?"

Max shrugged. In German, the word "*Ami*" was slang for an American. He thought it boorish and never used it. Now he'd use whatever it took. "Not exactly," he said. "The *Amis* are persistent, to be sure, but not in that way. Especially in New York. They won't listen to reason. They follow their own paths, I suppose. But the longer you're there, the less you know . . . "

A moment of silence crept in. They all knew less these days.

"You mentioned success," Pielau said. "Did you find it?"

"Let's just say I'm still looking," Max said. Stalling. Thinking. They were offering him some kind of opening, and he sure as hell would take it. Yet to come up with a plan, he would have to survive first. He knew what he had to do, for now. He'd pull out all the stops. The Nazis liked a show. Bombast was their milieu.

"Gentlemen, if I may say something?" Max said.

"Go on."

Max stood and met the eyes of all, fists at his sides. He let one knee wobble, in anger. "I hate America," he said. "I despise her. It. It knows no culture. It breeds contempt for others. It's a bourgeois wasteland of fat cats and unruly sheep. This all threatens the National Socialist ideal. The only threat worse is Communism. May the two rot in hell. So if I can help make that happen faster, I stand ready." The lieutenants nodded. Max turned to Pielau, clicked his heels, gave the Hitler salute and practically threw his arm out doing so.

Pielau gave a half-salute. "Fine, admirable. I'm sure you'll have your chance. Our intrepid commander—code name, Doktor Solar—will need such enthusiasm from all of us on this mission. We're all a part of this now."

So Pielau was jumping on the bandwagon. Smart man, the captain. Anka should have been this smart. "So, you speak English too," Max added in English.

Pielau stared. He nodded, and then began to shake his head—

"*Ach*, but of course, you do," Max blurted in German, helping the poor soul out. He turned to Rattner. "And you too, I suppose," he continued in English—

Rattner snorted a laugh. "Speaking of tongues, I bet you'd like to know about the guards here?" he said in German, changing the subject with as much skill as a rhino diving into a creek. "They're Ukrainian SS. Don't speak German well enough to know what's what. You see? We don't want our guards knowing a thing, going into town, getting too full of beers or brandy and spilling the beans. Now do we?"

"You don't trust your own men, sir?" Max said.

"That we will soon find out." As Lieutenant Rattner spoke, Max glanced at Pielau. The way Pielau's flabby jowl had tightened up, it was clear whom the lieutenant was addressing.

That evening, Captain Pielau sent for Max. Pielau met him outside on the parade ground alone. Max saluted and the captain clicked his heels. Pielau was smiling, his teeth glowing in the moonlight. He lit cigarettes for them. He handed one to Max.

"Let me tell you the greatest secret. Doktor Solar? Our commander? He is none other than SS Lieutenant Colonel Otto Skorzeny. You have heard of him, yes?"

"Of course. The man is a legend." Max didn't want to know. Surely, this was top secret.

"So I must warn you. What you said to me about fleeing to the Western Front? You must never say it to anyone again. Especially not here."

What about divulging top secrets to enlisted men? How did that fit in? Max shuddered, but it wasn't from the cold. He grimaced and hoped it was a smile.

"I mean it, Kaspar. Less astute SS officers would have had you shot for less."

"Rattner, for example. So I should thank you." Max clicked his heels.

Pielau stomped. "This is no joke. The war can change now. I can see how it can." He grasped at Max's wrist, his voice rising. "There are new weapons. The grandest plans. And we, here, are a part of that. We can win this. I tell you we can. When will you understand it?"

Max pried Pielau's hand from his wrist and stood back, locking eyes with the captain. "Oh, I understand, dear Pielau. I understand all too well." His cigarette hung from his lips, a cold dead stem. It had already gone out.

Three

October passed into November. In the west the Americans entered Germany and took Aachen. This once-grand city—the seat of Charlemagne—was reduced to rubble and thousands of Germans surrendered after the bloody fight. In the east the Red Army kept closing in, raping and killing German civilians along the way according to rumors—the bitterest revenge in full blossom, while in the south the Allies crept up from Southern France and Northern Italy. A sinister end was nearing in Germany, and you didn't need the BBC to grasp it. Old men were called up and issued bazookas. On street corners, the burghers wrung their hands and promised each other wonder weapons that were sure to turn the black tide.

In Grafenwöhr the snow fell early and piled up—never a pretty sight when you're in the army. Banks of icy and rock-laden brown snow lined the roads and the barren fields became pristine white tracts, a quicksand that swallowed men up to their crotches. The forests were no friend either. One nudge of the branches from man or bird or wind made the cold whiteness reign down in piles. Against it all, Max's old uniform was little protection, and he wasn't able to score a new one. SS Lieutenant Rattner told him he'd have no use for it soon.

As the dark days wore on, the lieutenants preached secrecy like missionaries the gospel. No one spoke of the code name Doktor Solar, so Max kept Captain Pielau's blathering to himself. The captain's gossip habit would have to stop, Max knew. The penalty was too high. This Doktor Solar had to be receiving orders from the highest level. Who else could call in German soldiers from all over the Reich? Surely the Führer was head producer, possibly even playwright.

The script they were writing had a clever angle, Max had to admit. The officers encouraged and even ordered the men to speak among themselves in whatever English they knew. It was fast becoming clear that theirs was a military operation that relied on one cheap motif—any knowledge of American English.

The snow didn't stall the hustle and bustle of Grafenwöhr. Hordes of soldiers were arriving by the day, and Captain Pielau confided in Max that they had close to 1,500 men. The place had become a giant rehearsal for portraying US Army life. They got US Army Field Manuals and learned American tactics, such as how to turn when ordered, raise a weapon, march. The hardest part was adopting the casualness with which Americans did almost everything. Standing "at ease" in the US Army was not a less stiff form of attention but rather slouching with your hands clasped behind the back. Americans smiled when they talked, even when at ease. And their speech? The hard Rs were toughest to sound out. Only the handful raised in America had it down. The rest complained that the *Amis* chewed on their words and the constant hard Rs made every sentence sound like this: "Are, are, are, are . . ."

Worse still, few in camp had been near the front lines, even fewer had seen combat, and yet their combat training was now being rushed (a very un-German thing). It was as if the army were sending out snipers who'd never shot a rifle before—as if it were opening night and the actors had not memorized one line. Yet the soldiers around Max showed the same childlike fervor as the burghers on the street. He hadn't seen this much frenzy since he performed at a League of German Women rally. Even the ones raised in America believed Germany could still win the war. Did they not see the vast industrial might of America and her still untapped reserves of men and spirit? America simply dwarfed Germany, Max wanted to remind them, and that was all that mattered in the end. Yet he held his tongue. And bided the time.

One evening they were showing a double feature with Betty Grable and Lana Turner and the barracks was near empty. Max reclined on his bottom bunk reading prewar American magazines, thumbing through *Colliers* and *The New Yorker* for mention of productions he'd auditioned for. Felix Menning was up on his top bunk. In the far corner, a group of Luftwaffe privates was playing cards. Apart from them, no one else was in the barracks. Max had been wondering if this little misfit *Aussenseiter* Felix was a man he might be able to confide in? A man he could trust? Were there even any left? He flipped the pages of a *Life* magazine, skimming the photos and ads. Americans devoted full-page ads to hair tonic and tiny ads to typewriters, while in Germany it was just the opposite.

He made a clucking sound with the top of his mouth. He was sure to smile when he spoke even though Felix couldn't see him. "What we're up to here? Let's not kid ourselves. Has to be a secret mission. Behind the lines surely. That's some dicey stuff. Don't you think?"

Felix didn't answer right off. His bed squeaked, once. "You tell me. Sure, and then tell me about your big combat days. Go on, Max." Felix had never called him Max before. It had always been *Herr* von Kaspar, with a smile or a joking bow. He should have never told Felix about the stage name.

"If I must. I was on the *Ostfront* for six months. Always on the front lines."

"How many times you fire your gun? How many you kill? Any face to face?"

"How many?" Now Max snorted a laugh. "Who was counting? My God, we were too busy getting shot at, and bombed..."

"You never killed anyone. Right? Right. So spare me the Hitler School patronage. Your fake optimism. You think whatever we got going here is doomed. That's what you think. That's why you're prying just now."

"Prying? Me?" Max chuckled. Not Felix too? he thought. A deluded child, like all the rest? Then again, the little juggler was also an actor.

The Luftwaffe boys were still having at it, slapping down cards and shouting. Max spoke lower. "You were never on the front lines. I didn't mean to question your ability, dear Felix, if that's what you mean. So please, temper the finger pointing. It will only get you—us—into trouble."

The top bunk creaked. Felix leaned over and stared down at Max, blocking the light. Max stared up. Felix climbed down and knelt next to Max. His small, narrow eyes locked on Max's, and he wagged a finger. A narrow finger. Everything about Felix was slender, from his shoulders to his eyebrows, from his lips to his skinny bowed legs. Even his Berlin accent was tinny. He was like some mythical forest imp. Max stared back, blank-faced.

"Don't give me that. I got your number," Felix said. "No one else here does, but I do." He whispered now. "You don't believe in any of this. You don't believe in the war."

"*Quatsch*," Max said, yet he had to shrug and look away.

Felix stayed at his side. Smiling now. Not letting Max off the hook.

Perhaps less direct was best, Max decided. He tossed the magazine to his feet. "In America? You said you were in the circus," he said.

Felix looked away, first at the Luftwaffe boys, and then at his hands hanging off his knees. "Why not, I figured. I could ride a unicycle, juggle, play the clown, dress up like a woman and play one even better. So I'd give it a shot. Cabarets were closing here. Not like your time over there, eh?"

Max shrugged. "Apples and oranges."

"So why give it all up for Germany?"

Max stared, a long time. How to answer this? With the proven old platitudes, or something more shrewd. Before he could respond, Felix jumped back up onto his bunk. He had to be smiling again, the way his voice was singing. "That's why you come here—why you play along. To find new roles, right? After all, you are an actor. And perhaps some new friends? From adversity comes clarity, isn't that the line?"

"Something like that . . ." Max rolled his eyes. Whatever was coming after Grafenwöhr, it might just give him a way out. And Felix was certainly giving him ideas. Had he meant to? Could this little forest imp read his mind? Predict the future?

"And you?" Max said. "Why'd you volunteer?"

"Didn't you know?" Felix said, adding a snicker. "It's to help you."

By their second week in Grafenwöhr, the clandestine materiel was arriving at a steady clip. Trains rolled in carrying vehicles covered with tarps. Underneath were US Army jeeps, a few trucks and a couple tanks, but mostly jeeps. The vehicles' olive drab paint and white stars were a shocking sight but one they'd have to get used to quickly, Captain Pielau assured them.

The captain assigned Max and Felix Menning to a warehouse that was open, on one end, to the stinging November air. The concrete under their feet was colder than the ice on the windows and the snow drifted in, swirling and gathering into small white dunes that refused to melt. The warehouse had rows of long tables, like in a beer hall. At one table, Max and Felix sorted the American tunics that had been delivered, accidentally, with POW triangles painted on the backs. Pielau had ordered them to try to scrape off the paint. They scrubbed and scraped, bent over the tables, their backs tightening up, aching. Sweat rolled down Felix's face despite the cold. The paint would not give way. (After all, it was meant to stay on forever.) It was thankless work, yet far better than cleaning up the "dog tags" of dead American soldiers. Pielau was doing Max a good turn once again.

Captain Pielau paced the warehouse with a clipboard, checking stocks and making notes. A couple tables over, their *Quartiermeister*, a former clothing designer (who'd worked in New York's Garment District), was hunched over a new shipment of uniforms diverted from the Red Cross by no small degree of trickery. The *Quartiermeister* called Captain Pielau over. Pielau held up a pair of trousers, huffed at them, threw them down, and then threw up his hands. He scratched at his clipboard and paced the warehouse muttering. All went back to work. Max kept an eye on the captain. Over in a corner, Pielau threw his clipboard across the concrete floor.

He ended up at Max's table, his jowls reddening. "Kaspar, you know what is happening here, don't you? Can't you see it?" Beside Max, Felix slowed his scraping to listen. "Those trousers over there? All British. Here we go and swindle the Red Cross for *Ami* uniforms, and we get British. Well, we can't use that, can we?"

"I wouldn't know, sir." Max added a smile.

"And see all that—and that?" Pielau went on, his voice growing shrill. He pointed around the warehouse at the crates and boxes and the tables piled with mismatched gear. Men looked up woodenly as if they were being complained about. "And that there? We have not nearly enough. We need belts, ammo cases, helmets, and more overcoats. We have no helmets."

"Helmets would be good, sir."

Pielau slumped against the table, whispering now. "*Mein Gott*, Kaspar, you know Doktor Solar is not going to like this." He glared at Felix, who resumed his scraping.

Max stepped sideways, closer to Pielau. He whispered, "Look, you have to relax. Tell you what—go on to your officers' mess, get yourself a coffee with two fingers of corn schnapps in it. That'll make you feel better."

"You don't understand," Pielau said. "I mean, what will people think?"

Pielau often took weekend trips to Nuremberg. He had friends and girlfriends there. If he were boasting of great things, Max could not know about it. He gave the captain a long, hard stare. "Sir, people are not supposed to think anything—let alone be aware of it," he said.

Pielau stiffened as if at attention. "You're right as always. Thank you." He lit a cigarette, patted Max's shoulder, and strode off into the cold and gray afternoon.

Max and Felix scraped on. As they worked, four sailors two tables over began laughing at them. The four had been merchant sailors before the war. Their American English could be clumsy, and thick with accent, yet they knew all the slang and could say what they needed. Max heard them now.

One nodded at Felix and said what sounded like: "Piece a' chicken." Another pointed and said, "Pantywaist."

Felix kept scraping, but he had stopped sweating. His forehead grew red.

Physically, the sailors were Felix's opposite—stocky and thick and even the wiry ones had muscle. The widest of the four, a balding redhead with a broad smile, kept the others laughing with new words. "A real Nancy," he said, "that fella's a flit," and what sounded like "Fag-got."

Max glared at the sailors. "Should I translate?"

"No need," Felix said under his breath. "What did I tell you about the lieutenant? Same goes here."

"Very well . . ."

Felix stopped scrubbing. He looked up at the sailors. They laughed louder. They whistled. Felix grinned. "Hiya boys," he said in American English, practically shouting it.

The sailors laughed harder. They flopped their wrists.

Felix added with a slippery lisp, "Why don't ya come up and see me sometime?" He put his hands on his hips and wiggled the hips.

Others in the warehouse laughed and pointed at the sailors, who glared back now, rattled by the implication of this. Felix kept it up. The red-haired sailor got special treatment. Felix blew a kiss and rubbed at his crotch. He shouted: "And who's that next to ya, sailor?"

Next to the red-haired one stood a sailor with prematurely white hair. He had a discreet goatee beard. The two stared at each other.

"Gets lonely at sea, no? So tell me, Red, how long you been screwing the goat?"

Laughs boomed and echoed in the warehouse. The older sailor glared at the red-haired sailor, whose face hardened. The red-haired sailor showed Felix a fist.

Felix marched over, past the first table.

"Menning, wait," Max said, following.

The red-haired sailor came around the front of his table. Felix kept going. The laughs turned to jeers and shouts.

They met on open floor. Felix swung at the sailor. The sailor ducked. Yet he didn't punch. He let Felix have another go. Felix caught the sailor in the right jaw.

The sailor hardly flinched. Max stepped in to break it up, but others held him back and the men gathered from all corners of the warehouse.

Felix swung again and missed. The sailor spat, smiled, and then undercut Felix in the stomach. Felix bent over, his mouth shaped like an O, and a rushing sound shot from his mouth. The sailor moved to sock Felix under his jaw, but stopped. Felix was still bent over. The sailor pushed him back with a thumb, and Felix stumbled back and landed on his butt. The cheers peaked. The sailor bowed. He hollered something in Northern dialect and sat on Felix as if pretending to ride him.

Felix tried to bite at his knuckles.

"Who's the goat now?" the sailor said, to more cheers.

Humiliating. And yet Felix grinned, and the cheers rose. Men clapped. Felix loved any audience, hostile or no. It was the way he got back at the world, Max thought, clapping along (while for Max, it was the way he made love to the world).

"You're all right," the sailor said to Felix. He dismounted and helped Felix up. The two bowed together.

"He's coming," someone shouted.

"Look alive."

The clapping had stopped. The sailors sprang to attention. SS Lieutenant Rattner was pushing his way through the crowd. "What the hell you pulling here, boys?" he yelled, glaring at the sailors. He had his cap clenched in his hand as if ready to swat someone with it. No one spoke.

"Where's Pielau?" Rattner shouted at Max. "Don't know, sir," Max muttered.

Felix was gasping for breath. His uniform was a mess. Rattner saw him and sneered. He marched over and stopped inches from Felix's face. Felix grinned again.

Rattner slapped Felix hard across the temple. Felix stumbled but sneered back, defiant. Rattner slapped Felix across the jaw, cutting his lip.

Felix, wobbling, stood at attention.

Rattner turned to face the men. All eyes met his. "That's for your own good," he said to Felix. "Haven't learned a thing from my combat training, have you?"

Felix shook his head. Blood rolled onto his chin, mixing with sweat. "Not yet," he muttered, "but just you wait and see."

Four

Late November now. One Monday morning, Captain Adalbert von Pielau did not return from his weekend leave. The same day, Lieutenant Rattner assumed Pielau's duties. On Tuesday Rattner became an SS Captain. He roamed the Grafenwöhr compound with his overcoat wide open, showing off his new insignia.

The stout red-haired sailor who'd scrapped with Felix Menning led Max out behind a storage shed. The sailor's name was Zoock. Zoock said Captain Rattner deserved a flogging for harassing Felix to no end. "I can't take his swagger. Just say the word, Mac," he said in impressive American street English, "and me and the boys we'll give him the works."

"I'm not Menning's keeper," Max had to say in German, disappointed that he couldn't think of the American way to say this. "Why don't you ask Felix himself?"

Zoock asked Felix, but Felix passed with heartfelt thanks. "Things will take care of themselves, my good man," Felix told Zoock, patting him on his balding head.

On Thursday, after midday mess, the men were ordered to stay in their barracks. They watched from windows as a glossy command car and motorcycle escort rumbled through the compound. In Max's barrack, the men traded hopeful stories about the visitors. Some suggested it was *Reichsmarschall* Goering, or Admiral Doenitz, head of German intelligence. Others were certain of a captured Allied Commander in the flesh, either that "gangster clerk" Eisenhower or that schmuck Montgomery. Felix couldn't stay on his bunk. He paced the room, retelling their fantastic hypotheses and trading them for more. He then proposed it was the Führer himself, though many fell quiet at this prospect. Max so wanted to tell them: It was Doktor Solar, of course.

Outside, boots crunched on the pathway pebbles. Lieutenants came and called selected men out, one at a time. In Max's barrack these were mostly the sailors. Zoock got the call. They returned smiling and grinning, holding their caps at their waists like wedding bouquets. They fended off all inquiries. "I can't tell what it's all about but just you wait and see," Zoock said, bouncing on the balls of his feet.

At evening mess cases of beer were set out and each barrack got enough for three bottles a man. They hauled off the cases, and back in the barrack, they settled down to long card games and talk of busty pinup girls. Max sipped from his second bottle, holed up in the darkness of his lower bunk. He was certain he'd get the call. Could it be his association with Pielau? Or his looks? Perhaps he was too handsome for the role.

An hour before lights out, the door flew open and Captain Rattner filled the doorway, his hands on his hips and his cap set at a jaunty angle. "Kaspar! Come with!"

About time, Max thought. Then his heart started knocking at his ribs and his legs went weak. The men helped him. They cheered and clapped as he passed, the cigarettes hanging from their mouths. Felix stomped his feet and hollered. At the door, Max gave them a merry bow. Hadn't he been in this spot many times—the last act on?

Outside, the wind pulled the door out of his hand and slammed it shut. The gusts stung his cheeks. All was dark. "Ready?" Captain Rattner said. He stood against the wall, slouched in a manner Max had never seen. It was almost, well, American.

"Certainly, sir." Max saluted.

Rattner only tapped his heels together, as Pielau used to do. "Time to meet Doktor Solar," he said and strode off.

Was it a test? Max blocked out the response. He started walking. Waited a beat. "Who, sir?"

Rattner pivoted and faced Max, waiting for him to catch up. He pulled two cigarettes and lit them in his mouth. "A crack answer," he said, and inserted a cigarette between Max's lips. "Just the sort of acting talent we'll need in the days to come."

In a corner of camp, deep in a small wood, stood a stout villa with large ornate wrought-iron lamps and gate. Parked outside were the shiny command car and motorcycles. Max heard the crunching feet of guards but couldn't see them.

Rattner led Max through to the front steps. "On your own —for now," he said and patted Max on the back.

The front door opened. An SS adjutant in a white coat and gray gloves led Max through a marble foyer and down carpeted hallways with floral wallpaper and polished wainscoting. The adjutant left Max in a den lined with dark wood bookshelves. A fire crackled in a broad stone fireplace and deep, wide leather chairs sat before it. A standup antique globe in the corner. Orchids stood on a buffet and Max could smell them. He walked over and breathed them in.

Footsteps. In the hall someone said, "Kaspar." Max stepped away from the flowers.

An SS officer—a lieutenant colonel—strode in and they shared a quick salute. "Evening, Corporal Kaspar," the lieutenant colonel said and, to Max's surprise, shook Max's hand with both hands. He was well over six feet tall and Max had to look up to meet his eyes. His rugged face had a deep scar down one cheek, a line that ran from ear to mouth to chin. This was his *Schmiss*—his dueling scar. He could only be SS Lieutenant Colonel Otto Skorzeny, the crack commando who'd freed Hitler's Italian ally Mussolini from a mountaintop prison. In Germany, now, men like this were the real stars.

Skorzeny beamed at Max as if reading his thoughts. "Please, sit," he said and they took the leather chairs by the fire. The dueling scars glistened orange as the fire's warmth worked its way through Max's crusty, coarse uniform. Only his fine clothes would really do here, he regretted. At least no women were here to see him like this.

"So. Captain Pielau is out of the picture," Skorzeny said.

He'd said it like a producer announcing a casting change. It could mean anything. "Out?" Max said.

"Dead. Yes. He's dead."

Dead? The flames were warming Max's cheeks, stretching them tight. He felt weary. He couldn't think.

"Went on leave, died in an air raid," Skorzeny added plainly as if ordering a salad with his entrée.

Max shook his head. He liked Pielau. Truly. And in the long run, Pielau might have made things easier. He might even have gotten Max out of this altogether, if things got too hot. "That's t-t-terrible," Max stammered, "Why, Captain Pielau, he—"

"You mean 'von Pielau'? Isn't that what you mean? Eh, *Herr* Maximilian von Kaspar?" Skorzeny chuckled.

Before Max could answer Skorzeny barked, "Arno! Make it two." Skorzeny grinned for Max. "I do hope you like cognac."

"What? Oh, yes, naturally."

"The problem with Pielau was the man was too naive. You mustn't be too hopeful in life, even in your most private dreams. Mustn't even be optimistic. You'll start believing your own bullshit. You see?"

"Yes. Yes," Max said, stalling for the right line.

"One must be rational. Work things out. Wait and see. Give nothing away. And shut his trap, for God's sake." Skorzeny's lips tightened as if he wanted to spit. His big hands met and folded into each other and he held them there, like a priest considering a misbehaved acolyte. "The most perplexing problem with Pielau was he wanted others to believe his own bullshit."

"One should keep one's own bullshit to one's self," Max said.

"Precisely. It's a personal matter. Spiritual, if you like."

Max nodded, shifting in the warm leather. When was that cognac coming? Perhaps this was the famed Skorzeny's unique brand of torture—offer a thirsty man a fine drink and then watch him suffer when it never comes. Max's thoughts were piling up fast, colliding. Pielau was probably put up to a firing squad, if he weren't in some Gestapo prison. Skorzeny himself had probably ordered it. Though you could never tell from the way the lieutenant colonel was entertaining Max in this bourgeois villa. His nasally Vienna accent didn't fit his brutal physique in the least. His eyes sparkled as he spoke. A definite charmer. Yet so was the Marquis de Sade. "Spiritual," Max added. The fire seemed to grow hotter. The sweat itched under his hair.

"Feel free to unbutton your tunic, Corporal."

"Right. Thank you." The unbuttoning helped. Max also took his cap off and hung it on a chair to warm—that would come in handy in the cold barrack. Good thinking. He was coming around.

Skorzeny continued, "We cannot—will not—tolerate leaks or dissension from within the unit. Traitors could be anywhere. Turncoats. American spies. The mission must be protected. Certain types, they resort to their own ways, and ends. Think they know better."

The adjutant was standing over Max, offering him a cognac. The glass was oversized and warmed. Max drank from it. It went down as fine as he imagined, all fumes and caramels. He wiped the sweat from his forehead.

"Let's get you away from this fire," Skorzeny said and stood. Max followed him across the room cradling his glass. Skorzeny opened wall-to-floor red curtains, revealing French doors. They looked out at the black night full of twinkles from snow falling. "Most men here, they volunteered," Skorzeny said. "But you? They say you can act and sing in English. You did just that in America. So you see we had to send for you, find you at all costs. You're our German Chevalier, what?"

"Ah, if only . . . Let's call me our German Kaspar for now." Max fought a blush. "In any case—had I seen the order for volunteers, sir, I certainly would have—"

"You're one of the few who didn't see it." Skorzeny slapped at the door glass, his face hard and his eyes black with rage. "An uncoded order goes out to all German units, on all fronts, soliciting English speakers? What were those twits thinking? Surely Allied intelligence saw it. Might as well have put an ad in *The New Yorker Time.*"

"*New York Times,*" Max blurted in English. "—Sir," he added in German.

"Certainly. Now here's the thing, Kaspar—I'm putting together a special unit culled from the troops here. Cast, if you will, with the best American speakers. Sort of a spearhead force. Most of the sailors are in. Get the picture? Just the production for you. Sort of a, shall we say, a touring show. Ha ha. You're in, of course?"

It wasn't really a question, of course. How could it be? Max was the one who'd auditioned, yet he didn't even know the script. A special unit, Skorzeny said. It was already top secret. If Max said no, he could very well end up like Pielau —on leave and caught in the next air raid. Still, he had to admit? it couldn't hurt the plan he had in his head, the one he'd been developing in the dim obscurity of his lower bunk. It had him sliding through on just enough ability, and then? Perhaps, somehow, he could get far enough behind the US front lines. Get to New York if the role had any legs at all. That was where he belonged. Hadn't he told himself that so many times? Germany had fooled him. The Fatherland was a trickster. Promised success and a grand life but delivered the Grim Reaper and a *Götterdämmerung*. He could go AWOL. Defect. Hopefully he wouldn't have to fire a shot. It was to be the greatest role in his life. It was indeed true what the masters said of the best performances—they had to be lived.

Max's eyes had filled with wet heat. He glared off toward the fire.

"I can see you're moved." Skorzeny was rocking on his heels. "What if I was to tell you what's next, eh? Give you a taste. Could you keep it mum?"

Max's head and shoulders rose up, with fervor. "You forget, I'm an actor, sir."

"Yes, I was just thinking that . . ." Skorzeny studied Max, tapping a thick finger at his cognac glass. "Despite that, I think I'll trust you. We start with a test run. Any day. We're running a number of you out in teams. Various speaking levels. Could be dangerous."

"Teams?" Max said. It was the only word that sounded harmless.

"That's right. Teams of four. You're probably a good judge of abilities, by the way. Anyone you'd like along?"

Max thought a moment. Stalled. "Is Captain Rattner going?" He was taking a chance here, but he had to find out.

"Who? God no. Man can barely say thank you in English. Besides, I need him here getting the men in shape. More than a few butts need kicking—"

"In that case—I propose Corporal Menning. He's in my barrack. Spent time in America. Physically, he's got it down. He was once a circus performer, so he understands the American body language like few here do—"

"Ah, yes. The Americans, they're always slouching, yes? Hands in their pockets and such?" Skorzeny chuckled again. "Very well. Anyone else?"

"Zoock. One of the sailors."

"You'll have him." Skorzeny grinned again.

Max wanted to grin too. In another time, they might have got on well. Skorzeny would have made a bulldog producer of the first class.

Instead, Max looked up somberly. "Permission to speak, sir?"

Skorzeny nodded, the grin fading.

"What are we up to? We're not doing *Babes in Arms*, I take it?"

Skorzeny laughed, as Max anticipated—even soldiers liked the show biz talk. "Don't they wish, some of the hams we've attracted here. You'll see soon enough. We're aiming to put the fear back into the Americans. And with any luck, might just make them shit their pants."

"Excellent. That's genius, sir."

They drank in silence. Skorzeny opened his mouth as if to say more. Instead, he held up a finger and pressed it to Max's chest pocket. "There is one matter. This old army kit of yours is a shambles. I'm putting you in Waffen-SS uniform—if we pull this off, it might just be good for propaganda."

Waffen-SS? So what if the pay was better. This was not part of the plan at all and certainly not good for the role. There was nothing more feared and hated than the SS, even within Germany.

"But sir, the army treats me fine," Max muttered. Think, Max, think.

"Nonsense. We'll do the swearing in if—when—you get back." Skorzeny clicked his heels and gave the full Hitler salute, his arm ramrod straight. "Corporal Kaspar, you are hereby inducted."

No choice. Max clicked his heels and returned the silly salute, and yet he added a little bow for the memory of Maximilian von Kaspar. Cognac splashed on his wrist. What a waste, he thought.

Five

Two mornings later at 3:30 a.m. sixteen of them crammed in the back of an Opel troop truck and headed out on their test mission. They kept the rear tarp closed tight and huddled for warmth as the road jostled them, black figures in the dark, yawning at the floorboards, in and out of half-sleep. At least I'm off the Eastern Front, Max thought. At least he was keeping Germany's gruesome end at arm's length. As long as he did that, hope lived for him. His deliverance would reveal itself.

They'd go in as four teams of four. Max got Felix, the sailor Zoock, and a young army orderly named Braun, who had floppy ears and a fleshy nose he hadn't grown into. In their fifteen-minute briefing the previous evening, Captain Rattner had called out their American disguise names:

"Kaspar! Your name is—Mike Kopp. First Sergeant. You drove a tank."

"Zoock! Your name—Jim Zook. Technical Corporal. Artillery."

"Felix Menning? Fred Musser. Private First Class. Infantry."

"Braun!—for you it's Roger Braun. Private First Class. Infantry."

The German-American names would explain any language problems, Rattner had assured them. They got dog tags, American uniforms, and blue handkerchiefs.

Max, for one, could not play a part without some understanding of the character. In all his time in America he'd never even seen an American soldier. So he held up a hand. "I think I can speak for all when I say that we've got some questions. Where's my character from? America's a vast land. And what does he want, this Mike Kopp? Need. Crave? Does this Mike Kopp have a wife and child back home? A farm? A pet fish perhaps—"

"Spare us the thespian jerk-off," Rattner snarled.

"What about these blue hankies, sir?" Zoock said.

"I'm getting to that. This is crucial. If it gets too dicey you'll use the signal—your blue handkerchiefs—to extricate yourselves."

Extricate? It made them sound more like guinea pigs than some spearhead elite. "Sir, I don't know the first thing about a tank. Really, how can I be expected to play this?"

"You're not gonna be in a tank," Felix interrupted— thoroughly out of line. And Rattner said, "Exactly. What, baby actor boy doesn't like his lines? So improvise, Kaspar—that's the whole point . . ."

There were perks. They now had American uniforms— for Max, tankers coveralls and windbreaker, a wool GI overcoat that was too short for his taste but thick as a blanket, a warm cap, and decent boots. Felix got the standard GI field jacket, wool pullover sweater and a knit helmet liner cap—a "beanie," the *Amis* called it. Felix liked his beanie—"makes even my toes warmer," he said, and he even liked the sound of the word.

Two hours into the journey, and still pitch dark out. They were traveling on smoother road now—a mild thump every few seconds, which Max took for an autobahn. Few of them slept. Rocking and rubbing their cold hands together, they muttered their memorized identities to themselves. And they spoke English, frantically and all at once, trying things out.

"Send us out like this?" Zoock was saying in English. "Here's your hat what's your hurry—what kinda bull is that? Really putting our dicks on the table if you ask me."

Max, Felix and Braun gaped.

"Right. My thoughts exactly," Max said.

Zoock spat. "Ah, fuggetaboudit—whaterya gonna do?"

And Braun opened his mouth but came up with nothing.

"Look what rags they gave me?" Felix said, tugging at his sweater. "Can you believe it?"

"No, I can hardly believe it," Max said. "What a mess you look."

And Braun blurted: "Roger Braun, Private First Class, serial number three-two-two-four-seven-three-nine-four."

They sounded like madmen. They were madmen. Soon they fell into a grim silence. Quite a long way from Doktor Solar's cozy camp villa, Max thought. He had returned from there with that warmed cognac smile on his face, just like the others. Then it wore off so quickly when lights out came. Of course, everyone who had an appointment with the "Doktor" received the same treatment. That sly Skorzeny probably didn't finish one complete glass of cognac the whole night—Arno the adjutant just kept topping off the same glass. Put him in a special unit? Induct him into the Waffen-SS? Skorzeny was only making it harder on Max. This was why he kept Felix close to him. Felix may be playing the keen one now, but what about when they were in a real pinch?

Zoock was teaching Braun how to say "squirrel"—one of the hardest English words for a German.

Felix nudged Max. "For this you have volunteered me," he whispered in English. "Didn't you not?"

"I haven't the faintest idea what you're talking about, young man."

"Yes, you do. You hoped to protect me away from Captain Rattner—or him from me, I should say."

"What? Well, I—"

"It's okay," Felix said. "Actually, I find myself glad you did. And do you know why that is? That day when Zoock wanted to hit me? You moved to help me. No one does this. I'll not forget that ever. I always had to fend for myself, you see?"

"Oh? It was nothing. Still, I regret I failed to do anything about Rattner."

"Please, I beg you. Who could?"

Zoock was shaking his head at them. He slapped a hand to his forehead.

"What?" Max said. He turned back to Felix. "You know, your accent is good but you need to work on your word order."

"Thank you," Felix said. "I will. And as for you," he added, smiling, "I'm not so sure you speak like the tank drivers."

They fell silent again. One by one, they tried on their blue SOS handkerchiefs. Max tied his around his neck. Felix wrapped his around his wrist, and Zoock let his hang out a back pocket. And Braun blew his nose into his.

"Mike, Mike." It was Felix, nudging Max. Max had fallen asleep, his head back against the truck's tarp roof. He remembered—his name was Mike now, Mike Kopp. "Mike, wake yourself," Felix was saying.

"It's 'wake up'—not 'wake yourself.' Get with it," Zoock said.

They had the rear tarp pulled up. It brought a chilling wind and the gray morning light. They saw guard towers with spotlights and high barbwire fences, surrounding a barracks camp that seemed to stretch across the horizon. The truck was turning around and backing up, the gears jolting, and a barbwire gate opened for them. A sign read: "Stammlager VII A."

The German guards walked shepherd dogs—"German shepherds" to Americans—along the barbwire fences. The truck halted. A guard peeked in. They waited, listening to more voices and gates closing. "Prisoners, inside!" someone shouted in German.

"Roger Braun, Roger Braun," Braun muttered, hugging himself from the cold.

And Felix gave Max a careful rub on the shoulder as if, Max couldn't help thinking, Max was a child and it was his first day of school.

Stammlager VII A was a POW camp for American enlisted men—for GIs, in *Ami* words. As falsified new prisoners, the sixteen were herded into a hut with a sign that read "Interrogation." Windows were boarded shut, but enough light showed through the seams between the boards. They got a quick briefing and some stale coffee. "The camp guards know of you and of your blue hankies," an elderly German captain told them, "but you should not rely on a soul. Clear, boys? Now don't fuck up our lives too much."

The captain gave them cards showing their barracks numbers. Max's group got 13. The captain left, and some of them fell asleep sitting up. They awoke to a far-off voice barking at measured intervals. "I'm guessing that's roll call," Zoock said.

"Roll call?" someone said.

"'*Appell.*' Stand up and be counted. Shit, are we in for it."

Footsteps. The door flew open bringing a shaft of daylight. Two guards in overcoats stared at them from the doorway. They were middle aged with old-fashioned Hitler-style mustaches. One waved his hand as if to say, come on, come on. The other yelled "*Herauf! Raus! Raus raus schnell!*"—for the benefit, Max figured, of any American prisoners listening on the other side of the fence.

Daylight hit them like stage lights and they had to shield their eyes. Yet this helped the role—made them look like prisoners. The guards began a fast march toward the front gate, not bad for two old guys, and Max and the rest had to shuffle out in front. More guards joined in. All were older, it seemed, with the same stubborn look of aging schoolmasters or streetcar conductors. One shouted, "Have a nice stay, *Meine Herren*," and they laughed. Max and the rest stared in shock as if they didn't understand.

Guards opened the camp gate and let them through. Before them, about a hundred feet away, stretched the largest horde of unkempt men Max had ever seen, all dressed in various shades of olive drab and brown. American GI Prisoners of War.

They'd sent them in right at the end of roll call. A wave of prisoners was moving toward them. A thousand eyes on them. Max never had such an audience. They plodded on toward the horde, deeper into camp. Zoock slouched and thrust his hands in his pockets, and Max did the same. Body language was everything. "Loosen your backs, stoop your shoulders, that's it," Max whispered to Felix and Braun.

The wave of prisoners began to form a loose gauntlet. Max could make out faces, the abundance of hardy Nordic features. They looked young but haggard and unwashed, like the "Okies" from *The Grapes of Wrath*. How far they all were from Kansas, Iowa, Nebraska.

Max, Zoock, Felix and Braun stuck close together while the rest of the sixteen broke off into their groups of four, off in search of their barracks. No one looked back. "Good riddance," Zoock muttered. He'd taken the lead. They were passing through the gauntlet, the prisoners lining up for a look.

"Where ya from, Joe?" someone shouted.

Max hadn't decided. Somewhere no one was from was best. He blurted "Idaho" and realized he probably couldn't find it on a map. Was it a state? Or was that Iowa?

"New Jersey—where else is there?" Zoock was shouting. Felix and Braun didn't try. They walked with their heads hung. Suddenly they were fine slouches.

They passed barracks, long rectangular buildings of graying wood. Max peered at the white numbers above each door. They passed Barrack 4, then 5. The gauntlet stretched on.

"What they do, boys, do yer laundry?"

Their uniforms were far cleaner than those of the prisoners. "No. How dare they," Max said and stomped to show he meant this—whatever it was he said.

"Oooh, get him," someone shot back, flapping a wrist. Men laughed.

"Hey Mac, how'd you all score a shave?"

They were clean-shaven, too. So many blunders.

"Good luck," Zoock said. "See how lucky we are?"

More laughs. The four kept walking, determined as if walking was the only thing not giving them away. Max patted Zoock's back, pushing him along. A couple men were shaking their heads. They picked up the pace, passing barracks 8, 9, 10, and the gauntlet thinned.

Barrack 13. The door was open. They strode up the steps and in. The long and vast one-story structure was so crammed it looked like the inside of a messy closet after a great quake. Zoock charged on into this mess and the other three followed, dodging the many obstacles. The double wooden bunks of cheap, splintering wood. The chairs and tables so undersized they could have been built for *Kinder*— these stood everywhere, at every possible angle. Laundry hung on lines strewn in all directions, forcing them to duck every few feet. Piles of blankets and cans and boxes, so many rough edges and barriers. Max caught a shin on a bunk corner; Felix held onto a bunk ladder and got a sliver; Braun staggered into a pile of wood scraps and sent them flying.

The barrack was empty of occupants as best as they could tell. No one had followed them. "Where are we going?" Max said finally, and Zoock stopped them about halfway through. They stared at each other.

Felix threw up his hands. "Where does one sleep?"

"I am so tired," Braun said, his eyes wide, his face ashen. "I am Roger-er."

The clop-clop-clop of footsteps and the front door swung open with a grating creak. The barracks' occupants filed in. Max and the three turned to them showing broad smiles that felt strained and sickly on their faces.

A short and wiry American with black curly hair led the line of prisoners, which seemed to number at least forty and they kept coming. The curly-haired prisoner touched and stroked every angle and corner he passed as if this grim barrack was his beloved submarine and he the commander. Max thought of saluting but saw no visible rank on the curly-haired one, so he waved. The man nodded, kept coming. His jaw had hard angles, just like the bunks. His skin was pocked. His exact age, unknowable—somewhere between mid-twenties and late thirties? Five feet away now. Max held out a hand and the man shook it. Max held up the card with "13" on it.

"Morning," he said. "Mike Kopp. It would seem we're your new guests."

"That it would. How-do, Kopp. Cozy, huh? These huts were built for twenty. With you boys, that makes it about sixty." The curly-haired man had a strange accent to Max—it was slow and rich, taking its time. He placed it somewhere in the American Southwest.

"At least sixty," Zoock said, staring at the men still filing in.

"Say, could ya try the next hotel?" a prisoner said from behind the curly-haired leader. It was a joke. Satire. Irony. American jokes were like that. Max blurted a laugh and the rest followed, overdoing it.

The curly-haired one never gave his name, Max realized. It seemed very un-American. The prisoners gathered around the four, filling the barracks and cutting off the only exit. If trouble started there'd be little chance of calling for guards, for showing the blue hankies. Then again, the *Amis* would have to be smarter than just attack them. That would only bring greater punishment. All these thoughts raced through Max's head as the curly-haired one asked the standard questions. Where ya from? How's the front? They rough you up any?

Braun's accent was showing, so Max explained that the private was from a German community in Minnesota. "Braun, that bumpkin," Zoock blurted, then something about Braun being Amish, and Max hoped that didn't make the curly-haired one suspicious, since most Amish people lived in Pennsylvania, Ohio, Indiana.

"What's the word? We really home by Christmas?" a prisoner said.

"I cannot see why not," Max said. "Look, we have the krauts on the run. We took back Aachen, the last I have heard. We're in Germany now. Must be only a matter of time." Max played this up, smiling and slapping his hands together.

Zoock, Felix, and Braun stared, grimacing. It wasn't widely known inside Germany that the war was going that badly. Pielau had told Max. Pielau listened to the BBC.

"Let you get settled some," the curly-haired one said and stepped aside. Prisoners were clearing off a double bunk for Max and the other three. It meant they would have to double up or find places on the floor. Depressing. Were they going out of their way to keep them together? Could they be isolating them?

The Americans left them to their new bunk, and the barrack routines began. Men played cards, read, napped, wrote postcard letters. Many knitted, to Max's wonder—it turned out the Red Cross sent balls of yarn and needles, of all things. And Max noticed the smell of this place—a gritty, oily, greasy aroma that had worked itself into everything. At least the odors of the front were different every day, while this place had the same stale reek all the time.

Soon Zoock was sleeping up on the top bunk, and so deeply that he snored. This seemed to bother no one but Max. Braun curled up on the floor before the bunk, like an old dog. Before long he slid under the bottom bunk facing the wall, which also seemed to bother no one. Meanwhile, Felix flipped through old US magazines and spoke with Max in English, but they found little to talk about that was harmless. Max thought it best to be interested in the POWs' world, so he called a young private over and started asking questions about life in a prison camp. The private was helpful, but most of his answers involved slang not even Zoock could have known. "Ferrets" were guards who came at unexpected times and searched the barrack for contraband or tunnels. "Readers" were select POWs who listened to the BBC secretly and visited various barracks, updating the men on the war. "Goons" were the German guards, most of whom had wacky nicknames such as "Schmuck Mug" and "Turkey Neck." And Max asked about the smell—POWs only got showers twice a month and usually cold water at that.

At mess the four endured more questions and avoided the petrified stares of the other German undercover GIs. Their meal was a thin gray soup and some dry brown bread. Back in the barrack Max pretended to nap on the bottom bunk, his eyes cracked just enough to watch the prisoners. Men stared and studied them, and others seemed to talk about them in dark corners. All the while, the barrack seemed to have many visitors who sat with the curly-haired one.

Evening came to the barrack, at long last. The electric lights came on, brown and flickering. Braun was back on the floor under the bunk. Zoock and Felix watched prisoners play a card game called Blackjack. Prisoners tossed an oblong American football down the long room yet managed to hit nothing, not even a clothesline. Someone put on a record—Django Reinhardt playing "Stardust," of all things, and other men began dancing. Max thought of joining them. That could be fun.

The curly-haired one was standing before Max. He was not smiling. Max opened his eyes fully and smiled.

"Have a seat," the curly-haired one said. He nodded toward a table two bunks down—well out of earshot of Zoock, Max thought. Men had been knitting at the table. Now they were clearing away their yarn and needles.

Max stopped smiling. "All right."

Max's knees banged at the bottom of the table. They sat opposite each other. "Must be your office, I take it," Max said.

Curly-haired nodded. "Espinoza."

Was this a slang word? Max nodded.

"I never told you my name. It's Espinoza. Manny Espinoza."

"Oh, right. Kopp. Mike Kopp."

"So you told me. I'm a First Sergeant too, Kopp. Not that rank matters much inside Thirteen." Espinoza lit a Lucky Strike, and aromas of fine Virginia tobacco filled Max's nostrils—better smokes in here than Germans had at home.

Espinoza handed Max the cigarette. "Splendid," Max said. "Thanks."

"Thank the Red Cross." Espinoza watched Max smoke, then hand the Lucky back. "You new kriegies are always cause for excitement. And some head-scratching."

"Kriegies?"

"Short for *Kriegsgefangene*—POW—just another kraut word that's about three syllables too long."

Back over at the bunk men had gathered around Zoock and Felix, peppering them with questions. A couple others were talking to Braun, who was still under the bunk.

"I can't imagine why heads are scratching," Max said. "We're just average Joes."

"Yeah." Espinoza picked tobacco from his front teeth. He watched the men talking to Zoock, Felix, and Braun.

Say something, Max. Anything. "Say, what's your unit?" Max said.

"Super Sixth." Espinoza added a smile—the tobacco still between teeth.

Super Sixth?—Max needed more, a clue. He smiled.

"Sixth Armored," Espinoza said.

Max slapped a knee. "Hey, I'm from the Armored Forces too." The Armored forces? What was he saying? "I'm a tanker, I mean. Second Armored—'Hell on Wheels.'" It said it on his sleeve patch. "See here?"

"Knew a lug in that outfit," someone said, off behind Max. They had good ears in here. "Oh?" Max said, not looking back. "Swell."

"Knew a couple guys," Espinoza said. "More than a couple, fact. Lot a guys come through here since '43. I been in that long. On account a Tunisia. That and a wily kraut named Rommel. You?"

"Siegfried Line," Max said. Hoping it was vague enough.

"What's yer hot box?"

Max stared.

"Your hot box. Tank. Panzer, krauts call it. You know."

"Sure, sure. Hearing's not the best, sorry. It was a Sherman."

Espinoza stared. Now he needed more.

"Drove the goddamn, mothersuckin', thing," Max added. "It was hot in there, boy. Steamy."

"Steamy. Right . . ."

How long was this to go on? Max gazed over at the men dancing. "You probably got a theater in camp? I would like to help out. Keep my mind off things."

Espinoza didn't answer. Someone had handed him a metal mug. He passed it to Max and nodded. Max drank. It burned and Max's eyes welled up and his head became light, as if a woman's hands were cradling it. Someone laughed, a piercing cackle—probably the cad who brewed this swill, Max thought.

"Potato likker," Espinoza said. "Well?"

"Think it tastes of petrol," Max said, swallowing hard. "But she'll do the trick."

Espinoza drank. "Petrol? You mean gasoline." He smoked and inhaled deep, and he leaned forward, across the table. He exhaled as he spoke, into Max's face. "Here's the thing, Petrol. We're having a little ball game tomorrow out on the *Sportplatz*. Why don't you play?"

"Ball game?"

"Baseball. That's the kinda game for us tankers, all we ever played and I'm sure it was the same in your outfit."

Baseball. A small white ball and a club-like hitter called a bat. Some men hit the white ball and others stood around waiting to catch it. Lou Gehrig. Babe Ruth. Brooklyn Dodgers.

"Your friends are in," Espinoza added. "My pals are making sure of that right now. Fact, it's something of a tradition here for the new Kriegies."

A crowd had surrounded the other three. New York Yankees. Home run. How many bases were run, Max wasn't sure. But he knew one thing: Americans played their baseball in the summertime, not in the winter.

He reached for the potato schnapps. "Baseball, hey," he stammered, "That sure beats the dancing, doesn't it?"

Six

The next morning after roll call Max, Zoock, Felix, and Braun used the cover of a heavy fog to meet outside behind the latrine shed. Icicles hung from the roof. Steam puffed out their mouths as they spoke, and they hopped in place for warmth—all except Braun. Dark thoughts must have oppressed him during the night. He moved lazily, as if a zombie, and his blond locks hung in his face, a truly wretched version of the model Hitler Youth he'd likely been once.

"It's no use," he blurted in German. "These brutes had us fingered the minute we come through the gate."

Zoock punched him hard on the arm. "Where's your English? What the fuck's wrong with you? Don't you wanna make it outta here in one piece?" Braun muttered something. Zoock lunged at Braun. Max and Felix jumped between them.

"It's not here I'm worried about," Braun said, slumping against the gray, frozen planks of shed wall. "It's what comes after."

"Gentlemen! We need whispering," Max said in English.

"All right, all right." Zoock turned to Max. "So. What kinda questions that Espinoza ask you last night?"

"The standard things, you know. Seems he only wanted to hear me talking—"

Zoock spat. "He wanted confirmation, you mean—that there's something fishy. Probably takes you for our leader. You got that look, sure. All spiffy-like. That's why they isolated you. They're targeting you."

"Me? My God." Again, not what Max wanted. Obscurity was the plan. Yet he had certain gifts, and what can one do about nature? He threw up his hands.

"Don't give me that. It's that way you talk, too—like the swell in some picture show."

"The what?" Felix broke a smile. Max gasped at him. Zoock took a deep breath and faced the three of them. His bushy red eyebrows had thickened with an icy frost. "Now look, boys, this baseball thing has gotta be a trick. A test. Luckily, I've played some ball in my time, so just do what I do. Got me?"

"I got you, yes," Max said.

"Got ya," Felix said, his beanie pulled down low on his forehead. He too knew baseball, he'd whispered to Max during the night. In America, with the circus, it was all the men did between shows besides drink, play cards, and make passes at the midget women. He'd said, "This baseball is strange, an agonizingly slow game marked by rare—and not nearly enough—moments of extreme excitement and panic. It's a taunt and I despise it."

And Braun? He nodded for Zoock and stammered in English, "I will, yes, do my best, sir. I want you to make it out in the one piece."

Zoock cocked his head at Braun, smiling. "That's better. Okay." He gave the kid a rub on the head.

The four stared at each other, breathing steam, in silence. As if on cue, all felt for their blue SOS hankies, but cautiously as if about to draw guns in a Western movie.

Espinoza and a crowd of prisoners were waiting for Max, Zoock, Felix, and Braun in front of Barrack 13. On the front steps were a bundle of baseball bats, a bucket of balls, and a duffel bag. Espinoza had on an oversized leather glove that made him look as if he had elephantiasis of the hand—it was a "baseball glove," Max realized. A prisoner was throwing a ball at Espinoza fast and hard from about twenty feet away. The ball traveled in a straight line. Espinoza caught it in his big glove with a slap and flung it back for another go, and another, and another. They did this mechanically, yet rhythmically, like automatons. One of the prisoners made a clucking sound. As Espinoza turned to see Max and the three walking up, the thrower accidentally released another pitch —and yet Espinoza still caught the hardball with his bare hand. Max and the three passed through the crowd. No one mentioned the blue hankies on their arms. Not even a glance.

"Boys. Morning. Ready?" Espinoza said.

"You betcha," Zoock said. "Let's do it," Felix said.

"Nice catch," Max said.

Espinoza tossed a ball underhanded at Max, who ducked. In the same instant, Braun lunged—and caught the ball a foot from Max's forehead. "Thanks," Max mumbled as Zoock and Felix gaped in wonder.

"Top-notch, kid," Espinoza said, and exchanged glances with a couple of his most trusted prisoners.

The light morning snow settled over the icy ground. The men slid and skated on the slippery powder as they trudged on over to the *Sportplatz*, tossing balls and swinging bats. The fog had cleared, revealing high clouds. A harsh white daylight reflected off the snow and the ice. The *Sportplatz* occupied a far corner of camp. Guard towers surrounded it on three sides. Prisoners laid out the diamond-shaped baseball field. At each angle of the diamond, frozen burlap sandbags served as the bases. Espinoza clapped like a stage director, and the men gathered around, shuffling their feet. He pointed to bases and said, "Okay. That's home, first, second, third. Outfield, all the way to the fence . . ."

This *Spiel* called baseball was coming back to Max—from home base, the "batters" hit at the "pitcher's" throw, sending the ball out into the "outfield." There was one problem Max saw. At the outfield's far edge stood the so-called Warning Rail, a one-foot high bar of wood that ran the length of the camp's two tall parallel fences of barbwire. The five-foot gap between the rail and the fences was a no-man's land. Signs along the Warning Rail read:

ANYONE MOVING OVER THIS BARRIER WILL BE SHOT

"Questions later," someone had scribbled on one of the signs.

Espinoza was still shouting out instructions, his voice a pitch higher in the cold air. At the edge of the crowd, Max looked to Felix and nodded toward the Warning Rail. Zoock and Braun were doing the same. All their eyes met. Zoock gave Max a shrug.

One of the prisoners raised his hand high and cleared his throat, as if on cue. Espinoza waved for him to speak. "What if the ball goes past the Warning Rail?" the prisoner said.

"Then you go an' get it. Right? You know the drill. Goons won't shoot at us for fetching some measly ole' Red Cross baseball. What do they care?"

Was it really the drill? Zoock's instincts were dead on. This was more than a game, and everyone knew it—any real American prisoner would already know how to handle the Warning Rail.

Two thick-necked prisoners were standing next to Max. One grinned at him and said, "That's okay with the likes a youse, ain't it, pal?" The other one patted Max on the back. "Sure, sure, okay by him," this one said. Both wore arm patches for the Second Armored Division, Max now saw.

"Okay by me," Max said.

"Sounds good," other prisoners were saying, nodding along and trading smiles, "Sure thing," and, "Checkaroo, Sarge." Others patted Zoock, Felix, and Braun on the back.

"Because the goons up there? They trust us. And we trust them," Espinoza said. Max looked up at the guard towers, one, two, and three. He saw dark outlines of helmets, and made out the long barrels of MG 34 machine guns.

"Krauts ain't even watchin' anyways," a prisoner said. "They hate baseball."

Were they watching? Max couldn't tell. He didn't see any binoculars. He peered around the ground in desperation, his shoulders tensing up, not caring if his fear was obvious. Out on the grounds, there were no guards anywhere near them. And Max found it tough to swallow, as if one of those hard baseballs were lodged in his throat.

If only the four of them could meet again, come up with a plan. Behind the home base another crowd of prisoners gathered to watch, no more than thirty. Max looked for other undercover GIs but saw none. Even Zoock seemed seized by shock. He stared at his feet, his hands deep in his pockets.

Espinoza split up teams. Zoock and Felix ended up on the team batting first, while Max and Braun ended up on Espinoza's team. Espinoza was their pitcher.

Max's throat was constricting as if filled with a swelling, sticking yeast. Desperate acts blazed in his brain. This was no place for him to try to defect. What if one of them feigned illness? Or simply started running and calling for guards? What could happen? The problem was, Max and his three weren't the only undercover fools in camp. Someone could catch a knife or a poison in the confusion. Max's whole abdomen area rolled and thumped, great big butterflies in there flapping and scraping at his ribs, stomach walls, intestines.

He had to get a hold of himself. As he always did before going on stage, he closed his eyes a moment and breathed deep. The tower guards would see the blue hankies, he told himself, sure they would. Probably already had.

In the duffel bag were more of the baseball gloves—some made from pillows cut up and re-sewn. Espinoza passed them out. Max and Braun each got one. The other team led Zoock and Felix away, and Max's team huddled around Espinoza, hopping up and down for warmth and punching fists into gloved hands. It was all happening too fast. Espinoza barked orders and plays in words that Max couldn't understand.

"Kopp, Braun—you got outfield too," Espinoza was saying, "Kopp center and Braun the left."

Max nodded, his big glove hanging off his trembling hand.

"Okey-doke, coach," Braun said and slapped at his glove.

Espinoza went to the duffel bag and pulled out jersey tops dyed blue. "Looks like we're the blue team again," he said and handed them out. And he winked at Max.

In the harsh white snow light, the blue tops would wash out the blue hankies completely. Max thought of running now, but Braun nudged him and took him aside. He helped him with his jersey, pulling it over his head for him. The kid's heroic change of attitude was astounding. He had pushed the hair out of his eyes, he was smiling now, and he gave Max a rub on the shoulder. "I played this game, too—one of the few things I like from America," he whispered in German. "You're going to be all right, Kaspar."

Over near home base, Zoock and Felix's team were pulling on red jerseys and swinging bats. Zoock and Felix made no moves to run. They were all on their own.

Max and Braun followed the third outfielder far out past the bases, yet they stopped far short of the Warning Rail. About 75 yards stretched between Max's back and the Warning Rail. Quite a distance, he thought. He hoped.

First inning. Max watched from his spot, the snow crunching cold under his feet. The blue players around him murmured a strange chant—"eh batta eh batta eh . . ."

Espinoza threw. A red player swung at pitches and missed. One out. Next up. This red player hit the ball low. It skipped past a diving Espinoza and right for Braun, who, again to Max's wonder, scooped the ball up and flung it straight to the first base as the running hitter slipped and fell on a patch of ice.

A cheer went up from the crowd. Braun gave a little bow and doffed an imaginary cap for Espinoza, who gawked from the pitcher's mound, his arms slack at his sides. So this kid Braun was a ball player. It could save them. He could prove they were Americans. Max punched his fist in his glove and shuffled his feet.

Another red hitter—this one Felix. He swung, missed. One strike. He hit the second pitch but poorly, yet the ball skipped and jumped across ice and snow and Felix ran safe to first base. More cheers.

"Eh batta eh batta eh . . ." Another red hitter struck out. That made two.

Another hitter. This one missed two of Espinoza's pitches, but he struck the third with a great crack and the ball soared high over Espinoza and then Max, losing itself in the snow white of the sky.

It showed up again at the other side of the tall barbwire fences, bouncing to a halt. Great cheers now. "Outta da park!" someone yelled.

Max's heart tightened. This "home run" was proof the Warning Rail was well within range.

Running past second base on the way to home, Felix glowered at Max with hard eyes and wagged a finger as if to say, Don't go after any ball past the Warning Rail. It's not worth it.

Max nodded. He looked to Braun, but Braun only winked and slapped his fist into his glove once more.

Another red batter—Zoock. He swung hard at Espinoza's first two pitches and missed mightily. He'd done it on purpose. Brilliant.

Before the third pitch, Espinoza turned and looked to Max and Braun. He stared a moment, his face stiff and blank. Then he threw. Zoock went to swing hard again, but the ball struck him in the thigh and he dropped. Jeers went up now. Some of the men in red shouted at Espinoza, raising fists. But Espinoza had outfoxed Zoock. A prisoner acting as referee walked Zoock, limping, to first base.

Another hitter, one of the thickset Second Armored men. Espinoza wound up but released a soft throw, and the hitter struck it hard and low.

The ball lifted and sailed high over Espinoza, over Max, and over Braun, traveling between them. It landed before the Warning Rail and then bounced under and through into no-man's land.

Men cheered. Max looked to Braun. Braun was already gone, sprinting for the Warning Rail. But the hitter had not taken off to run the bases. He stood and glared, as did Espinoza, his hands on his hips.

More cheers. A few jeered. Max ran toward Braun yelling "No, wait, no."

Braun slid to a stop before the rail, and he turned. He looked back at Zoock and Felix behind home base, and then at Espinoza, and finally at Max.

Men stopped cheering. Silence now.

Something had changed in Espinoza. He dropped his glove and took a step forward, his face as gray-white as the ice.

Braun stepped over the rail, moving backward, still facing them.

"Don't kid, don't, it's okay," Espinoza shouted. "All right now." He raised a hand.

Braun smiled, and then gave his little bow once more. He walked to the fence and picked up the ball.

"*Halt!*"

From the towers, the machine guns cocked.

"*Nicht bewegen!*"

Max jumped and waved his hands and tugged at his blue jersey. "No, don't shoot don't!" he screamed in English, and Espinoza started in with the same, the whole game yelling now, Zoock and Felix and the fans and the referee, "Don't shoot, don't shoot!"

Braun lunged to throw back the ball.

The machine guns burst out from three towers, ripping the air and twisting and turning Braun in a crazy dance, and he fell, a dark lump on the snow. An elbow stood at a bizarre angle, pointing to the milk-white sky.

Seven

The steam rose from Braun's mangled body in shimmering billows as if released from some snowbound mineral spring. Max had dropped to his knees. The baseball glove slid off his hand, into the snow. Prisoners rushed past and swarmed the Warning Rail and the guards descended, their guard dogs barking and howling.

Soon after, Max, Zoock, Felix and the other phony Americans found themselves abandoned out on the ground. Prisoners kept clear of them. Guards gave them the cold shoulder despite their blue hankies, which were out and clear to see now. They were lepers. Nonpersons. Max, Zoock and Felix regrouped on the deserted *Sportplatz*. They spoke little, the cold scraping at their cheeks. A foul heaviness ached in Max's chest.

"What's this shithead *Kommandant* going to do?" Zoock sputtered in German.

A half hour later the *Kommandant* ordered a lockdown but didn't call in the undercover Germans. Max, Zoock and Felix ended up in Barrack 13, where at least it was warm. Inside, the American prisoners spoke with hushed voices. Espinoza sat alone, in a dark corner, and read from a thick old book. Perhaps the American had pity for them. Perhaps he thought them part of some twisted Nazi experiment. Zoock and Felix took the double bunk: Zoock up on the top, his eyes moist and puffy red; Felix down below sitting with his hands clenched in his lap and his face taut with hate. Max sat at a table alone. After a while a prisoner set a metal cup of potato schnapps before him. Max nodded thanks and sipped, letting the swill burn all the way down. And his thoughts began to darken and distort. Good Pielau was gone, and now young Braun. And what had Max done? When that hard white ball bounced into no-man's land, he had frozen. He might have reached the rail at the same time as Braun. Surely he'd have thought of something there. He'd always been able to improvise on stage. And yet he left the trap wide open. All he did was hop up and down and shout in English. Still in character. Never showing his true self.

Another sip, choking it down. Braun probably thought he was saving them with his senseless act. Or? Perhaps Braun was the smartest one. Perhaps he saw all too clearly what lay ahead for him, for Germany, for all those he loved still living. The kid had saved himself. Cashed in. Gave in. He was no fool. Only fools had hopes and dreams. Only fools kept secret plans. Max, in that case, was the biggest fool of all.

A gulp, his tongue numbing. And yet, what else can I do? Max thought. The sad fact was he'd have to be even more foolish if he was going to make it—if he was going to save himself. Set yourself free, Max. He raised his cup in a toast.

"Here's to the fools," he blurted in English.

Around the barrack, deadpan faces turned his way. "Here's to 'em," said a prisoner. "Said it, Jack," grunted another.

The guards came minutes before lights out. They pulled Max, Felix, Zoock, and the other undercover Germans from their barracks and kept them safe in the German section of the camp. Others had not fared well, they learned. One was knifed in his bunk (a flesh wound, luckily) while another had the gall to make a pass at a prisoner. This one was bound with wire and tied to a post in the shower hut—naked. The sorry tale had made Felix smile for the first time since Braun's death.

Nevertheless, the *Kommandant* vowed to keep the remaining fifteen in camp until their two days were up—

Doktor Solar's orders would be fulfilled. The solution? Compulsory language lessons. The next day the *Kommandant* offered rare ersatz beer and meat rations to any American who came to the auditorium and spoke their brand of English with the camp's mystery guests. The prisoners came in droves. Even Sergeant Espinoza stopped by. "You got to lay off the stuffy Mid-Atlantic talk,'" he told Max, tugging on his watery beer and making it last.

"Thank you." The heavy ache in Max's chest was back. He lowered his beer. "You must tell me. Why Braun?"

"Why? No why. The kid picked himself. Might as well have had 'kraut' stamped on his forehead, the way he was talking and acting—till he got a baseball glove on, that is." Espinoza shook his head, took another sip. "To be blunt? Rest of you were little help. Amish? My ass. He's Amish, I'm a goddamn Rockefeller."

The language sessions were helpful, yet the day left Max with an even greater ache in his chest and head. The prisoners could have refused to take part. After all, weren't they aiding and abetting the enemy? Yet it didn't seem to matter to them. Max saw it in the way Espinoza and his gang smiled at him. They must be thinking: *These undercover krauts are so moronic, so doomed, they aren't even worth the fight.* It was only worth the bad beer.

By the last day in Stammlager VII A, Max had fallen into a blue funk. He needed to get back to Grafenwöhr and move onward. The show must go on. As they waited outside for the truck that would haul them away, Max nudged Felix and they shared a cigarette alone by the fence. "Don't tell anyone how off I was," Max said, speaking German again. "How rotten. My God, if that was not the worst performance of my life."

"I won't," Felix said. Max huffed and smoked, glaring out beyond the fence. Did Felix have to be so callous? The least he could have done was ask the same of Max. "Look, don't fret it," Felix added, placing a hand on Max's shoulder. "You'll have the chance to make up for it. We all will. I will. Not all *Amis* will prove so sly, of that I can assure you."

The fifteen exhausted and humiliated agents-in-training returned to Grafenwöhr late at night. The sky was still and pitch black, smothered by low heavy clouds. Max and Felix said goodnight to Zoock and trudged off to their barracks, Felix leaning into Max they were so tired. They headed up the steps, opened the door. All dark. All quiet. Max shut the door behind them, letting his eyes adjust. The lights flashed on.

"Hurrah! Hurrah! Hurrah for the Special Unit Pielau!"

"Long live our Pielau commandos!"

The whole barrack had stayed up. Max and Felix stood at the door, stunned. The men clapped and stomped and knocked on the tables and bunks. Max smiled. Felix grinned. Max bowed. Felix gave Max a playful punch in the ribs. Max grasped Felix's hand and they bowed together.

"*Zugabe!* Bravo!"

"On to victory with Special Unit Pielau!"

The big news from camp was the fifteen were now part of an elite new unit—named after the dead man Captain Pielau himself. The men surrounded Max and Felix, asking questions all at once. Said one, "Bet your English is stellar now, eh? Tell us."

Max placed a hand to his heart, with fingertips. "Well," he began in English, "ours was a tough mission. But that was the boat we were in. And it was a bad one."

They stared. "A poor ship?" muttered one. "Must be an idiom," mumbled another.

Someone tossed Felix a pack of cigarettes and lighter and he juggled them. "It's like this. We showed the *Amis* who's boss, really had them spinning—just like this," and they passed him more to juggle—pack of cards, bullet cartridge, a knife. "Shame we can't give you the juicy details. But just you wait and see what we got in store for them." The men shouted and stomped some more. Felix kept it up. "These fool Americans, they can bomb us but they can't stop us. When the going gets tough, such a bastard and lazy nation stands no chance against the likes of us." Men hollered and punched fists in the air. They lifted Felix and carried him around the barrack like some Egyptian prince.

Max clapped along. He shouted, too. Of course, they were no elite force. Yet to these young men in the barrack, he and Felix were the one great hope. And why not? Their illusions were probably healthier than Max's own.

By the morning, Felix had totally rewritten the script. "You want to know what went wrong in that POW camp? Nothing. It was the *Amis'* fault," he told Max on the way to mess. It wasn't the *Amis'* fault that Max forgot the American word for petrol. Yet Max held his tongue. "See, they set us up from the start," Felix continued. "Like true dogs they tricked us. Only a sly and degenerate—no, evil—race could concoct such a scheme. We all agreed—you heard it last night. So how can it not be so?"

It certainly drew the greatest applause. Max shrugged. "All I know is, Dear Felix, war will do strange things to people."

The first week of December. The snow was falling nonstop. The camp linguists had determined that out of all the supposed English speakers in Grafenwöhr, roughly twenty could speak fluent American English. Zoock belonged to this group, while Max and Felix belonged to the next range of twenty or so who'd mastered near-native American English. Another good hundred could speak the language, but their accents gave them away. And the rest? Beyond redemption. In a casting call, they'd barely make the cut for background extras. Once behind American lines they would not speak unless absolutely necessary, it was decided. If forced to speak, they would stick to grunting words such as "yes" and "no." By no means would they utter any American words containing "th" or "w." If pressured they would act crazy, shell-shocked, nauseous or even diarrheic, in which cases they might escape by holding their stomachs and wandering from the scene.

For those who could master limited pronunciation, prepared scripts would provide stock slang phrases soldiers could employ to stall and run away—or get off the first shot. With his background, Max was recruited to help draft the scripts. One went like this:

Situation: You face an American sentry.
American sentry: WHO GOES THERE?
You say: IT'S OK, JOE.
If the sentry repeats the question, you say: IT'S OK, JOE. DON'T MIND ME.
If the sentry is not satisfied, do not try to understand his demands, as this will only give you away. Respond in one of four following ways:
1.) GO ON, DON'T BOTHER ME.
2.) SAYS YOU. LAY AN EGG.
3.) COME UP AND SEE ME SOMETIME.
4.) SO IS YOUR OLD MAN . . .

For Max, the language problem was only the tip of the iceberg. They'd studied US Army handbooks and could march American-style, but how good was any of that at the front, under fire? Then there was Max's own plan. He would be a crude and perverse sort of double agent—betraying Germans and conning Americans at the same time. Would he have to kill Americans to get free? Or would it be one, or more, of his own? When, how, where to act? The risks were multiplying faster than he could grasp them.

Grafenwöhr, December 10 now. Their world had turned white. They trained on packed snow and ice. That evening, Max went for a stroll. He lit a cigarette and let himself daydream, if only a little. He had a woman here, he imagined, and he entertained her in Skorzeny's villa. As always, he was careful not to have her be too much like his Liselotte. This time she had a deep and silken voice like Dietrich and her hair was long in the style of Veronica Lake. Max proved the old raconteur. He sang her songs. She took him right there in the den . . .

Strolling on, the fresh snow barely swishing beneath his feet, Max rounded the front of the mess hall—and heard something. He stopped. Put out his cigarette between fingertips, let it fall to the ice. Someone was whispering, and then another, and so heatedly it sounded like hissing. It came from around the corner, from the side of the mess hall. Between the hall and another building was a dark and narrow alleyway. During the day some used it to duck from duty. Yet now, so late? From there Max heard:

"So-called secret mission quite a fiasco, eh? Couldn't even handle some filthy Yankees in a POW camp. So who screwed it up, then? You? I'll bet it was you . . ."

This sounded like Captain Rattner.

Max heard a hollow bang—someone pushed up against the wall. He tiptoed forward, and took a peak around the corner.

Two figures about halfway down the alley. It was dark, but the one doing the pushing was definitely Rattner—Max could tell by his thick shoulders. The one Rattner pushed was Felix.

"Why should I tell you?" Felix shot back. "Why tell you anything? You're just envious."

Rattner slapped Felix on the side of the head.

Max pulled back, squatting low. He heard Felix say, "You wouldn't have stood a chance in there."

Rattner slapped him again.

Max could break this up. All he had to do was whistle and stroll on by. Despite his early stumbles, Felix Menning had made it into Special Unit Pielau. He'd taken part in a reputedly heroic operation. And yet Captain Rattner's wrath over Felix had only increased. At the same time, Max had noticed a strange parallel—the worse Rattner treated Felix, the more fervent Felix grew about their looming mission. Max had judged this to be the result of longstanding, unrealized drives lurking in each of them and imagined it a sort of mutual father-son complex—only through a glorious victory might Felix the son prove himself to Rattner, the father.

It had gone quiet down there. Max turned to look. Felix had grabbed Rattner's cap. He tossed it. Felix kicked Rattner at the ankles and knocked the lieutenant to the ice. Crouching, Felix twisted Rattner's arms behind his back and pushed the lieutenant farther down the alley, into the darkness.

Felix was knocking Rattner around. And Rattner let him?

Rattner was on his knees. Felix pulled down his trousers, slapped Rattner on the side of his head and pulled the lieutenant's face to his crotch. Max heard a giggle, and it wasn't Felix.

Max pulled back, picked his cigarette stub off the ice and hustled off on tiptoes. He was no prude. A man's company was one thing, he thought, and he'd seen it often enough in the theater world. This was something different. This was where love and hate spoke the same language.

Next morning at mess, the men's zeal was peaking. The rumors and theories turned so grandiose, Max found it hard to keep up. They were to capture the American General Staff, went one rumor. No, no, they would retake Paris in American uniform, said another, and push the Allies back to Dunkirk just like in 1940. Even Zoock got in the game. They were to sail to England and bag that old navy man Churchill, of that he was certain.

"Ask me, I say we're going to take out Eisenhower himself," Felix shouted.

Max was sitting at Felix's right as always. What he'd seen the night before did not happen, he'd reminded himself three times this morning. "That sounds about right," Max said, smiling. Then he picked at his potatoes and sipped his cold ersatz coffee.

That evening, SS Lieutenant Colonel Skorzeny addressed Special Unit Pielau in his villa. Numbering about forty now, the commandos of Special Unit Pielau had packed into Skorzeny's dining room. They sat shoulder to shoulder on chairs set out in perfect rows as if they were about to hear a baroque quartet. Skorzeny stood before them, where the quartet might have been, and Arno the adjutant served the men champagne glasses filled with thinned beer just like they got in the POW camp. Max was near the back, next to Felix, yet they didn't have to strain to see the tall Skorzeny. The man wore the combat fatigues of an American Colonel, a tight-fitting and much drabber costume than his tailored SS finery. Skorzeny raised his glass and they all raised their glasses and stood on the tips of their toes. Skorzeny said:

"Congratulations, *Kameraden*—you brave men in this special unit are the spearhead of what is now called *Panzerbrigade 150*. We move out in two days."

"Hurrah! Hurrah! Long live the Führer!" shouted the men. They drank and beamed at their colonel. Skorzeny beamed back, nodding, and bade them to sit. He continued:

"Before we embark, there's one last matter to address. Enemy uniforms. General Staff High Command West has noted that the wearing of American uniforms could make one a spy under the rules of war."

Spies were shot when captured. It had always been that way in war. Yet this had occurred to no one, it seemed—not even Max. The men gaped at each other, murmuring.

"Bullshit!" someone yelled in English. "Let's see them try!" shouted another.

"That may well be, men," Skorzeny answered in German. "In any case, General Staff has ordered a solution." As he spoke, Skorzeny began pulling off the US Colonel's garb to reveal his SS uniform. "We wear our German uniforms underneath. Like so, yes? In case of a fight, you simply peel off your *Ami* tops and start shooting."

Bullshit indeed, Max thought. To the Americans, an SS man had to be the only thing worse than a spy. All had fallen silent. Even Felix.

Skorzeny's eyes found faces around the room. He grinned. "Chins up, good old comrades. So what's two sets of uniforms—it'll only keep us warmer, isn't that right?"

"Right," someone yelled. "Splendid solution," another shouted. Some more hollered, but most stayed silent. Max's hand was forming a fist around his glass and he wanted to pitch it against the wall. More men were shouting now, drowning each other out. "Brilliant," Max blurted in English, "just genius."

"Gentlemen, *Kameraden*, as your good Doktor Solar, I introduce you to our bold new mission—Operation *Greif!*" Behind Skorzeny stood a large easel draped with silk. The shouting died, and the men began to sit. Skorzeny downed his glass, handed it to Arno the adjutant and pulled away the silk to reveal a broad map crammed with unit symbols, dotted lines and black and red arrows so packed together that Max had to squint to make out their operations area. It was the dense, vast Ardennes Forest of Belgium, a dark and cursed province and a long, long way from America in both miles and fortunes.

Eight

That night Max tossed and sweated in his bunk until the bedding twisted into a ball between his calves. He lay on his back and stared at the slats of Felix's top bunk, loathing the hours he'd wasted worrying instead of sleeping. He'd gotten free of the war, only to face it again as a two-timing spy? He was a double agent of his own design. An impostor. Did he really think he could make it back to America this way? He was not sure who was crazier—he or his decadent friend Felix. If only he had hours—days, no, months—to sleep. If only he could wake up somehow back in Manhattan with Operation *Greif* and the whole war over. His stomach pinched and gurgled. The blood pulsed hot in his veins. His temples twinged. He never felt this bad before a first show or a big casting call. He'd always slept well before a performance. Only once had he been so rattled—when he made the move to New York City.

It wasn't the normal route, but what was? *Familie Kaspar* emigrated from Kiel in 1928 and soon settled in Manchester, New Hampshire, a declining industrial town. Max's father was a baker, his mother a seamstress—Manfred and Elise. He had a little brother, Harry. All his *Vati* and *Mutti* knew of *Amerika* came from Karl May westerns, silent films, and letters from relatives. Yet the Great War and its aftermath had left them penniless, so they'd saved for a boat over and never looked back. Max had stayed in Germany on a baking apprenticeship his father had set up even though young Max was already taking acting classes in secret and hitting every movie and play he could. Learning songs. He reunited with his family in America when he was eighteen, in late 1931. He could barely see New York City coming into port because of a blinding white fog. They'd missed seeing the Statue of Liberty. At the railing, people gathered around a man pouring champagne. A pretty young woman handed Max a glass, and as he drank a stray sunlight ray shot through the fog, illuminating his golden bubbly.

"Look," someone yelled. Men shuffled backward, their heads jerked upward and children gaped, paralyzed. A woman fainted. "Mountains!" someone screamed in Dutch, as others screamed in languages Max didn't know. "Icebergs! We'll collide," someone shouted in German.

Monstrous dark shapes loomed like colossal crates and boxes, shafts and spires piled high upon one another. The Manhattan skyline dwarfed their mighty liner.

"All's well, good people," a man shouted back in Queen's English, "it's just the colonies." People laughed, shook hands and hugged, and the champagne flowed again.

As they'd inched into port the tallest buildings disappeared into the low clouds. Not even cathedrals could do that. How high could they go? Max wondered. Children rushed to the railing, pointing and calling out the names of buildings. How did they know so much?

Mutti and *Vati* and his little brother Harry got him on a train straight to New Hampshire. Some who came over at that age were able to shake much of their accent. Young Harry already sounded like an *Ami* in English. Not Max, and missing high school didn't help. He gave baking a shot in Manchester but he knew he was not meant to be a baker. He and his father fought about it. How could Max know what he wanted? His *Vati* told him he was only a kid, and he was running from a good solid life. He took more acting, singing and dancing classes by night and tried out for small roles in local theater productions. But by day it was early hours and tough dough and the other bakers were immigrants too and spoke only German to him. To top it off, Manchester was a burg and a burg was a burg. His only way out was New York City.

The year was 1934. Early spring. Max and his father had one fight too many. He hugged his crying mother and young Harry and was out the door. Max spent his first days just walking the streets. This wasn't Manchester and it sure wasn't old Deutschland. He marveled at the massive city blocks, the vast sidewalks, the giant billboards for gum and tires and hair tonic. Every sight was a superlative. So many carefree and laughing people he saw! He must have appeared the astounded immigrant, but not for long—soon he would throw himself into their struggle, the daily round of punch and jab and charm. This city was a country of its own and just made for him. America had become the cradle of all that was modern, and what could be more modern than American show biz? Dreams were life here. The musicals promised it. Hadn't he told everyone on the ship it was so?

Many German writers and actors, producers, and publishers were choosing America. Most were Jewish and had little choice, of course. Still, if they could do it, why couldn't he?

Six months in.

Certain realities had set in. The worst thing about Manhattan was the subtropical heat. There was little escape from it. People sweated and fanned each other and walked with long slow steps, conserving energy. And yet they kept going. Bustling. The hustling. Max tried the English-speaking theaters, but he had little luck. All the émigrés had tried. How many accents did Broadway need? No matter what he tried, he was an émigré. He was neither Jew nor Communist yet all Americans assumed he was both. And why wouldn't they? He'd arrived on a growing wave of persecuted émigrés.

Like zombies they trundled about Manhattan with their tired stunned pale faces and rumpled clothes.

All the while, Americans didn't let them forget that World War I and the Great Depression were far from over. They yelled at Max on the street:

"All you *Yids*, nabbing all the good jobs."

"Go back to Heini-Land, Hitler lover."

He took French lessons. Maybe he could pass himself off as French? It only got him more laughs, more jabs.

His money was running out. He told himself he'd done the right thing. Things could be worse. At least most émigrés had their shabby rooms and menial jobs while many of the American-born artists had to sleep on park benches. That was the downside of the shimmering, optimistic, industrial mindset. You're on your own, Jack, so deal with it.

A year gone.

Max couldn't afford Broadway shows. He almost never made it into the grand theaters of the Great White Way, and yet he made sure to stroll the theater district as many nights as he could, taking it all in. Who were these people in their fur overcoats and silken hats? Of course they were laughing. What he hated most was waking from an afternoon nap, dazed, and then realizing, in a dark slam of truth, where he was. The cheap cafeterias he frequented doubled as drug stores, so Max had to eat his greasy egg sandwich next to displays of ointments, bandages, elixirs. And he began to resent the little differences all over, just as he had when he came over in '31. He started seeking out more Germans, for the comfort. In the émigré coffeehouses they traded complaints. Here the doors have knobs instead of handles. How can you open the door with your hands full? Not only that, the doors opened the "wrong" way, that is, out of the building rather than into it. And peanut butter? Disgusting. What kind of a people could love that brown goo? Then there were the women. They were beautiful, to be sure, but why were they all so prim? It seemed absurd to Max that here, in modern America, it wasn't considered polite to start a conversation with an attractive woman on the bus or subway. What could be more modern and gentlemanly? Every time he tried it he got a cold stare or a slap.

One early evening in Greenwich Village, Max was waiting for a bus outside Haus des Kuckuck, a cheerless new cabaret full of émigrés and outcasts hoping to recreate Weimar Berlin. What a hopeless endeavor. Beer was served in tin pitchers. The political jokes were ten years old. A young and nubile dancer from Bohemia was giving it her best, but the horrible lighting refused to cooperate. Outside, the streets had quieted for that calm time between work and play. Max was alone out on the sidewalk. He'd leaned against the bus stop pole as American men did but the pole bit into his ribs. So there he stood, his feet together as if waiting in an imaginary line, when a young woman—a "gal"—strolled up and stood next to him.

She was smiling. She clicked her heels together. Was she mocking his stance? Max could play along. Slowly, he turned his head and let his eyes move up her fine leg—a "gam," they called it, and onward and upward, all along her splendid curves until he found her face. She had dimples and thick red lips and blondish curls that refused to stay under her hat. Lovely flapping eyelashes shrouded her eyes. He said, "Beg your pardon, Miss, can you tell me what bus you're riding? I should very much like to join you."

She turned to him. He added a tip of his hat. Her eyes were sky blue with little silver flecks. *Wunderschön.* "Well, Fritzy, aren't you the fresh one?" she said.

"Fresh?"—like this it meant *"frech."* Max shrugged. "Perhaps. One must not behave like a monk."

"Oh, so it's frisky Fritzy, is it?"

"Actually it is Max—Max Kaspar. Although I do like your name for me."

"Good thing." She held out a hand gloved in red and said, "How do?"

Max shook her hand, once tenderly, and gave a little bow from his waist.

"So, Max Kaspar—what did you think of the stripper?"

"*Bitte?* What?"

She laughed. "The stripteaser—the dancer, in the Kuckuck. Silly. If that wasn't you I saw in there I'll eat my hat."

Max smiled. "Please, you wouldn't want to eat such a pretty hat." He removed his bowler and offered it to her. She laughed again. Max flipped his hat back on. "I was in there, yes," he began, "but I've decided I must quit living that life."

"Haven't we all?" She sighed. "I, for one, felt sorry for that dancer. No one can afford to live it up in a joint like that. It's too depressing."

"The owner's from Cologne," Max said, as if this was an excuse.

A bus was coming, turning into their street two blocks down.

"Sure, and don't I know it? Guy doesn't even know you need a liquor license. Wanna stay open? Just wait till the bulls come in for the take. Get me?"

"Bulls?"

"The coppers."

"Ah, as in '*Bullen.*'" Max wagged a finger. "How do you know all this?"

She opened her purse and held it open for Max. "See a check in there? I was in to pick up my first check. Supposed to be their cigarette girl—ha! Now I got no check, and I need no check like I need a hole in my head." She shook her head. "What's a gal gonna do? Joint's going under any day now. So I quit, see."

"And the pig let you? What a fool."

She tilted her head at him, and her curls bounced and seemed to unravel down to her chin. "Ah, now ain't that sweet?"

Did she mean it? Max hoped. Americans spoke with so much sarcasm, so much irony. He shrugged, smiling. "*Ach*, what can one say?"

The bus coming was his, he saw.

"Anyway, a gal's gotta eat," she added.

The bus kept coming and passed Max by, so full that men stood in the doorway. He waved his hat and cussed in German and English. "Goddamnit all to heck! Heck, heck you!"

Her head had pulled back. She chuckled. "Hey, you got to relax."

"You're right. Maybe it's not such a bad thing to miss my bus," he said. He offered her a cigarette, one of his last two. She took it and he lit it.

"Name's Lucy," she said and walked off down the street, rocking her hips.

Max watched her. He could watch this a long time. He would have given his last ten dollars to watch her cross the next intersection.

She stopped and turned to him. "That was my bus too. You coming or not?"

Lucy Cage was one of the few Americans who spoke to Max while looking him straight in the eye. The others were always moving too fast, looking for the next street corner, or thinking of the next three things to say.

For Lucy, Max tried harder. He avoided the dark coffee houses full of his melancholy émigré friends. For lunch, he gave the automats a go. He strolled into one on Eighth Avenue and gazed at the bright chromium and Bakelite—a wall of clear plastic doors. "How does it work?" he asked a passing attendant.

"See the little doors? Reach in one, grab yourself a sandwich, piece a pie, anything you want we got it."

"Pie?" For lunch—Max never understood it. There was a time and place for treats.

"Sure, an' add a slice of cheese if you want. Any door you like."

Max got a piece of blueberry pie. It put a bounce in his step, but an hour and a half later he was hungry again and he needed a nap. He complained to Lucy, but she only shrugged. "A guy's gotta adapt," she said.

Max kept trying. He changed his stage name to Maximilian von Kaspar. He thought this would help. That's what you do in America, keep changing the game—one of the more successful émigrés had told him this. It helped little. His agent could only get him parts playing silly continentals in off-off Broadway shows.

"If I wanted that, I might have stayed home," Max complained.

"But that's what you are," his agent shot back. "The continental. Look at the name you gave yourself, for God's sake. So work with it. Work with me."

That agent lasted another month. The next one could only get Max roles in B-Movies playing insipid Prussians wearing monocles or crude Nazis with hate burning in their eyes. All they saw was a Hun. A Heini. The worst part was, they required that Max move to Hollywood—half a world away. Hollywood? One émigré called it that "candy-coated hell." Many Germans who tried it fled back to Manhattan broken, hobbling, alcoholic. To them, and to Max, America was New York City. The rest was just a colony. Yet he too was somewhat of a colonial, forgotten in Germany and unknown to America.

Nine

December 15, 1944. Night had fallen around Münstereifel, a forest-bound town near the intersection of Germany, Belgium, and Luxembourg. Deep within the forest, Max, Felix and Zoock sat perched on crates next to their American jeep, smoking and shivering as they waited for the attack launch —set for 5:15 in the morning.

If only Max could have known that leaving America would someday lead to this. Their crates and jeep sat on a vast clearing of cold mud. Above them, the branches hung so densely intertwined Max couldn't make out the stars in the sky. It was a dim catacomb of pine and birch. The forest dripped and trickled. The constant pit-pat pounded in Max's head. He closed his eyes and imagined he was sleeping in a grand high bed, with a feather bag a foot thick, and he was wearing silk pajamas. A young warm maiden cuddling up to him . . . His eyes popped open. If only it were true. These woods housed an armed camp. It reeked of freshly churned mud, acrid like a salt, and the bitter fumes of blackened exhausts. Then there was the constant racket of guns being cleaned, of wrenches clanging, of boots sloshing mud. Soldiers coughed and sputtered nervous laughs. Engines roared alive, then cut out just when Max got used to their drone.

He'd even stuffed paper in his ears. It did no good. He'd sleep sitting up if he could. But who could sleep? So much had happened that day. At the Münstereifel train station Special Unit Pielau was split into teams and attached to the various regular units that would escort them into battle— and cover their infiltration behind American lines. Max,

Zoock, Felix and their jeep ended up here in this clearing with the First SS Panzer Corps. They were one small cog in a monstrous wheel. It seemed the whole German army had ended up in this remote border region of Northwest Germany. The latest rumors told that tent cities and masses of tanks, half-tracks, and artillery had filled every forest. Even Max's most unmilitary mind could grasp what was about to go down. For months the Allies had been racing toward Germany. They controlled the air. They had the troops and unending supplies. Then the weather turned worse for the winter. The thick fog, clouds, and snow would make fighting a grind and air superiority moot. For American and British commanders, it was the perfect time to let supplies catch up and the fighting men rest. Their armies were hunkering down in Belgium, Luxembourg, and pockets of Northwest Germany. Besides, they need not hurry. Germany was practically a corpse, and corpses weren't going anywhere. The Allies could afford to be complacent in victory. So Hitler and his band of generals cooked up a wild plan. Beyond the Münstereifel woods loomed Belgium's mighty Ardennes Forest, through which German armies had marched into France both in 1914 and in 1940. France had been taken by surprise, and the Allies had buckled. So, why not once more into that breach? It would have to be the West's largest offensive since 1940—a massive, surprise drive through Belgium and on to the coast of France seizing Allied posts, depots and bridges along the way. As in 1940 they'd push the Allies to the English Channel, which left Paris open to them on the left flank. The window for opportunity had to be small, Max also knew. The victories of 1914 and 1940 required good weather. With its narrow muddy roads, rushing rocky streams, and tight confining ravines, the Ardennes in winter would be a cramped route at best. Hitler's band of lackey goons probably had less than a month to get it right. Still, as all good Germans knew, Hitler and his lackey goons always got things right on the money.

After midnight now. December 16. Less than five hours until the attack. Felix passed Max his GI canteen. He'd filled it with something called Jägermeister, a sweet and sticky herbal liquor that, Felix said, had kept noble German hunters warm for centuries. Another Felix fib. Even Max knew that the stuff had only been around since about 1935.

"Better drink that up," Felix said. "Not too many GIs around with herbal liquor in their canteens."

Max wiped the opening with his sleeve and took a tidy sip. "Thanks, Joe," he said, practicing his best American. "Thanks lot."

They still sat on their crates, surrounded by the muck. Felix had calmed down a great deal. When they'd first showed up in this forest with their American jeep and uniforms, the regular soldiers of the First SS Panzer Corps only stared and shook their heads. What these fake *Amis* were up to with their tricks and subterfuges they didn't want to know—and Max, for his part, didn't want to be asked. SS Lieutenant Colonel Otto Skorzeny had called their mission Operation *Greif*. Fitting name, Max thought. A *Greif*, or Griffon, was a mythical monster with the body of a lion, the head and wings of an eagle, and a back covered with feathers. In other words, a sideshow freak. Which is exactly what they were. Felix, on the other hand, had probably expected an ovation. He had glared at the soldiers and refused to juggle anything.

Now it was Max who'd fallen into a grim mood. His own private little production was looking like a total rewrite. He had planned to make contact with the Americans carefully, correctly, and without malice. Anonymity and self-reliance were the keys to a stellar performance. Talk about a hopeless run. At first Skorzeny had kept him in the uniform of the feared and hated SS—and underneath his American garb at that. Nevertheless, he was hoping to be made a lowly GI corporal or private. When they arrived in Münstereifel Captain Rattner had issued him the uniform of a US lieutenant. Everywhere Max turned his plan was coming unhitched. He had intended to sneak off into the woods and go it alone once the mission was underway. Yet they were to be crammed into a jeep, riding at the spearhead of a massive surprise assault that would panic and enrage the Americans. And to top it off? His jeep team included Felix and Zoock. How was he to shake his good *Kameraden* without betraying them?

As midnight neared, most of the regular soldiers left for a nearby barn where there was a fire and hot soup. Their songs and laughter echoed through the trees.

"They can go to hell," Felix said in American. "We're the elite fighters, not them."

"Goddamn correct," Max said, giving it his best. The linguists in Grafenwöhr had learned that front-line GIs swore incessantly so they'd encouraged the jeep teams to curse in American, the cruder the better. They also produced updated scripts. Zoock the sailor was a great help here. One went like this:

Situation: You face an American sentry.
American sentry: WHO GOES THERE?
You say: JUST ME, JOE. WHO THE FUCK ELSE?
Or you say: JUST ME, JOE. WHAT THE FUCK?
If the sentry is not satisfied, do not try to understand his demands, as this will only give you away. Respond in one of four following ways:
1.) FUCK IT. I'M LEAVIN.
2.) GO FUCK YOURSELF. OUTTA MY WAY.
3.) LOOK WHAT WE GOT HERE—A REAL FUCKIN EGGHEAD

4.) FUCKIN FDR—WHO YOU THINK?

As Max and Felix drank and smoked on their crates Zoock was over fussing with their jeep, arranging the gear just so as if this steel and olive drab equivalent of a donkey were his sailing ship. Their donkey was definitely laden. Tucked under the front seat was a counterfeit wad of five hundred US dollars and another of British pounds. American, German and British guns, explosives, and grenades filled the storage spaces. They had exquisitely forged papers, a topnotch American field radio, and Zippo cigarette lighters that each hid a vial of swift-acting poison. The jeep bore the insignia of the 5th US Armored Division. Its hood had a white X on the corner—so that German soldiers in the know could recognize them as German agents. Zoock was to be their driver. It was good news, except for one snag—the sailor had been acting odd ever since the POW camp fiasco.

Now Zoock was pulling a tarp over the hood of the jeep. He got under the tarp with a flashlight. The tarp rose and fell as Zoock grunted and chuckled, his feet clamped to the bumper, his thighs rubbing against the grill.

Felix sat up and watched. "He's painting something. I can smell it."

"Painting?" Max said. He went over and lifted the tarp and the strong whiff of fresh paint hit him. Zoock smiled, made room for Max, and pulled the tarp back over them.

On the hood, painted in white outline, was two-thirds of what appeared to be the Confederate States of America flag.

"Careful, don't touch it," Zoock said.

Max's mouth opened in horror, but even his German failed him.

"It's the Dixie flag," Zoock added, wiping specks of paint from his jaw. "Y'aw like er?"

"What?" Max said, even though he had heard clearly. Zoock, Max recalled, had gone to see the last American movie shown in Grafenwöhr—*Gone with the Wind*. He had watched both showings. Ever since, he'd insisted on calling the *Amis* "Yankees." He talked of "avenging Atlanta" and "General Sherman's March"—for which the Sherman tank was named, he pointed out. Now Zoock was attempting an American southern accent? It was horrible, and hokey. It destroyed his near-perfect colloquial accent. He sounded to Max like a Chinese man trying to speak English.

Zoock's smile faded. "Y'aw heard. Shore. Aw reckon aw said, y'aw like er—"

"Yes, I heard you." Max added a smile. This would take some tiptoeing. He moved close, despite Zoock's warm schnapps breath, and put his arm around Zoock. He spoke in clear and firm German. "Listen, sailor, I think you're going to have to lose that accent. You'll have to trust me on this one, for I am an actor."

"I see," Zoock said in German, staring at the rebel flag at his fingers. It only needed more stars. "Aw reckon aw have to think on thatta one."

Two o'clock in the morning. Only three hours left. Max grabbed the canteen and let the rich brown schnapps ooze down his throat. Max and Felix had each pulled a couple crates together and laid on them, staring up into the black branches, smoking and drinking and pretending like Zoock really hadn't painted a Confederate flag on the hood of their jeep. Zoock was sleeping, in the driver's seat. He was not their only problem. Every jeep team was to have four commandos, since they only had so many jeeps. At Münstereifel station, Rattner had promised their fourth man would be sent directly. That was twelve hours ago.

Max tried to remain hopeful. "I'm rooting for another sailor—good English is the only thing that counts," he said.

He and Felix had spoken little for the last hour. When they did speak, it was in German. Who knew when they'd be able to speak it again.

"You mean like our man Zoock there?" Felix said.

They heard sloshing footsteps in the dark, and growing louder. Someone was coming. Max hoped it was a cook's orderly bringing some of that hot soup though he expected only another private seeking a tree to pee on or a secluded spot to vomit.

"A fair point," Max continued. "What we really should have done is have you use your influence with the captain . . ."

With a pop, Felix exhaled a stream of smoke. "Care to explain that, Kaspar?"

"Explain? *Moi?* I . . ."

"Bickering again?" said a voice. It was Captain Rattner himself.

They jumped to attention. Zoock rolled out of the driver's seat.

"Stop, no—at ease," Rattner said, waving hands. As the captain stepped closer they saw he wore the unkempt uniform of an American GI. He held a GI helmet at his hip. "I don't mean the German 'at ease'—I mean the American 'at ease.' Like we taught you." Rattner tried it himself, slouching his shoulders—a little wooden but it would do. "Like this, *meine Herren.* You see now?" He was speaking with greater patience, as if addressing the children of prominent upper-class bosses. He hadn't looked at Felix. He faced Zoock and Max, who had moved close to Zoock at the front fender. "See, I'm afraid you'll—we'll—have to get used to it. Because I'm your fourth man."

Max slumped against the fender. Anything but this. He'd take one of the former chefs, the ballet dancer, anyone—

"Great! Just fuckin' swell," Zoock said in English, adding a grin.

Felix glared at the black ground, his cigarette hanging.

Rattner grinned. "What, no cheers? No toasts?"

Max held up the canteen. "Here, sir. Break a leg."

Rattner grabbed the canteen. "That's the spirit. Besides, I can't let you drink all my hunters liquor, can I?" he said, giggling, and added something in dialect about this being his hometown drink, seeing how he was from Braunschweig. Max guessed he had given it to Felix as a bon voyage gift. He gulped it down, what must have been five shots' worth, and passed the canteen to Felix.

Max's knees loosened, and he stooped, the fender digging into the back of his thighs. He wanted to drop right there in the mud.

"That's it, how Kaspar's doing it? That's the 'at ease' I'm looking for."

"But, sore, yaw speakin' German," Zoock said, retreating to his Chinese Dixie accent. "Ah reckon we best be speakin' English."

"What was that?" Rattner grunted in German. "That English?" he said to Max.

"After a fashion," Max said.

"Ah." Rattner put on the GI helmet. Clearing his throat, he tried in thickly accented English, "Please, I am not so vell understanding."

Felix shook his head and grumbled something. Rattner let it pass.

"Besides, you need a radioman—and I'm top certified," Rattner said. This much could be counted on. Electronic devices seemed to be one of the captain's few chaste joys. He had even overseen the field radio operators' training. Yet it also meant he could keep in closer touch with HQ.

As their radioman, Rattner also wore the insignia of a common technical corporal. Max, however, was a lieutenant now. He had the bars on his shoulder. He'd almost forgot. He stood up tall and faced Rattner. "From this moment on, Corporal," he said in crisp American English, "we're going to have to speak American-style, whether it's only a grunt or a yes or a no. Understand?"

Rattner straightened. He nodded, shook his head, and looked to Felix. Felix looked away. Rattner said, "Juss me, Joe. Vaaht zee fuck else?"

Zoock spat.

"Corporal, let's have only yes or no answers, shall we?" Max said—

"Yeah, you stupid moron you," Felix blurted. In German.

Zoock started. Max expected a tirade, but Rattner surprised them all. "Understood," he said in German, and he grinned and wagged a finger at Felix.

"Very well, then," Max said. He handed the canteen back to Rattner.

Rattner hugged it under an arm so he could light a cigarette. The lighter's flame created a ghastly effect with shadow and made Max take good notice of Rattner's features. Eyes too far apart. Broad forehead, with a hairline only inches from his thick eyebrows. Flabby lips. Gaps between his teeth. He'd probably shaved that afternoon, yet black stubble was already showing on his heavy jaw. Physically, at least, the man looked the part of the stereotypical *Ami* dogface. Max would have cast him.

Rattner clicked the lighter off. "So my English is no good," he said in German. "So what? Half the brigade can't speak it."

A pause. This didn't explain what the captain was doing there. They needed more explained to them. Something to give them hope. Max needed a PhD in it.

"That's where you'll come in. Anyone can shoot a gun, that's clear, but not everyone can do an accent," Rattner added to Max. "Can they, Kaspar?"

"No. Bravo to that."

"That's why I opted to join you all. At least with you I'll stand a good chance. Plus, I can keep my eye on you, can't I?"

Rattner had meant it as a joke. No one laughed. Felix reached in the jeep and turned back around holding one of the poison Zippo lighters. He strode over to Rattner, snatched the captain's Wehrmacht-issue lighter and tossed it off into the mud.

"This one's just for you, Corporal," Felix said and stuffed the poison lighter deep in Rattner's trouser pocket.

Ten

Four thirty in the morning, December 16. Darkness. Freezing. Zero Hour. In their American jeep, Max, Felix, Zoock and Rattner rode near the front of the German spearhead. Three hulking Panther tanks rolled ahead of them, while behind them the column seemed to stretch back to the eastern horizon. For ten minutes they had been inching westward, in single file. The clanking panzers and droning armored cars slowed, and halted, then restarted with a jolt, only to stop again for no reason they could know. Engines revved and roared. Exhaust fumes burned in their eyes and nostrils. The Panthers blocked Zoock's view of the road ahead. All they saw was the beast's steep rear end with its steaming grilles and two fat pipes pumping out the black smoke.

They had their collars up and scarves over their mouths to block the soot and cold. No one spoke. Reality was setting in, and no comparison to a theater production could help Max now. This column was heading straight into battle, and the four of them were undercover German agents. Max's new American cover name was Lieutenant Julian Price. He sat up front wearing olive drab combat trousers, one of the better late-model American tunics with concealed buttons, and a wool overcoat. He had actual lieutenant's bars. The overcoat, he couldn't help noticing, had two holes near his left underarm. The other three were enlisted men. Zoock's name and rank was Sergeant Bert Ignatius. Behind him sat Felix, who was now Corporal Herb Fellowes. Next to him rode Captain Rattner, or, Technical Corporal Curt Mauser.

All wore SS tunics under their GI garb so that, as SS Lieutenant Colonel Otto Skorzeny had promised, they wouldn't be shot as spies.

Zoock's left hand clamped the steering wheel while his right hand and legs worked a crude ballet of shifting, accelerating, braking so they didn't ram into the rear end of the Panther. Ever the sailor, Zoock hated tanks. "Rather face an *Ami* firing squad than get sucked under that monster," he'd shouted. He'd also proved stubborn about his Confederate flag on the hood. Zoock's Dixie mania could get them killed, Max had warned Felix, yet Felix only joked, "Me, I like it. We could mount a pirate flag on the back." Rattner also approved. He called it a "crafty ploy" and ordered that it stay. That was the last order Rattner gave. He then finished off the last of Felix's canteen and started on another bottle of the hunters' schnapps. Now he appeared to have passed out in his rear seat. His helmeted head slumped forward, and he swayed with the bumps. At least this gave Felix a break. When they first got in the jeep Rattner sat close to Felix, and Max saw the captain trying to grope for Felix's hands. Felix resisted it. Finally, Rattner gave up and rediscovered his schnapps bottle.

Close to five o'clock in the morning, and still dark. They were heading uphill. The jeep's engine growled in low gear, the front wheels shimmied. The temperature seemed to drop and a wind picked up, biting at Max's ears. Straw covered the road, to keep the convoy quiet. It didn't help the ride any. They lurched and rocked, bouncing along. Max checked his compass. They were heading due west, straight into the American front lines. His stomach tightened up. His throat constricted so it was hard to swallow. This was like stage fright—but more violent in its fury. Who knew what minutiae of dress and habit would give them away? All questions could not be known and they had no end. He only hoped his thin mustache fit the role of an American lieutenant. A cold sweat spread to his palms, forehead, and upper lip.

They stopped again. Max checked his watch—the second hand passed 5:15 a.m. They started up with a jerk and hit a full speed sprint out of the forest, the rush of wind smacking their taut faces. This was it. The column raced forward, the jeep wanting to overtake the slower Panthers ahead and Zoock, shouting again, kept her steady by downshifting, braking, spinning the wheels sideways.

The road widened. They hurtled onward, a storm of metal, the tracks clanging, the ball bearings squealing. Max was plastered to his seat, his hands stiff on his thighs. He closed his eyes. He heard a thump and his eyes popped open.

The darkness burst open with blinding light—hundreds of searchlights shot upward like giant fingers, white beams that lit up the American positions ahead and the low clouds above. The air had lost all moisture. Artillery thunked and rocket launchers screeched and tracers cut through the light, raining down on the Americans in orange and white and red, a horizon of erupting volcanoes. And they sped right for it, back onto slippery mud now, the Panther before them slinging the muck at their windshield. Awesome, horrific, ghastly. As if they were plunging down a narrow cavern of limestone in which bullets raced and ricocheted in all directions.

A glob of mud smacked Max on the tongue—he was screaming and didn't realize it. The Panthers before them halted and Zoock had to wheel the jeep sideways to stop. One Panther fired and then another, and they continued on.

Was it time? They gaped at each other, their faces flashing white and black from the blasts. Rattner was sitting up, his eyes wide and not blinking. Felix nodded to Max. Max yelled: "We're on, let's go!"

Just in time. The tanks were coming up fast from behind. An armored car raced right around them, shredding the low hanging branches. Zoock punched it and drove on with his head low, staring through the steering wheel spokes. Up ahead, to the left, was the road crossing—just like on the maps.

From then on, they would be Americans.

Zoock steered for the crossing as the column of tanks plowed on forward into the convulsion of light and explosion. Their side road led southward into the woods. Zoock floored it. Shards of wood and metal landed in their path. Zoock swerved, they bounced high, Zoock almost fell out, and Max steered. Zoock grabbed the wheel again.

"Everyone okay?" Max shouted in English. "Bert? Fellowes?"

"Okay here, sir," Zoock and Felix shouted. Rattner grunted. A stray burst hit the trees behind them, igniting trunks and branches, the sparks cracking and popping. Rattner thrust his head between his legs, but Felix didn't so much as flinch. He gazed out the back of the Jeep as if watching a fireworks show, his mouth hanging open.

Zoock drove on, skirting the main thrust. Max wiped drool from his chin. He checked the compass. They were still heading west, flanking the American front lines.

"Made it, we made it," Zoock shouted in German.

Max nudged him and said "No more Deutsch" in English. So much for the stage fright. His bodily functions seemed to have ceased altogether as if his cavities were filled with a gelatin. The adrenalin enhanced his senses. He could make out individual tree trunks in the dark. He could hear far-off voices among the shelling.

They rounded a narrow bend and their headlights flashed on a green figure up ahead, crouching in the road. A motorcycle lay at his side as if he had simply pushed it over. Max saw his olive drab helmet.

"Shit," Zoock blurted. Rattner, mumbling, grabbed at Felix's sleeve. Felix drew his American Colt pistol.

"No," Max said. "You wish to damage any chances we have?"

"You're right," Felix said, "all right," and he lowered the Colt to his lap.

"Keep going, to the same tempo," Max said to Zoock, "we'll just pass him by."

Zoock shook his head and shifted down, maintaining speed. Within yards now. The American soldier stood. He held out an arm to halt them. Max saw the sergeant stripes on his sleeve. The sergeant yanked a stubby cigar from his mouth.

"Stop there! Hey stop," he yelled.

"The Germans they're coming!" Max yelled as they passed, so closely that Max could smell the cigar.

"Retreat! While you can!" Felix shouted.

Speeding on, they saw American soldiers retreating through the woods beside them. They were running for their lives, sprinting and zigzagging and jumping over fallen trees and streams, like so many Daniel Boones. Some had tossed their weapons. This scene in a newsreel would have made Rattner, Felix and even Zoock whoop and hurrah but now they only gazed, incredulous. For they were heading in the same direction.

They rounded another bend, heading northwest, and the road glowed orange from the flames of burning American vehicles ahead. The flames licked upward, as high as the treetops, heating up their faces and stretching their skin dry. Zoock navigated the horrid, blazing carnage with care, slowing into low gear. Trucks, jeeps, and trailers stood at odd angles. An ambulance upside down. In the mud, blackened corpses flickered with orange and blue embers. The stench of burnt rubber and flesh quickened Max's pulse. Such mayhem seemed to portend victory, but Max knew better from what he'd seen in Russia. The greater the mess, the slower the advance.

New German bombardments tore into the woods around them. They ducked. Splinters and who knew what whacked at the jeep as Zoock drove on.

"Help us! Slow down! Need a ride!" GIs ran out to them from the trees waving their arms. Some slipped and fell, yet more came from all sides. "Krauts'll kill us," one screamed, "SS are coming, Mac, gotta roll back," yelled another. One got within inches of the rear fender. He lunged but missed and tumbled.

Up ahead, GIs were hauling an antitank gun into the road. Some broke off and started for the jeep. A GI landed on their hood. His helmet bounced off but he stayed on. Zoock swerved to shake him. The GI grabbed at the windshield. Max pulled him in by the collar. It was a kid, no more than 18. His blonde hair flapped in his eyes, and he gasped for breath. "Thanks mister, sir, thanks much," he panted.

"Okay, it's okay," Max said—

A boot struck the kid in the face and he toppled out the jeep. Rattner's boot. Rattner was standing, clutching at the back of Max's seat. "See that *Ami* half-pint?" he shouted in German, "That's all they're fighting with?" He cackled and fumbled for his bottle, but Felix pulled him down.

"Will you stop with the German?" Zoock shouted.

The horizon turned purple. Dawn. Up ahead a dead GI lay on his back, still clutching a pack of cigarettes. They slowed to nab the pack. Inspired by the prize, Felix suggested plundering the wreckage and dead for American gear but Max argued it was too risky. The rest agreed. Rattner mumbled thanks to Zoock for his fine driving, then nodded off. Up front, Max and Zoock smoked the American cigarettes. They were Pall Malls. Max had smoked the very same in New York City. For a moment the fine musky aroma took him back to his apartment on the Lower East Side, back to the stoops and drug store diners and salary men in the elevators, and even back to that strange automat where he ate pie with a slice of cheese. And then the moment was gone. It didn't take him back to Lucy. She smoked Camels.

The sky became a heavy, dark gray mass. The morning mist formed drops on their olive green wool. It was time to consider the mission, and Felix took the lead. He checked the maps as they drove on. As planned, they had been dodging the major crossings and villages. They passed only minor crossings and checkpoints. At every signpost Felix had Zoock stop so he could jump out and switch the signs backward. Ideally this would send any unwary or retreating Americans right back into the advancing Germans and, similarly, any counterattacking Americans far to the rear. It was vaudeville to the death. And with every switch Felix jumped back into the jeep giggling.

They headed downhill, and the fog thickened. A stream had washed out part of the road, revealing the tops of rocks through the mud. Zoock shifted down to cross the water. Max peered through the fog. Something was ahead, at the base of the hill. He grabbed the binoculars.

It was a roadblock. Two jeeps, an armored car, and a squad of roughly ten American soldiers stood ready. The silhouettes looked unreal in the fog, like two-dimensional cardboard cutouts. Seeing them, Felix cocked his Colt pistol. Max shook his head at Felix. "Don't worry, Lieutenant. I'm all right," Felix said.

"Good," Max said, and to Zoock, "So. We'll just proceed slowly."

Zoock nodded, slowly.

This was the first semblance of order they had seen. It meant they had to be well behind American lines. I could end it here, Max thought. Just step out of the jeep, stroll over and tell these Americans that German soldiers were with him. Then he'd be free. Wouldn't he? He looked again with the binoculars. The Americans' helmets had horizontal white stripes. They were Military Police—MPs, they called them. Could it be that easy? Max wasn't sure. Logic and sentiment clashed and sputtered in his head.

Felix passed around American chewing gum—Black Jack gum. Zoock refused it, but Felix and Max chomped on theirs, smacking and sucking down its weak licorice sap. Any prop would help. Luckily, Rattner was still passed out, his head hanging to one side.

The MP jeeps were parked angled into the road, creating a narrow passageway. The armored car stood behind, its gun aiming down the road. "Easy," Max said, "easy." As they approached, slowing, an MP each moved to the hoods of the two jeeps. They had Thompson submachine guns—"tommy guns" like Chicago gangsters used. They raised arms to halt the jeep. Zoock came to a stop.

One MP was a lieutenant and the one on Zoock's side was a corporal. The MP corporal stepped forward. Seeing Zoock's Confederate hood flag, he rolled his eyes. Then he gave Max a lazy salute, which Max returned with only a nod and a smack of gum. Only now did he realize he was smoking and chewing gum. Frightful.

"Kill the engine, please," the MP said to Zoock. Zoock did so, and they heard the distant thudding of battles. It was much louder without the whine of their jeep. Zoock and Felix straightened in their seats. The MP winced at the loudest bursts. He had thick eyebrows. "Man, you boys look lost," he said.

"Yes, yes," Max began. Zoock blurted:

"Ah wreck-on we done gone da wrong dang way."

The Chinese Southern accent had returned in force.

"What?" the MP said. He pushed back his helmet and cupped a hand to his ear.

"Ah sayde, we done—"

"He thinks we're misplaced," Max shouted over Zoock.

"Come again, sir?" The MP stepped closer.

"Go lay an egg," someone blurted. It was Rattner. His head was down, his chin at his chest. He was so stoned he hadn't sounded German but simply drunk.

"Excuse me?" The MP stepped back and glanced over at his lieutenant.

"Real fuckin egghead," Rattner said, snickering.

The MP glared at Max. "Where does he get off? Sir?"

Max glared at Rattner. "Shut your snout, Corporal."

Zoock added, "Ah, doen mine heem, massa Joe. He's mahty fine."

"Jesus," said the MP, glaring at Zoock now. "You sure speak a funny kind of English."

Rattner's head had raised up. He was grinning. His mouth opened. Felix slapped him, hard, and then again. Rattner groaned and slumped back.

"It's the goddamn shell shock, see," Felix said in fine American English, "thinks the war's a gas. Imagine that?"

"Yeah, imagine," the MP said. He rubbed at his chin. Felix offered him some gum. The MP took a stick and slid it in his breast pocket. He patted the pocket, staring at the four of them.

"Look here, corporal," Max said, "I can explain." He stepped out of the jeep, and to his relief, no one made a move from the jeep or the roadblock. He felt the power of the stage now, infusing his brain and heart, a poise he could only know while performing. Hearing the rhythm of real American English stirred him. He understood these Americans. Sure, they wore olive drab wool and steel helmets, yet weren't they still the men on the streets he'd passed day in, day out for years? And now? He was an American lieutenant. A salary man. He strode around the hood of the jeep, tossing his cigarette butt in the mud.

Over at the MP jeeps, the MP lieutenant nodded. Max walked up to the MP corporal, handed over his papers and took the corporal aside, a yard or two away. They had their backs to the jeep. As the corporal checked the papers, Max stared off into the woods. More GIs were gathering in there, staring back from the branches and trunks like so many wolves and owls.

Max spoke softly. Fatherly. "We are a long way from our unit, as you may read in my papers here." A sigh. "We became cut off, and we lost a good deal of men. In an instant, they were all gone. Cut down. We are among the few left."

The MP corporal stopped reading. He looked up. "I lost two pals this morning."

"I'm sorry about that, son. Truly. However, we are going to find our way back, aren't we? Aren't we, son?"

The MP stared, his eyes wet.

"Yes, we are. As for our driver, old Bert Ignatius over there, well, there is no explaining his type. He is from Louisiana, you see, and he took too many bombs too close to the head. And, he always was a little, well, let us say, cuckoo. A fair driver though. And as for the one in back? Pity." Max added a smile. He drew his plundered pack of Pall Malls and, careful to smack it against the back of his hand American-style, slid one in his mouth. He lit it and offered one to the MP.

"No, thanks, sir. I'll bet he is that—your driver, I mean. The loony ones can always drive." The MP handed Max back the papers and gave his lieutenant a thumbs-up. He shook his head at Max's jeep, at their mud-caked windshield and dented fenders. "You saw some tough stuff this morning, didn't you?"

"We did, yes. I'm afraid the Germans are coming in fullest force." Max started back for the jeep. The MP followed.

Felix was leaning out the rear seat waving at them. "Say, Corporal," he said to the MP. "We're a bit lost. We're in Belgium? How far we from the front lines?"

"About twenty miles. It's definitely Belgium. You're good and safe now—for now. Krauts are throwing everything they got at us. Say they even got planes in the air. Trying to split us north and south, we're hearing. Making lots of headway too."

"Gawdang bastahds," Zoock said.

"Fuck it, I'm leaving," Rattner muttered.

The MP turned to Max. "For your shell-shock case there? There's a field hospital up the road a stretch, take the first right. Then look for the signs."

"I will. Thank you."

"And good luck, sir. Hope you make it back safe."

"Thanks, son. You as well. I'm guessing we'll all need much luck in the days to come."

Eleven

Ten o'clock in the morning. They had infiltrated over forty miles behind American lines yet had another forty to go, ever westward, toward the town of Huy on the Meuse River. Huy's bridge was their goal. They were to confirm the bridge was intact, cross it, and report back on conditions. Seizing the Meuse bridges was supposed to be crucial. By the end of this first day, the surprise panzer columns were to cross the river and race onward for the Belgian city of Antwerp. After Antwerp the countryside opened wide, and France beckoned. It could be 1940s' Blitzkrieg all over. A German Europe. Fortress Europa. Wine, women, and song. It was all crazy talk. The successes of 1940 had also been a delusion and would never come again. Even taking Antwerp was a pipe dream.

All Max needed was to get over that river. Once their jeep crossed that bridge at Huy, he'd make his move and be long gone. It was a good thing he hadn't tried to defect at that MP roadblock. The Americans were rattled. So why would they reward him for turning in his friends? Wasn't he one of them too, and wearing the uniform of a US lieutenant at that? Once a kraut, always a kraut—hadn't he heard people say it in America? Besides, how could he betray Felix and Zoock like that? He was no traitor, not to his comrades. Until he got over that bridge, perhaps he could help them help themselves. He certainly couldn't let them destroy themselves. He'd already let that kid Braun destroy himself. He would make his own way but only when the time was right. In the open country west of the Meuse he'd go on the lam. He knew enough French, and Paris was not far. If only they could get there. The Ardennes was proving a tangle of thick woods and craggy ravines. The roads were so narrow and tricky and the main crossroads so clogged that every jammed mile seemed to take an hour.

At the same time, Max couldn't help but get engrossed in his new role. After they made it through that MP roadblock they raved about it like school kids who'd just visited the zoo. They compared the ways the MP GIs walked, talked, stood. They analyzed the fit and wear of the uniforms and debated whether the repainted olive green on their jeep was close enough to the real thing. Mostly, they raved about Max's performance. Fantastic yet balanced, they called it. "Subtle, you know?" Zoock said, abandoning his Chinese Southern English for the moment. Subtle—there was no better compliment for an actor. Max took great pride in that. Even Rattner came around. "Nice work, truly," he said in German and added a careful pat on Max's shoulder. Then there was Felix—Felix the Sphinx. For the first couple miles after the roadblock, he had grinned at Max, smacking his gum.

"You really went out of your way there, didn't you, von Kaspar?" he said finally. "For the team. I am truly in wonder."

"Thank you. Thank you," Max said. "I do what I can." It was a grand scene, he had to admit. He had changed the mood of that MP corporal completely.

And yet, as with all great performances, the thrill could not last. A few miles down the road and Max was regretting his bravado, his recklessness. He had totally ad-libbed his lines. What if the MPs had checked them out closer? Zoock's cover identity wasn't even from Louisiana—his papers said Delaware. It might have been a slaughter. Only by accident had it succeeded.

By noon, Felix had led them in switching five signposts and cutting two telephone lines. He boasted of blowing up a transmitter station or a munitions depot—if only they could find one. They passed a minefield along one side of the road. Felix asked Rattner if he could remove the warning signs. Rattner consented. He then ordered Max to help and Max had no choice. Rattner was sobering up. He tried radioing HQ but the weather and battles, ravines and hills made it impossible. With each failed try he grew darker. He slumped in his back seat and scowled at the trees rushing past, his left temple twitching. Max liked him better drunk and violent.

Felix came up with a new con. In one village they pulled it off brilliantly. The place was little more than a fork in the road. A team of GIs stood guard there. Zoock raced up and started honking, and the four of them were waving their arms before the jeep had stopped. The GIs raised their guns. Zoock screeched to a halt and they yelled:

Zoock: "Thangs at the front, they jawst gown apeshit boy! Gown apeshit!"

"Huh? How do you mean?" said one GI, his cigarette trembling between fingers.

Felix: "You heard him. Those krauts are nuts. Crazy!"

Zoock: "Fixin' to scalp us, they are."

(Rattner mouthed along, stammering "R, R, R . . .")

Felix: "Hey what outfit you from? How many strong are you? Where's the front?"

Max sat tall and looked official as the GIs answered to the best of their knowledge.

Zoock: "You got that wrong, boys, all wrong. Thaw front's thataways."

Max: "Men, we must find our way to the Meuse. Are we still holding it?"

"Better be," said one GI, his voice breaking. "If not we're surrounded already."

They did the routine at four junctions. It was a hit every time. They accumulated lots of minor, constantly fluctuating information, of which Rattner took copious notes. Any sign of officers or MPs and they'd speed off.

Around one o'clock in the afternoon, they came to a crossing blocked by a long ragtag column retreating from the front. MPs lined the crossing. One stood in the road directing traffic. Before Zoock could turn around the MP waved them on into the stream of vehicles. Zoock merged in behind a troop truck. Traveling behind them was an armored car. More MPs guarded the turnoffs ahead, crouching with their guns slung low in their hands.

"At least we're heading west," Max said. No one laughed. Behind them, the armored car's cannon extended only a few yards from Felix and Rattner. The truck ahead was so tall Max's eyes were level with its muddy taillights.

Zoock tapped Max on the knee. Crammed in the back of the truck were German prisoners. They'd rolled back the canvas top's rear flap and were staring out. Some were bandaged and bloodied, their eye sockets dark and hollow.

"They're ours, the poor dogs," Felix muttered. Rattner sat up, silent with rage.

Most were old men and kids. Max tried nodding at a middle-aged private. The private gave Max an American-style middle finger. An SS captain appeared wearing a thick dirty bandage wrapped around his head like a turban. Seeing him Felix removed his helmet, pulled out his blue handkerchief and tied it around his neck. Zoock, meanwhile, pointed to the telltale white X on the corner of their hood. The SS captain grinned and whispered to the men around him, and they stared now too, incredulous. They smiled and pointed.

"This is no good," Max blurted in German, "They're going to give me away—"

"Give us away," Zoock said.

"They can't help it," Rattner said. "We are heroes to them."

Still grinning, the SS captain ran a flat hand across his throat, like a knife cutting a jugular. Then the truck hit a bump and the captain toppled back, never to appear again.

"What's that supposed to mean?" Felix said. "He can go to hell."

"Just find an open road, goddamnit," Rattner growled.

Soon Zoock found an unguarded turnoff onto a forest road. A heavy wet snow started falling and they stopped to put the roof up, saying nothing.

With twenty miles left to the Meuse, the sounds of battle had dimmed. This was not a good sign. It meant the lead panzers were falling far behind schedule. As Zoock drove on they watched the snow fall in silence, each considering, in his way, what total failure might bring. They smoked their German Ernte 23 cigarettes with care, breathing deep, smoking them right down to the end.

The snow thickened and stuck to the windshield. They saw the sparkles of ice forming on the road. The cold ached in Max's knuckles and in his knees. He put on his gloves and sat on his hands.

Rattner tried the radio out in a field, atop a hill, and in a ravine. Zoock drove straight inside the woods so he could try it there, the tires whirring on freezing earth. Among the static Rattner could hear the cries of desperate Germans in battle but they couldn't hear Rattner, who pleaded with them to hear him.

They stopped to eat rations along a raging stream. On the opposite bank a steep wall of ravine rock rose up, blending into the thick branches above. On the other side of the road stood a wall of broad fir trees. It was like they were in a cave. Their voices seemed to echo and the water made a hollow roar.

Rattner tried the radio again. All he got was static. He burst out of the jeep, ran down to the stream, crouched before the violent current, and got on his knees as if praying.

"Maybe he'll jump in," Zoock said.

Felix went down to Rattner. Max and Zoock watched from up in the jeep. Felix spoke softly and put his arm around the captain. Zoock looked away, but Max had to watch it. After a couple minutes Felix trudged back up to the jeep.

"The captain, he wants us to turn back," he said, almost whispering it. "Just head home. He's losing it, gents. Losing faith. So much for the vaunted SS."

For Max, heading back now was as bad as being caught spying. He got out of the jeep, stood in the road, and shook his head—pondering the right response.

Luckily, Zoock said, "And what would heading back accomplish? Tell me that. We'd be retreating without authorization. Besides, might be worse medicine than anything the *Amis* can dish out."

They were all speaking German now.

"He's commanding officer," Felix said. "As long as he's with us, he gets final say."

Zoock got out and joined Max and Felix in the road. They stood in a triangle for at least thirty seconds, thinking.

"The question is—has he acted like a commander?" Max said. He was pushing it, but this was no time to hold back.

"Of course not," Felix said. "The real question is, what to do about it."

Zoock threw up his hands and slogged over to the nearest tree trunk, to urinate.

Down at the stream Rattner kept staring into the raging water, still on his knees. He appeared to be muttering. "Look at him," Felix said to Max. Rattner was gesturing now, pleading with hands, rocking his head. "He does that a lot. It's his family—he thinks he can talk to them."

Finally, Rattner and Max had something in common. For a time Max had tried to reach his lovely Liselotte like this, he missed her so much. He tried it at her grave.

Felix's lips had scrunched up as if he'd eaten mud off his boots. He added, "I know what you're thinking—he's cracked."

"No. I don't," Max said. "Far from it." He held out his pack of Pall Malls for Felix. "It was an air raid. Am I right? He lost some kids, a wife perhaps . . ."

Max wanted to tell Felix about Liselotte, but held off. This wasn't his show now. Felix gazed back with hard and narrow eyes. He nabbed the Pall Malls and lit one. "You're right about the air raid, and the loss part—oh, you're right on target there. Braunschweig was bombed all to hell. It was his parents, and his grandparents, and six of his relatives. Flattened the house he grew up in. You see, our Captain Rattner never married, Kaspar. As you might imagine. He lived at home when on leave. He had no other home."

Max lit a Pall Mall, although they only had two left. He put a hand on Felix's shoulder. "Look, I was thinking. Why don't you go back over there and talk ole' Rattner into sticking to our guns, eh? Inspire him. Whatever it takes."

Felix inhaled. He stared. He blew smoke out the side of his mouth.

"If, you know what I mean," Max continued. "I know you can. I . . . I've seen you—I've seen what you two do. So, take your time. I could take Zoock on a little walk, if you like—"

Felix released a nervous giggle. He patted Max's shoulder. "Way to take charge. You've really impressed me, you know. You're earning this. Truly, a fine performance."

"Oh? Thanks. Thank you." Max didn't ask exactly how he was impressing, and what exactly he was earning. It was best not to know. He wanted Felix safe. He wanted him happy. But he wasn't about to die for the little juggler.

Max took Zoock on a walk. They scouted the road ahead for ten minutes and turned back. Back at the jeep Rattner was standing tall in the road, his hands clenched on his hips like that first day Max met him. He announced:

"The Meuse River is within our grasp, comrades, so let's waste no time."

They found a main road and drove a few miles but daylight was thinning fast, so they spent the night at a hikers hut deep in the woods. Zoock and Max slept in the jeep while Felix and Rattner took the hut. It was a dark, wet, and cold few hours. Each rose often and paced around to keep warm, and Max couldn't help feeling like they were doing it out of mistrust. It was like in an American Western movie—the robbers must camp out, and as soon as the campfire dies, they eye their accomplices all night from under their horse blankets. They needed each other, and yet they were poison to each other. Max, for his part, could not sleep. He considered leaving again—just walking off into the trees and never coming back. He didn't. This was all about tomorrow, and the day after that. So he rolled up in a ball on the back seat and closed his eyes, squeezing them shut until he'd fooled himself into something like sleep.

Twelve

The next morning—December 17, 1944. At dawn Rattner tried the radio again with no success. Felix had their maps out on the hood of the jeep. They had bypassed the towns along the main attack route—Stavelot, Trois Ponts, Werbomont, Ouffet, Seny—and traveled almost a hundred miles. It might as well have been one thousand miles. Their jeep was a banged up, mud-caked bucket. Their fuel was on reserve. Their limbs ached from the night in the cold, their uniforms were damp down to their skin, and their feet wet and freezing in their boots.

They hit the main road. At the first crossroads American tanks, artillery, and troop trucks were heading east to the front, stalling all cross traffic. With only ten miles left until the Meuse River, they had to sit and wait and watch the mighty columns pass, a seemingly unending supply of replacement materiel and men.

"Look at the fools," Rattner growled from the back seat. "Throwing in the very last of their forces. And what are they to do when that's all gone, eh? Send in the donkeys? Or their Negroes?—be lucky if their Southern slave drivers even give them guns. Sorry, Zoock, but it's true."

Zoock nodded, wearily. Felix coughed. Max said nothing. All three knew the truth—America's resources were endless. They had been there. They had seen it.

The traffic kept them from Huy on the Meuse until almost ten o'clock in the morning. A narrow forest road carried them to the crest of a wooded hill that overlooked the town. The dense forest obstructed their view, so they parked the jeep next to a thick fir they could climb for a better look.

Rattner went up first. He stayed there a long time, saying nothing. He climbed back down with ashen cheeks, his binoculars loose in his trembling hands. "Good God," he mumbled.

Max grabbed the binoculars and headed up. He saw a medieval fort atop a hill, the spires of a minor cathedral, and a town hall plaza. The Meuse River curved through the center of old Huy. Huy Bridge was stone and arched, centuries old. American soldiers, armored cars, and machine gun nests packed both ends of the bridge. The Americans were going to hold this at any cost. Even entering the town looked impossible. Soldiers manned key intersections and rooftops. Sandbags, tank traps, and barbed wire blocked all roads to the bridge, and anyone who dared approach got the third degree from the MPs. Max watched as a staff car bearing the flag of a two-star general was searched and the general questioned at length.

He lowered the binoculars, stunned. What a fool he was. Any real soldier would have known the river had to be crossed at some remote place. Swimming it was probably best. Max didn't even know how to swim. Making it across would be risking hypothermia, pneumonia. It might also require boldfaced treachery and possibly killing. Who was he kidding? He was a better swimmer than a killer.

A black mood seized him. His chest filled with a dull pain. He should have bolted when he had the chance.

He clambered back down, grasping at the cold and slippery branches. "Well, that's that," he said.

Felix waved at him to be quiet. "*Psst*," Zoock said. Rattner was hunched over the radio down behind the jeep. When Max went up the tree, all he'd heard was crackles and fuzz. Now he heard German voices, and Rattner spoke back to them in a modified code of which Max understood little. Water drops from high branches hit Rattner and rolled down his neck, but he didn't flinch nor wipe them away. He had gotten through.

Max was a fool, without a doubt.

Rattner glared at them. "You're disrupting my signal," he sneered, "so go on, take a walk, why don't you?"

The three shrugged and strolled off in search of water. They returned with full canteens twenty minutes later. Rattner was sitting in the mud before the jeep, his back against the rear tire, staring into the mud with his hands hanging off his knees. He spoke to Felix:

"I told them the situation. Huy's a fortress. The bridge is there, and it's there to stay. We have nowhere to go but backward."

"And?" Zoock said. Rattner kept looking at Felix. "And?" Felix said.

"I requested permission to roll back—request denied till morning, they said."

"Till morning? What are we going to do meantime, just sit here? Freeze our asses off." It was Zoock again. "Son of a bitch," he said in English and punted his canteen up into the branches. It didn't come back down.

Felix spoke softly. "No. Now listen. We'll just get more intelligence. Confuse the *Amis* some more. Put some real fear into them. Isn't that right, Hartmut?" He had called Rattner by his first name.

Rattner shrugged. "Yes. I suppose. What else is there?"

"How? We'll need gasoline," Zoock said.

"I'll get it," Felix said. "All right? So how about it?"

Rattner shrugged again, this time violently, practically throwing out his shoulder sockets. As if he cared for nothing now. It gave Max a chill down his back.

"They told you something else, didn't they?" he said to Rattner.

"Is that true?" Felix glared.

Rattner started to speak, then stopped. He did this twice. "Yes," he said finally. "It's way behind schedule. All along the front, from fifty miles north of here to all the way south of Bastogne. We're doing some real damage, but it's stalling. And the whole thing depends on schedule." He cleared his throat and spat, but the attempt misfired and mucous hung from his chin.

Zoock leaned against the hood, shaking his head, his hands balled as fists. Felix stood over Rattner, as if ready to knee him in the face. "That all?" he said.

"That all? That all?" Rattner snickered and wiped at his chin. "No, that is not all. Operation *Greif*, if you must know, has been compromised. The English speakers, the *Ami* uniforms, our jeep teams, all of it. Special Unit Pielau. Top that off, *Amis* are using passwords now, and they're changing from unit to unit, hour to hour. Something happened. Someone was found with our plans, something. The upshot is, the *Amis* know about us and they have ways of spotting us. And that, my dear Menning, is all."

Felix pulled back, his arms slack at his sides.

Max rubbed at his raw, itching eyes. Of course it was true. American intelligence had to have suspected something ever since that armed forces-wide request for English speakers was issued two months ago. Now they had all the details. If Max was a fool—if they were all fools—then the commanders at the top were the true jokers.

"All of which means," Max said, "that we don't know what the *Amis* will be looking for—that is, which telltale clues will be giving us away."

Zoock banged on the hood. "Always have to be so goddamn correct, don't you *Herr* Know-it-All?" he said to Max.

Rattner let his head hang, and his cigarette dropped into the mud between his legs. Felix let out an anxious, incredulous snigger that sounded like a pig's snort.

"I'm only being realistic," Max muttered, a bitter saliva forming in the back of his mouth. His sore, surging heart seemed to rise up into his throat. He could not go back home, nor flee west, it seemed. And yet he had to keep his comrades together. He had to lead them. It was the only way to find a way out—so that he could betray them.

They spent the rest of the day traveling along the Meuse, skirting the open valleys and sticking to the forest roads, south then north again, clinging to the hope that the panzer spearheads would catch up to them. They didn't even hear the distant battles for long stretches. The thick clouds glowed fluorescent, pregnant with snow. Then they grew denser and darker and it started to snow, heavily, the fat flakes blotching the mud white and clumping in the puddles.

In a village, Felix stole fuel cans from a parked American supply truck. "At least we have the gas now," Max said, hoping to lighten the mood.

"For what? To return? Return to what?" Zoock blurted. "Our last Christmas ever? Soon there'll be no Germany to return to. Better start learning your *Ami* English," he yelled back to Rattner, "because soon we'll all be chewing chewing gum."

No one answered Zoock. They let him drive. Felix offered Max the last Pall Mall. A couple minutes later Rattner said, "It's not over yet. It's not."

All the roads were looking familiar. They were going in circles. Now and then they heard the cracks and pops of gunshots. Artillery thumped again in the distance.

To the devil with correct—Max had to push it. He blurted: "I know—if we see an open bridge, why don't we just take it? Or we could make a raft. Now there's a ploy, comrades." He knew he was babbling, but he was scared now. He didn't really want to go it alone. This might be the only way out—simply get them all stuck on the other side, together. "Good? What do you all say to that?"

Felix was grinning. "That's bold of you," he began, but Rattner cut him off:

"Absolutely not. We are ordered to patrol and recon the eastern Meuse, and that is where we'll stay. Right here. For better or worse—"

"Wait, wait," Zoock said. He had straightened up. He let off the gas. Up ahead was a jeep off to the right side, its rear end between two trees and the hood sticking out into the road, as if it had emerged straight out of the forest. Steam billowed out the radiator grill.

A GI was slumped over the steering wheel, and another was hanging out the back.

Felix grabbed a Colt and passed one up to Max, while Rattner pulled out a tommy gun. Zoock dropped it into first, inching them closer. Bullet holes dotted the jeep. Its tires were flat. On the other side of the road, at the edge of the forest opposite, lay the bodies of two more GIs. Zoock stopped about fifty yards from the scene. They jumped out and spread out with guns aimed, crouching as they walked, peering into the woods for sounds and signs. Nothing. No one. The shot-up jeep's engine made pinging noises. Felix took the lead, while Max went over to check the two GIs across the road. One was on his side as if sleeping. Blood still ran from his stomach and into the mud, releasing steam. The other was on his back, his legs bent up high like a frog's, arms out straight. His eyes were open, staring up into the clouds. The snow already covered the eyeballs. The flakes filled the folds in their uniforms.

"Don't get it—why would dogfaces shoot at each other? And from this close?" Zoock shouted across the road to Max in English.

Max had been thinking the same thing. He crossed over to the shot-up jeep. Two more dead lay on the other side of the vehicle, curled up in balls as if they'd been shot trying to jump out and find cover. In total, four had been in the jeep. The snow was sticking to them too, dusting them white.

Felix, Zoock and Rattner went silent. They stood in a line, their guns pointed to the ground. Max thought he understood—none of them ever saw the dead so up close and freshly expired. He had. It was the only part of combat he knew, it seemed.

"You'll get used to it," he began to say—

Then he saw it. What they really saw. On the ground were a lieutenant and a corporal. The lieutenant was staring up at them with blue-gray eyes that were still melting the snowflakes, and his hands were clenching at his tunic, which he'd obviously tried to rip open. Underneath was the field gray uniform of an SS corporal.

Thirteen

They unbuttoned the other three's American tunics. All wore SS uniforms underneath. The jeep's hood had a white A in the corner. It was team A from Special Unit Pielau. Lightly, with fingertips, they brushed snow off the four faces.

"Poor Hasko—dear God," Zoock whispered. The driver was his sailor friend, Hasko, the one Felix had mockingly called "the goat" back in Grafenwöhr. The phony US lieutenant dead on the ground was a once-great ballet dancer, Scherling.

Rattner scurried back to their jeep to try the radio.

"Should we hide them, get their German uniforms off?" Felix said.

"What's the use?" Max said. Clearly, the GIs across the road hadn't bothered to question jeep A—somehow, even they had been able to spot the four as Germans.

Zoock carried his friend Hasko into the forest, a few trunks inside the tree line. He struck the ground with a shovel. It clanged at the icy earth. Felix started toward him but Max held him back by the elbow. Zoock sat Hasko up against a tree. Kneeling, he spoke a few words to his friend, in his ear, then he placed Hasko's cap over his eyes, which made Hasko look to be napping. Zoock reached in Hasko's tunic as if looking for photos and letters. He found none. They'd been forbidden.

Rattner strutted back smiling, the steam pumping out from between his gapped teeth. "I got through. The battle plans have shifted. We're to return at once. Check out any towns on the way, they said. Radio in enemy strength. So let's be off and fast."

They sped away, back east toward the German front lines. All knew what Rattner's news meant, though none of them voiced it. The surprise offensive had failed. When they made it back, they could be reinserted into another absurd and risky scheme. They might even be thrown into a regular unit.

Zoock drove hard and fast. After a couple miles he steered the jeep into the woods, stopped, got out and began scraping the X off the corner of their hood with his knife. Max helped him, and Rattner and Felix went to work scraping the X off the rear. They did all this without speaking.

The road turned rough and icy. The suspension clattered and knocked, and the tires spun on frozen patches with a ripping sound like the squeals of stampeding boars. Crusty snowflakes whipped around inside their canvas cab. Yet Max burned hot under all his wool. The sweat rolled down his chest and back and itched under his hair. With every mile they went, the Meuse—and Paris, and *Amerika*—lay further at his back. He was missing his chance altogether. He wiped the sweat off his neck and forehead and unbuttoned his overcoat. Even if he were to break free, how could he know the Americans wouldn't shoot him on sight? This would take more than an escape—it would take a miracle.

Now he was cold, freezing cold, and he wrapped a GI-issue scarf around his neck. He blurted: "We should've crossed the river when we had the chance. Shouldn't we? Swam it, stolen a dingy, what have you." Zoock kept his eyes on the road. Max glared at Felix and Rattner in back. "Am I right? *Kameraden?* So perhaps we should just split up now, eh? Go our own way."

Subtly, Felix shook his head at him.

Rattner snarled: "Corporal Kaspar, get a hold of yourself—"

"Least we should take off our SS tunics," Zoock shouted. "I'm not even in the goddamned SS, and neither is Kaspar here. Man's a goddamned actor. Look at him. And I'm a sailor." He banged at the steering wheel.

Felix turned to Rattner. He said, softly, "Sailor boy has a point, now Hartmut, it is a long way back—"

Rattner pushed at Felix. "How dare you call an officer by his first name? You heard what Skorzeny said—we'd be shot as spies that way. Who knows what happened back there, any of you. Maybe one of them lost his head? Betrayed the others."

As Rattner said this, he locked his scowl on Max.

Max glared back. "Just what are you implying, sir?"

"You know perfectly well. So don't feed me that gentleman shit-speak." Rattner grabbed at Max's collar, then heaved it loose.

Max turned around and faced the rough and icy road that was sending them further east. The captain must have been suspecting him the whole time. Perhaps his drunkenness was only a ploy. Perhaps they all suspected him. Luckily, Max still had the Colt in his overcoat pocket. And yet Zoock had a Walther pistol in his lap, Felix a tommy, and Rattner a tommy.

And they drove on, in silence. They might as well have been chained together, Max thought, like a team of escaped convicts.

Afternoon now, December 17. The snow fell in heavy, churning sheets. Their forest world had turned white. They got lost twice. They lost time. Yet already they were halfway back to the German lines. Max's heart ached and he imagined it black and clogged, barely pumping. His predicament was suffocating him, yet his indecision was worse. How could he make a break for it? Here the Ardennes was all slippery hills and snowbound streams and Zoock kept racing on, horrified of getting stuck.

Max gripped the Colt in his pocket. He slid off the safety. "This is it," he muttered as the snow whipped at his lips. Whatever he was to do he would do it for Lucy, to show her. And he would survive it for Liselotte, to love her still.

They passed a sign for a town, but the name was shot up. Only "Five Kilometers" was legible. Rattner, waving his tommy, screamed at Zoock to drive on.

The snow and the wind let up, and they heard the din of battle, growing louder.

Up ahead, a line of GIs was blocking the road. They saw the white helmet stripes—they were MPs.

"In English, and keep it short," Max said to the rest, "let's keep our guns down. Captain, I suggest you act drunk. You've done such a fine job in the role before."

Felix smiled at that and Rattner nodded, grunting. At least their canvas top was up—it would help cover Rattner. Zoock lowered his Walther to the floor.

Out in the road, two of the MPs moved forward with rifles raised. The MPs were black. American Negroes. Zoock's Confederate hood was free of snow and clear to see.

"Tell them this is not our usual jeep," Max said to Zoock out the side of his mouth. "Make up the rest. That clear? You can do it."

Zoock nodded, his knuckles white on the steering wheel. Yards away now. Zoock stopped with a squeal of brakes and a crunch of snow. One MP approached Zoock's side. He was a corporal and a lighter skinned black, with freckles on his cheeks. He had a thin mustache like Max's. He saluted for Max. Max saluted back.

"Where you heading?" the MP corporal said to Zoock.

Zoock grinned. "Hey there, I think we're lost." He'd ditched the Chinese Southern accent for good.

"See your papers," said the MP corporal. Zoock looked to Max, who handed over his papers. The MP corporal placed them on his wrist to read, still aiming the rifle.

The other MP was circling their jeep. He came around the back. Passing Max he gave a lazy salute and said, "'Tenant."

"Afternoon."

The MP corporal flipped the papers over, rereading everything, his lips pursed. The other MP stopped at the hood. Zoock pointed and blurted, "Hey, hey, sorry about the Dixie flag, gents," giggling. "Had a good ole' boy in our unit, he done it. But, well, he bought it yesterday. He was a sailor . . ."

The other MP stared, his rifle barrel resting on the hood.

"You see, since yesterday we cannot find our unit," Max said to the MP corporal.

"Uh huh." The MP corporal slid Max's papers into a pocket. He nodded toward the back seat. "You got a radio in the back there. Shouldn't be that hard. Sir."

"That's just the thing, Jack," Felix said, showing himself at Zoock's shoulder. "Can't receive shit in this damn forest."

The MP corporal was looking at Rattner. Rattner, wild-eyed, hugged at his stomach and gave a cheap little groan. The MP kept staring—the man could stare as long as he wanted. Probably make a great actor if America gave him half a chance, Max thought, and for some reason this thought terrified him. His heart raced, thumped.

They heard thuds of artillery, and the dull rattle of faraway machine guns.

The MP at the hood called over the other two MPs, and the three of them spoke within full earshot of Max. Max didn't understand their speech and, he suspected, many Americans wouldn't have either. They wore natty gloves with the shooting fingers cut off. They were unshaven. One chuckled at the Confederate flag, but another was glaring at the hood. This one said to Zoock: "Say now, driver man, what's that big ole' scratch on the corner the hood for? New too—metal still shiny."

"Oh, that—like I was saying, the lug who did it is dead anyway, see."

The MP corporal gave his three men a nod, and they spread out to the four corners of the jeep—one at Max's side of the hood, the other two at the rear corners. Only the canvas top stood between them and Felix and Rattner.

The bombings neared and they heard shells screeching in, probably hitting the town down the road. The MPs crouched and clutched their helmets on their heads.

And Max realized something that both terrified and inspired. By the looks of them, these MPs might too have lost their way.

The MP corporal looked beyond Zoock, over at Max. "Here's the rub, Lieutenant, sir. Our field radio went dead— we'll have to use yours. That all right?"

There were only four of the MPs, and four of them. The MPs had clunky Garand rifles, they had tommys, and the bombardment would cover the noise. Max only hoped Rattner—and Felix—had not realized this. He shrugged. "You are welcome to try, Corporal," he said to the MP corporal and then turned to Rattner, who'd stopped groaning and holding his stomach. "Private, why don't you reach me that radio from the back," he continued to Rattner, in a monotone.

Rattner's face hardened. He didn't budge.

Felix blurted: "I got it, sir," and handed the radio up through to Max, who handed it to the MP at his side. The MP stood the radio at his feet.

"Thanks." The MP corporal took a couple steps back. "Good. Now, a few formalities compliments of the boys in G-2."

G-2 meant Counter Intelligence. The other MPs stiffened and raised their rifles.

"Fair enough," Max said. "Shoot," Zoock said. "Can't be too careful," Felix said.

"What's Sinatra's first name?" the MP corporal said.

"What? Oh, it's Frank," Max said. "Mister Frank Sinatra."

"The capitol of Oregon?" said the MP corporal.

Silence. "Portland," Felix said.

The MPs eyed each other.

"Who knows Oregon—it's Salem," Zoock said. "Portland's the big city."

The MP at the hood said, "Where do you find a tight end?"

No one spoke. The MPs raised their guns, grasping them tight. The MP corporal said, "Here's an easy one—how much is a postage stamp?"

Any true GI would know this. Stamps and letters kept them human. Max had no clue, and he was sure the rest didn't either.

"Three hundred dollars," Felix whispered. He had placed three one hundred dollar bills on Zoock's shoulder so that only the MP corporal could see them.

Zoock froze still, as if a toxic spider had dropped onto his shoulder and he was deathly allergic.

"Afraid that's a little high," the MP corporal said. "Out of the jeep. All of you. Now." He'd said it calmly, as if routine. Was it really ending here? Max thought. Perhaps the man only thought they were deserters.

"All right. Out of the jeep, men," Max said. He began to step out, but the shells fell closer, a shrieking fury of rockets, mortars and artillery that shattered the woods along the road with a sound like breaking glass. The earth rocked and rolled.

Max recoiled, his head down. Squatting, the MP corporal waved them out.

Orange bursts lit up the cab. Rattner and Felix were firing out the back through the canvas. The two MPs dropped, their blood splattering snow. Hot shells clanked and bounced at the metal floor. Zoock had his Walther on the MP corporal. He froze, his hands up. Max's MP fired a shot, it bounced off the hood, and he ran. Max fumbled for his Colt and leaned out aiming. The MP was yards from the trees. Max had a clean shot.

He shot for the treetops. The MP lunged behind trunks and sprinted off.

"*Nein schiessen, nein schiessen,*" the MP corporal said in broken German. Bitter gunpowder smoke had filled the cab. Rattner and Felix climbed straight out the back, through the tears in the canvas. They tumbled out onto snow and stood over the MP corporal, their legs stomping like pistons, aiming and screaming, "Hands up hands up!"

"They're up—don't shoot him!" Max shouted in German.

The shells kept falling just out of range, killing all other sound. Once they caught their breath, they worked fast—their training had made them automatons. Max and Felix dragged the two corpses off into the woods to cover them with underbrush and snow while Zoock parked the jeep off to the side of the road. Felix stammered: "I had to shoot, I had to."

"You did the right thing," Max said. Anything to keep Felix levelheaded now.

Felix rummaged through the dead MPs' pockets but only found letters, photos, and two half-smoked Lucky Strikes.

Rattner moved the MP corporal beyond the tree line. He sat him up against a tree trunk, facing into the woods so he couldn't be seen from the road. Brandishing the tommy with one hand, he'd tied rope tight around the MP's arms and chest. The MP's face had lost color, revealing more of the freckles. He grimaced at Max and Felix as they trudged up.

Rattner struck the MP across the chin with the gun's butt. It was his show now. He ordered Felix and Zoock to keep watch—Felix out by the road, Zoock farther into the woods behind them—and told Max to translate while he interrogated their prisoner.

"I'll tell your boss all I know," the MP told Max, "but it's not out of fear, understand? Uncle Sam been giving us little reason to die for him."

He spoke with his chin high. A couple stray units had holed up in the nearby town, he revealed. They had been the only GIs on this road. The whole sector might have been cut off, but they weren't sure because their radio had gone kaput.

Max would have mistranslated any of it to help himself, but none of it could help him now. As the questions dragged on, the MP began to gasp for words, so Max demanded that Rattner loosen the rope around his chest. Rattner snarled but obliged.

"That MP who escaped—could he bring reinforcements our way?" Rattner asked.

"Little chance of that. That boy's sure to have run back into town. He'll stay put with the rest." The MP paused. He added to Max, "That's the good news for you. The bad news? The boy saw your faces."

The bombing had stopped, bringing an eerie quiet. Farther off, shattered trees creaked and snapped, and crazed birds fluttered in branches. Rattner left Max with the MP and went to try the radio. He'd handed off the tommy. Max slung it on his shoulder.

The MP shook his head at Max and gave a grim toothy smile. "So, looks like a good ole' fashion lynching. Eh, boss?"

The word was the same in German—*"lynchen"*—meaning a cruel and unjust vigilante murder. It had been borrowed from American English for lack of a German equivalent. Then the Nazis came, and the strange American word wasn't so strange anymore. Max shook his head. "No, not if I can help it—"

Rattner was back. He shoved Max out of the way and grabbed the tommy. Felix and Zoock moved closer so they could hear the interrogation.

"How did you know about us?" Rattner barked.

The MP waited for Max's translation. "Know what?"

"That we were Germans."

"That was easy—you were traveling four to a jeep. I was trying to finagle the radio out of you so we could call for help. We're cut off—out in left field—got me? You know how that is." The MP added another grim smile.

"I do," Max said.

Max translated the rest. Rattner wanted to know more about what gave them away. It was the four-to-a-jeep more than anything, the MP said. That was the dead giveaway. No one travels four to a jeep behind American lines. It weighed down the ride and was an easy target. Apart from that, it was just like G-2 had told them—look for code letters on the hood, any funny speech, suspicious wads of money, and any colored handkerchiefs—as worn by Felix. Any one of Max's crew fit the bill to a tee.

The MP continued to Max: "I'm only telling you this in the hope you'll spare my sorry behind. Tell your captain that, will you?"

Max told Rattner. Rattner grunted. "What tipped off your intelligence?"

"You mean in the first place? You really want to know?" The MP smiled again. "Captured a German captain with detailed documents, maps, everything. Just yesterday morning. Now those cowboys from G-2 are out looking to nab you all. One passed by here before we got cut off, heading east for your lines. Know what the man said? 'Thank God the krauts keep good records.'"

Max translated. Felix and Rattner exchanged sickened glances.

"Maybe you'll get to meet the man," the MP said to Max.

"Perhaps not, with any luck. I'm finished with this war."

The MP nodded. "Hey, hasn't your captain forgot something?" he said to Max.

"What's that?"

"My name, rank, and serial number—"

Rattner pulled a knife. The MP writhed, screamed. Rattner slit his throat, a thin line of red and a rush of dark blood hit the ground like a bucket being emptied. The MP opened his mouth. He could only wheeze. He was staring at Max. Then he was still.

Max's heart seemed to stop. The world stopped. He couldn't stop staring. Someone was yelling at him but he couldn't hear it.

It was Rattner: "Cut him down," he squealed. "Then search him."

Max shook his head. "No, no. You do it. You lynched him."

Rattner lunged and pushed Max to the ground. Max's Colt tumbled out of his pocket. It lay at Rattner's feet. Rattner shouted: "Who you talking back to? Has-been know-it-all actor, eh? Well, I got your number, Kaspar, had it all along. Now I got proof. You tried to give up our radio back there. You let that MP run off too, and I saw it—"

Rattner's head erupted in a flare of red and flesh. He dropped on his side.

Felix had fired. He stood only feet away. His overcoat was bundled around his tommy to quell the noise, and his GI tunic was half-open to show his SS uniform. Hot steam pulsed from his tiny mouth. He grinned at Max.

Max scrambled to his feet.

"Relax, Kaspar. You're safe with me. Now get his gun."

"Right." Max pulled the tommy from Rattner's clenched hand.

"Wait. Shit. No . . ." Felix's grin fell away. He was peering through the forest, crouching and pivoting in all directions. "Bert!" he shouted. "Ignatius, where are you? Goddamnit, Zoock, show yourself."

Fourteen

Felix and Max spread out to search for Zoock but it was little use in the dim and hazy forest light. After a few minutes slogging through snow and underbrush, Max found Zoock's SS tunic tossed in the cavity of a rotting log. He didn't bother telling Felix. Back at the lynching tree, Felix lit one of the half Lucky Strikes Rattner had taken from the MP corporal. They worked in silence. Felix cut down the MP corporal and lay him next to Rattner while Max gathered branches to cover the two corpses. Soon Max smelled a metallic bitter-sweetness. He had fresh blood on his overcoat, his hands, his thigh. He touched it. It was sticky, like glue firming up. A sour tang clung to his sinuses and throat, like syrup. His head spun and he had to lower himself down against a tree trunk. He strained to take long, deep breaths. He pulled off his helmet.

"That's the shock wearing off. Your senses want to punish you now." Felix sat next to Max. He cupped snow in his hands and washed the blood from them, seemingly unfazed by the icy cold. "Here, now turn to me." Felix took off his blue handkerchief. He dampened it with snow and rubbed at one of Max's cheeks, a temple, and an ear. "Had some on your face, too," he said.

"Thanks." Max put his helmet back on. "This must be the scene where I thank you for saving my life."

Felix chuckled. "I was saving my own. You were just in the way."

"Captain Rattner was in the way, you mean."

"Perhaps."

The crazed birds and creaking trees quieted down. A whirling wind rushed through the branches above, like a thousand brushes scrubbing.

Felix said, "You want to get rid of your SS tunic, I won't hold it against you."

"No, I'll keep it on a while," Max said.

Daylight was thinning, creating broad and dark shadows. Back at the jeep Felix spread the maps out on the hood. "So. We're closer to the front than we thought. We are lost, but not completely. Somewhere near a town called Malmedy. Here. Must be it down the road. But we can't drive through it, can we? I say we make our way around."

"Fine." Max just wanted clear of this place.

"Far as opposition goes, we'll just have to take that MP's word for it."

"I believed him. What did he have left to lie about?"

They would have to travel with the top down, since the jeep's canvas top was shredded. As an enlisted man, Felix would drive. The jeep did not start. They opened the hood and stared at the engine twice, for minutes on end, before realizing Zoock had somehow removed the distributor cap. He'd placed it neatly on top of the engine block.

Felix started up the jeep and, wrestling with the clutch, steered them off the road and on through the gaps between the trees. They drove through the woods to skirt the town, bouncing and bumping shoulders, Max grasping at the windshield frame. As twilight came a light fog set on the gullies and puddles. They passed through an area hit hardest by the bombardments, a wasteland of splintered stumps and black craters. The snowy earth had been churned up to resemble salt and pepper. Toppled trees covered foxholes, trenches, sandbagged artillery dugouts and timbered command posts. It was like a garbage dump. Emptied crates, spent shells, sandbags and satchels and helmets lay strewn about. Legs and hands pointed to the sky, frozen. They heard no cries for help, for the cold had taken care of those left whimpering.

The MP corporal spoke the truth. This sector was a forgotten land.

The mess created a labyrinth for Felix, and he steered them through in the lowest gear. Felix drifted into intense thought. His eyes seemed to stop blinking. He cleared the woods and found a road but still the journey was slow going. Patches of ice spun the wheels. Felled logs and charred vehicles clogged their path.

In two hours they traveled no more than ten miles. Darkness fell. The wind had picked up. It was snowing again. They stopped at a fire-scorched house with half a roof and a fallen wall. Felix backed the jeep inside. Stiffly they climbed out, and Max's joints ached and popped. One room still had a bed over in a dark corner. Max stretched out on it. Such cushy stillness was a divine luxury.

Felix joined him. He'd brought cans of American rations over. They sat up, their backs against the soft upholstered headboard.

Felix handed Max a Lucky Strike. Max just stared at it. "Why kill him?" he said.

"Who? Hartmut? You heard that MP—said *Amis* never travel four to a jeep. Not even three. That made us at least two too many. There's also the sad fact that he was going to get us nabbed before we could do some real damage. I told you. He was in the way."

"You've been planning this."

Felix lit his Lucky. His voice softened. "And you? You, Zoock, me—I guess we've all been planning."

Max said nothing.

"When we rode behind those German prisoners you said: 'I don't want them giving me away'—meaning only you. I remember that clearly."

"You have a keen memory. Congratulations." Max lifted an imaginary champagne glass. "Back to Rattner. I suppose there are many men to keep company with. Why him?"

Fritz shrugged. "He came to me. I didn't make him. Unfortunately, he was also a bastard. I'm telling you, sorry dogs like him will be hopeless in the New Germany."

"New Germany—you mean after all this? We'll be lucky if there's any after," Max said.

They opened their ration cans and shoved the cold bland beans into their mouths. Then they reclined and lay back, staring up through the gaps in the roof at passing clouds. "There will be a new Germany, and it might just be the best thing that ever happened to you," Felix said. "Did you ever think of that, my von Kaspar? Eh? You could recreate yourself. We all could. So you shouldn't fear the big change. Change is grand."

Had Max heard noises? He'd been sleeping. His eyes had popped open but he saw nothing. Where was he? On the bed. Still in the house. His eyes adjusted, and he saw Felix's silhouette in the dark, the glow of his cigarette moving up and down. He was standing over at the jeep.

"I was sleeping," Max said.

"Yes. Snoring, too."

"How long did I sleep?"

"Hour, maybe."

"What are you doing over there?"

Felix sighed. He trudged over to the bed, sat, and slumped. He began to speak, but his voice creaked. He tried again: "You know, I assumed that batty redhead sailor would stick around for the bitter end. He was going to come in handy."

"No. Zoock, he had it all planned out, right down to his silly accent. He wasn't losing marbles. That was just a ruse to throw off anyone who tried to track him down. Probably dyed that red hair already. I would have."

Max got up and wetted his face with cold canteen water, jolting himself awake, and the events of that afternoon came hurtling back. They had killed two American soldiers at close range. Max let the only witness get away. Then they'd interrogated and lynched their helpless prisoner. Max imagined the corpses hardening under the snow—those two young black MPs, their freckled leader, and even Captain Rattner, none more alive than carcasses hanging in a butcher's freezer. His little brother Harry had freckles, Max remembered.

Zoock was the smart one. The sailor had his one shot and he took it. He'd probably watched from behind trees as Max and Felix sped away through the woods. Soon, Max imagined, Zoock would hole up with some café owner's daughter, tell her he was an *Américain déserteur*. They'd share a wondrous night together. In the morning, he'd hitch a ride to the Meuse and on to Paris, where he'd make a good go of it and earn enough for a new identity—then a one-way ticket on an ocean liner. South America was an option. Maybe by then the war would be over. It was all just as Maximilian von Kaspar would have done. Yet von Kaspar was gone to Max now. His days in theater were dead and he could never bring them back. Passion itself was a pipe dream, a shot in the dark. He was being dehumanized— *entmenschlicht*. The only truth he knew was it was 7 o'clock in the evening on December 17, 1944, and outside the snow was dumping down and piling up. He was mechanical. He was *entseelt*—deprived of soul. He ran with goddamned murderers.

His eyes burned. A tear dropped on his thumb and he shook it off, sniffling. He dropped back down on the bed.

Beside him, Felix was sitting forward as if praying. "America, she chewed me up," he said.

"Say again?" Max wiped at his eyes.

"America chewed me up, and I hated America for that. Yes." Felix's voice gained clarity as if he were reading aloud to schoolchildren. He said, "And so I hated her for her ignorance, her piety, and her seediness, for her wild optimism, for her dog-eat-dog cruelty. And yet, I didn't hate Americans for what they are; I hated them for not shining even more than they do, and can. They can be so much more. You see, Kaspar?" Max nodded, why not. "Their potential is unlimited," Felix continued, "But they squander it. They could be supermen. Egyptians. Greeks. Romans. Conquerors."

Horse shit. That was the last thing the world needed. Max nodded anyway. "They are perfect for the part. But they don't get the role," he muttered.

"In truth? You want the truth? I was hating them for all the ways they're really too like me. Like us. By hating them, I was really hating myself—for holding back. Now I'm not holding back. You want to know why I fight on. Why I chant the slogans. Call for blood and victory. It's got nothing to do with Americans, or the Brits, the mongrel Reds invading from the East. National Socialism? That's just a banner. It could be any banner as long as it promised something . . ." Felix paused. "Max, sometimes I think I must be from another age. I want something nobler. Bolder. Not better. Not even idealistic, in the good sense. Just more, let us say, romantic."

Ruthless and primitive, were the words that came to Max. "That can be a bitter pill," he said.

"I'm not saying we're alike, mind you. While you were striving to be this cultured thespian of fine repute, there I was wasting away in the seediest clubs and cabarets—joints so degenerate, they easily survived the Nazi takeover." Felix snickered. "Now, with our Berlin-Rome burning, I suspect the old haunts are thriving."

They sat in silence. "America chewed me up, too," Max said finally. "Spit me out, as a matter of fact."

Fifteen

New York City, 1937. Over three years gone here and still in limbo. At least Max had Lucy Cage. They ice skated at the new Rockefeller Center. They picnicked in Central Park. Sure, these were the jaunts for tourists but they held such charm when he did them with her. (Why did the best memories always include women?) He'd go to her apartment after working late, and she'd be waiting up for him, keeping the bed warm, sprawled out on her back with one arm up close to her head as if she were waving. She called him Maxie. He called her Luce. She made him chew gum with her. She made him feel a part of this city. Instead of the din of cabs and sirens, he noticed the dew glistening on stoops and the toothy smiles of the shoeshine men, and how the steam danced and twirled from sewer grates.

Lucy was a model for advertisements. Cigarettes. Ice cream. You name it, she said. Once Max looked up on Fifth Avenue and saw her giant face nuzzling a giant pillow, two stories up and three stories tall, he couldn't even remember the ad it was so stunning. The gig went like this—she posed for an artist who drew her and painted in the color later. Sometimes they just took a photo and that was it, a half hour's work. She liked that best—the speed and convenience of it. Art was not a factor. Ambition barely played a role. It was just for the money. To her it was just a job.

Lucy got rejected lots of times. She just shrugged it off. How can you do that? Max wondered. In Europe we show the emotion, he told her.

"Apparently, you show it here too," she said.

"All you got to do is adjust," she said.

"Adjust, adjust—it's easy when you're born here. You can't adjust an accent." How many times had he ranted about this? It was the only thing they fought about. One time he threw a plate at the wall, and then a coffee cup. And why not? His whole block seemed to do it nightly.

And still the roles never came. His new agent was little help. Constantly he complained about the émigrés' stilted style. "Big European names, they said—sure, but the salt water it seemed to shrink 'em."

The only thing stopping Max was his accent. If he could fix that, all else would follow.

His new agent was skeptical. "The accent, it's got to be near perfect if you want to break out," he said. "Mocking is one thing. To be is another."

Max could be whatever he wanted, he decided. He went to the cheap matinees and watched the same films over and over, attuning himself to the American English sounds. Often he sat alone in the top corner of the balcony and sounded out the words. At home he repeated Lucy's sentences until they were dead on.

Lucy kidded him, "Honey, you don't want to sound like me. Who wants to see a German saying 'says you' and 'big lug.' It ain't right, you know? Got no class."

In America, class was only how wealthy you were. Heritage and profession played little role. He had to prove himself anew every day. Meanwhile, he had to eat, and it wasn't getting any easier. He had many jobs:

Funny waiter.

House servant.

Clothing factory—cutting buttonholes and pressing garments.

Guard in an insane asylum, of all things.

He could keep few of them. The funny waiter was in a club that still had vaudeville acts. He was expected to fall and spill on himself to get the customers laughing. He got the laughs, but they wanted him to wear an Imperial German helmet with a spike on top and a large Kaiser Wilhelm mustache. It was the only job he quit. The clothing factory job was tough. The steam and heat made his skin pink and tender all over, and the sewing machines made such a racket his ears rang. They told him not to come back one day. "My cousin needs a job," said the foreman, "and, well, you know how it is?" The strangest job was the asylum. It was an overnight shift. The hulking head nurse mistook him for one of the inmates once, and that was that.

Meanwhile, the émigrés were pouring in from a troubled Europe—more leftists and Jews from Germany and Austria, Italy and Spain. The more recent the arrival, the more bitter their take on the future. Many mistrusted Max. What was he doing here anyway, a gentile German? Some considered him an agent of the Gestapo, or in the least somewhat cracked in the head. Didn't he know there was a war looming?

Other émigrés talked of killing themselves. The writers were the worst. The older ones were serious about it. Max knew a middle-aged couple from Vienna who jumped together from their shabby apartment. She had a PhD. He'd won prizes for literature. Neighbors found them smashed into the roof of a Packard, still holding hands.

Nevertheless, Max's American English was improving. He'd lost the *ach* and *bitte* and *Mein Gott*, mastered the "th" and "w," and adopted a refined, Mid-Atlantic intonation that all the better actors were doing. Lucy told him so. "Oh Maxie, you sound so like Claude Rains. It's dreamy to be sure."

It was too late. The summer of 1939 was approaching and the scene was set—Germans in America were either bad Nazis or hopeless Jews. Max didn't look like a Jew. "So play a general or a spy," his agent told him, "that's the way it's been and the way it's gonna be for a while. Except in Hollywood. It has to be in Hollywood, Max."

Max stood his ground. New York City was the reason he came, and Lucy Cage was the reason he was staying. What else was there? He still had a hovel of an apartment on the Lower East Side, a small rectangle five stories up with one window facing the inner courtyard. Children cried nonstop. The elevated trains rumbled and clicked. To tell the weather he had to stick his head out the window and look up through the iron steps and railings of the fire escape. How many rides home had he declined so people wouldn't have to see how he lived?

One day, Lucy Cage picked up and left. She left Max this note:

I'm heading to California, Maxie. I'll be getting more work there, and you can bet I'll be seeing more sunshine. I'm sorry. I wish it could have worked out better for us, you know?
Love,
Your Luce

She might have been sorry, but she didn't even leave an address.

For weeks, then months, Max slept well into the day. He stopped looking for roles and started drinking rye whiskey like the tough guys did in the movies. Once he passed a prostitute who resembled his Luce and considered paying her to call him Maxie in her New York accent. But rye was overrated and so was sleeping late. One day, he began to snap out of it.

He didn't belong anywhere, but he was from somewhere. Was going back to Germany such a bad thing? After all, he was a German. So what if Germany was fascist? Many Americans admired fascism. Businessmen told him the fascist movement seemed a prudent and dynamic product of the modern age. Besides, who could appreciate the trains running on time better than an American? What better mirror of the efficient corporation than the resolute fascist state? Who else better represented the bold and decisive fascist leader than George Washington himself? Lots of Americans seemed to think so. Fritz Kuhn and the German American Bund thought so—they held a rally that filled Madison Square Garden, and who else should preside three stories high on the stage backdrop, between the stars and stripes and swastika, than that primeval All-American who could not tell a lie? For a time, American Nazism was more of an evolutionary certainty than many would care to admit by 1939.

Max was not political. He never had been. He was only seeing things for what they were, and the way things were going in Europe, he might not have another chance in a long time to make the jump. Hitler had annexed Austria. Then, he'd gone back on his word and taken all of Czechoslovakia even though he'd promised England and France he'd do no such thing. Max didn't blame Hitler for this. Of course, the little Austrian would overdo things in his first years of power. That was the way power worked, at first. Then he'd drink his tea and calm down.

Meanwhile, Max's auditions had dwindled to none. Hollywood wasn't an option anymore either, his agent told him on their last meeting—the place was now full of German speakers playing bad Nazis. Then his agent left town and hit California himself.

Max shrugged it off, best he could. He began talking to women again. A string of dime-a-dance gals kept him amused. He got a job as an elevator operator in a bank building. He heard American accents all day and perfected his American English in a frenzied rush.

In the back of his mind, he knew he was going back—and it wasn't back to Manchester. *Überall ist es besser, wo wir nicht sind*—"the grass is always greener," went the old saying in English.

One day an upper-class German man entered his elevator, and they struck up a conversation. The man said he was from the German embassy—a cultural attaché, he said. He invited Max to a nearby bar, and one drink became three.

Max was privileged this way, he knew. Most émigrés couldn't and wouldn't talk to embassy people. It felt nice to enjoy privilege. Max told the man everything. He loved America but it didn't love him back. He might have made a big mistake.

The man twirled the whisky in his glass and held it to his chest. He stared at Max a long while, peering into Max until the whisky was motionless, a straight brown line parallel to his manicured fingers. "In that case, you'd have to go back before it was too late," the man said. "Wouldn't you? And what's stopping you? The Jews had ruled German show business, and now they've all left. There's a great hole there. An opportunity. Think about it. You go back, make a real name for yourself. Return a hero to America someday if you like. This is the way to do it. So you think about that, *Herr* von Kaspar—or simply Kaspar if you like."

"I like. Maybe I like."

The man from the embassy frequented Max's elevator many times over the next weeks. The embassy would even cover Max's fare, the man told him. It was the least they could do for the serious-minded artist who appreciated the aesthetic opportunities in the new Fatherland.

"Times were changing, and you had to change with them," the man said.

August 1939. The subtropical heat was back. During these, his last days in America, Max wandered all over Manhattan as he had when he first arrived, taking it all in. The streets were hot and muggy like a steam, and he had to press his handkerchief to his neck to keep the sweat from soaking his last good shirt. He hoped he would run into Lucy. Maybe she hadn't really gone to California. Maybe he wasn't really going back.

Before he knew it he was aboard an ocean liner, which seemed too familiar, as if those eight years and change had only been days. This time, heading out of port, there was no fog or clouds. The sky was a crystal blue and the sun glared. This time Max saw the Statue of Liberty, shining jade green. They passed so close he could spot the tourists waving goodbye.

In the bar he had a rye, for old time's sake. Polishing glasses, the Irish bartender asked him how he liked America. Max told him:

"Funny you should ask me this. Because you know what I've realized? Everything I saw—the clothes, food, newspapers, door handles, drugstores, what have you—was different from what I knew growing up in Germany. But it was that way precisely—precisely—because they wanted it to be. And this was the very point. Why should they be like us? Do you know?"

"I'm afraid I do," the bartender had said, and then he'd poured Max another rye even though Max hadn't ordered one. Max drank it down, his hand trembling.

"Your American English, it's grand," the bartender had said.

"*Danke*," Max had said.

Sixteen

"I'm going to try to make it back there," Max said. He and Felix were still camped out on the bed, but the wind had started to rush through the fire-scorched house. They'd pulled their knees to their chests, hugging themselves.

Felix stared with his thin lips pursed. "You're deserting," he said. "That's what you're telling me." Of course, Felix knew of his plan. He'd known all along.

"That's what I'm telling you," Max said. "I've had it."

Felix nodded, in the dark.

"America spit me out because I let it," Max added. "I see that now. I didn't understand what was possible there. Anything is possible there, really. I probably began to realize this even before the ship put me back in Hamburg. Only later did I begin to understand that America in this sense—this promise of the possible—can happen anywhere. One must simply keep striving. One must not lie back down."

"So it's a state of mind. A worldview. That's rather romantic."

"Perhaps. I suspect we're more 'American' than most Americans, you and I."

A wolf was howling, from deep in the woods. Max told himself it was a wolf because he hated to imagine it a lost dog. Too often Max had wondered about the animals. How did they survive in war? Cities were being bombed. Food was scarce. All able men were called up. Yet zoos had cages and locks. Such thoughts horrified him. In war one had to keep the imagination hemmed in. And yet this was exactly how you lost your soul in war—by losing the capacity to imagine.

"Look, I'm going to make it easy on you," Felix said. "Just walk away."

Max stared. "What are you going to do?"

"I never got my munitions depot, did I?" Felix said. "Better yet, maybe I'll stumble upon a general. Farther north is a town called Spa. There's an American divisional headquarters."

Max had suspected something like this. It didn't mean he couldn't try to prevent it. "That's to the northwest, in the opposite direction. It would be against orders. We—you—are supposed to return."

"Then what? Reassigned? Slog on with the old men and boys? Cut down in the snow with the rest of the mob? That's all that's left. Our monocle-wearing generals are hardly romantics. Plus, you heard that MP—*Ami* Counter Intelligence is out here looking for us. No, there's no way I'm sticking to this sector."

"So you're the fanatic. The true believer."

"Perhaps. I want to go out in a rage of glory, as the Americans say."

"It's 'blaze of glory'—for once, I get to correct you." They shared a laugh. "You can have the jeep," Max said. "I've had enough jeep for a lifetime."

"I was hoping you'd say that."

"Take the radio, too. I won't need it."

"All right."

"I'll wait a few hours—till early morning."

"Splendid."

As always, Felix had been one step ahead. While Max was asleep, Felix split up their supplies. He was keeping the money, even though it was counterfeit and easy to spot under scrutiny. He gave Max the rations.

"Won't need food where I'm heading," he said.

He offered to shave off Max's mustache. The water was freezing, but his gentle touch made up for it. There wasn't so much as a nick.

"I told you I was here to help," he said.

Together, they scraped the Confederate flag off the hood. "Why did you stick around so long?" Felix said. "I mean really. You had your chances."

"Shame? A *Kamerad*'s bond? I thought I could help you first—you and Zoock. Then I'd go."

Felix made a tsk-tsk sound. "You got sentimental. That's a romantic's curse."

"I suppose so. I was also scared. And, I still am."

Four o'clock in the morning. After a couple shaky attempts at sleep, Max was ready. He had his overcoat buttoned to the top and two knapsacks crisscrossing his shoulders. Felix insisted he take a tommy gun—for authenticity's sake, he said.

"Rattner might have killed me," Max said. "He might have got us all killed. Truly, I'm indebted."

"Nonsense." Felix pressed something into Max's hand. It was one of the poison lighters. For Felix, Max smiled and slid the thing into a breast pocket. Felix placed his own into his breast pocket.

"So. *Der Vorhang hebt sich*," Max said—"And so, the curtain rises . . ."

Felix pulled Max's scarf tight around his neck, to better hide Max's SS uniform underneath his American tunic and overcoat. He pulled up Max's overcoat collar around it. "In another time? We might have made a good team, you and I. Grander souls would have seen the brilliance in pairing us together."

"On stage? I would have liked that very much," Max said.

"What the hell. Break a leg," Felix said in English.

"*Hals- und Beinbruch*," Max countered—the equivalent in German.

"I won't give you away, *Herr* von Kaspar."

"Nor me you."

Max gave his odd friend a little bow, and then a hug, and he was off, out into the expiring night. He trekked across a snowy field, clambered over a short rock wall and, checking his compass, entered the woods.

When the fire-scorched house was far behind him, well out of sight, he tossed the poison lighter far and high up into the trees. It knocked and clattered between branches, and was sure to land in the soft white snow without a sound.

Seventeen

The snow fell in heavy curtains, a white shroud that brought nature to a standstill. Fog evaporated. Wind ceased. The crows fled. By dawn all was white, and Max broke new snow traversing roads, fields, and woods. At times the snow reached his knees, yet it was powdery and resisted little. He saw humans only once—he'd emerged from woods to discover an American command car coasting downhill, tossing up the soft powder like a snowplow. As it passed, GIs stared from the turret with pale exhausted faces. They were coasting to save gas and didn't dare stop. And that was it. Max was alone. Free. The armies of Allies and Axis appeared to have vanished from his path.

His plan was to trek westward around the north side of Malmedy and on to the Meuse River. He had a long way to go. He had to pace himself. An hour after daybreak he stopped to rest. Within minutes his cold wet feet began to cramp up; he couldn't feel his toes, and the sweat under his wool chilled to ice water. Then a hunger started low in his stomach, piercing like indigestion, but he couldn't touch his rations, or they would never last. When he started up again, he began to lose confidence in his judgment. At one point he was certain he'd traveled in a circle, so he disregarded his compass and chose a direction on instinct—which really did lead him in a circle. After that he kept his compass pressed inside his fist, checking it every quarter mile. The thicker the flakes, the slower they fell. The snow hid everything. What if he was traipsing through minefields? Or right into a checkpoint of Military Police?

The forest seemed to grow denser, with no exit in sight. Thin shafts of daylight burned themselves out before reaching him. The snow became heavier and wetter, and fat globs of it smacked him at unknown intervals, trickling down his neck and chest. He shivered. His knees ached. He slogged on, getting clumsier. He had to climb over a fallen trunk but he couldn't feel his fingers grasping and he toppled down the other side.

Ten o'clock in the morning. For hours it had dragged on like this, a slow death. Then, the daylight formed patterns on the trail up ahead. The trees became skinnier and stood farther apart. He had to be close to something or someone even if just a village. He pushed on, stabbing his dead toes into the snow, flailing his arms, muttering like a madman, his heart pumping against his ribs. The forest gave way to a low valley that was hemmed in by more forest on all sides. In the middle of this white basin stood a boxy structure that resembled a factory or a modern train station—but upside down. A series of squares were set atop one another in the Bauhaus style, some held up by columns, others by sections of glass that seemed to have no girding whatsoever. A clean round tower rose from one corner. Flat stretches of roof bore puffy blankets of snow.

Max stopped at the edge of the trees and consulted the one map Felix had given him. This site was nowhere on it. He couldn't even locate the valley. Kneeling, he pulled out binoculars and scanned the snowbound grounds. No people, soldiers, vehicles, nothing. Closest to Max, statues, fountains, and dead shrubs poked through the white at symmetrical distances—what had to be a classical garden under all that snow. It meant the building had to be a villa. Max focused on the windows. Most blinds were closed. No smoke from any of the three chimneys.

Since he'd stopped, his sweat had cooled again. His shirts and underwear were soaked. Holing up a while might be the best thing for him. He could get a fire going. He tightened his scarf and buttoned up his overcoat to the top. He scanned the still scene once more, pulled his tommy gun off his shoulder, and marched down to the villa.

The double front doors—he guessed this was the front entrance—were black metal etched with gold, a Byzantine design of intersecting angles and swirls that reminded Max of monkeys tumbling down flights of stairs.

Why knock and announce himself? He was a soldier. He turned the handle and the door opened. He tiptoed through a foyer, and into the main room. Just enough snow-white light made it through the blinds and high windows to lend everything a dim, blue-gray hue. He passed chromium columns and semicircular partitions. The furniture was draped in white linen yet the protruding wooden feet and legs revealed to Max the antique styles of Louis XIV, Neoclassical, Empire. Even from under the linen, the pieces gave off the telltale muskiness of damp antique upholstery. The furnishings didn't match the villa's sparse and sterile design, and the effect was jarring. The curved modern walls held traditional tapestries, glossy plaques, and colorful coats of arms. Ornate rugs from the Levant covered the cold, polished tile floors. He descended into a sunken room and climbed short stairs into a higher room, and on and on, so that it became difficult to tell whether he was above or below ground without consulting the nearest window. He followed what sounded like a dripping faucet, only to realize he was hearing leaks within the villa's many skylights.

He caught what could only be the aroma of a fine perfume. Following the scent, he entered a room that looked like the den. The walls and pillars had elegantly carved woodwork. He sat on a settee before a window and, pulling back the linen, saw that it was covered in marvelous Belgian tapestry. "Wonderful," he muttered. He checked his watch.

Eleven o'clock in the morning. Only an hour or so before he dared deplete his rations—

"*Psst*. Why are you here? What do you want?"

"Who goes there?" Max bolted up aiming his tommy gun. He saw no one. The voice had been a whisper. It was a woman's voice, her English heavily accented. "Please, I won't hurt you," he whispered.

A desk was draped in linen, fronting a wall of built-in bookshelves. From behind the desk, a woman raised her head. Her blond hair was pulled back tight and her long, slender nose showed a faint crook at the bridge. The eyes were set so deep, Max couldn't tell their true color. They focused on Max and refused to blink. "I'm asking you, what is it that you want?" the woman said in Belgian French. "Speak up now, soldier Joe."

Max remembered—to her, like this, he was an American. "Sorry, don't speak much French," he said although he knew some. "And who you calling Joe? It's Lieutenant Joe to you." He lowered his tommy. He added a wide American smile.

The woman studied Max from head to toe, taking her time. Max kept smiling. The woman placed an old Luger pistol on the desk and stood. She was wearing a plain but elegant blue housedress with a faint pattern of orchids. She sighed and said in rough English, "You may have been killed, entering here without announcing. I might have killed you. But what is there to be done now? You are here."

"Yes. I seem to have lost my way," Max said.

The woman sat next to Max on the settee, and Max could smell her freshly soaped and scrubbed skin. For a moment, his hunger for food subsided.

"This is not an inn, you understand?" the woman said.

"I know. I understand. I was only cold." Max told her his cover story fast and all at once, dumping it in her lap just as any American would. His name was Price—Julian Price. His unit got hit hard east of Malmedy. The survivors were scattered and lost behind German lines. He had been able to escape. He just wanted to get home and go back to night school if he wasn't too old. He hoped to find a job where he could help people.

"I am Justine—Justine DeTrave," the woman said. She told Max she was watching over this, her family's country villa, along with her younger brother. Her brother had disappeared looking for food and she feared the worst, she said, bowing her head. As she spoke, the white window light revealed the soft curves of her face and long neck. She looked thirty at the most. He saw no wedding ring on her finger. She was beautiful even with her pinched features and curt manner—a hardier disposition than her noblesse upbringing must have wished on her.

"And your parents?" Max asked.

"They are dead," Justine said, sticking to English.

"Oh, forgive me," Max said, his confidence growing. With a Belgian, here like this, he could perfect his role. He could work on his mannerisms, and she'd notice few inconsistencies in his American English. Plus, the Belgians had to love the Americans for liberating them, for driving the hated "*boche*" back into Germany. "I should apologize," he added. "We Americans are always asking for a person's life story."

Justine gave a shrug.

They listened to the snow water trickling down the windows. They had no reason to hurry this. They weren't going anywhere soon.

"My compliments on your fine furniture," Max said.

Justine laughed, her head back, and she touched her neck. "Ah yes, but, the house itself? You don't like it so much?"

It certainly wasn't an actor's abode, Max thought. "These are smart, the modern Bauhaus designs—Gropius, Le

Corbusier. If one can afford them. Even so, one has the many water leakings to contend with, what with so many windows."

"So many, yes—don't tell me about it," Justine said, waving a hand. She cocked her head at him. "How did you know this house is a Le Corbusier?"

Max chuckled. "Yes, well . . . I went to college for a while."

"In any case, I quite agree with you. This house, it's not how *maman* and *papa* wished it. It turned out all wrong. But then have not most all things?"

"Indeed. You got that right, Ms. DeTrave."

Max drew a pack of cigarettes. They were Chesterfields— a surprise gift from Felix. He offered Justine one. She waved it away. From her hip pocket she drew a pack of Belgian cigarettes and placed one between her slim lips. Max offered a light, but she ignored it. She sat with her hands pressed to her knees as if ready to spring up.

"I will tell you about this house," she said finally. "The original structure, it is dated back to the 1400s. The French bombed it in 1916. Then the British, the American and— *mais oui*—even the German had a go at it before 1918 was over. So it was rebuilt, in the newer style. I despise the new style." She slapped at Max's knee and smiled. "Why can't they bomb it now? We could rebuild it in the old style, eh?"

"You must be careful what you wish," Max said.

"Yes, I suppose so. The furniture, that's from the original house—what we could salvage, in any case. Also this woodwork here in the, how do you say—*repaire*? Refuge chamber? Sanctuary?"

"It's a den. They just call it a den."

"They?" Justine straightened, her eyes hard again.

Max shrugged, smiling. "'Just an expression—figure of speech."

Justine was staring at his two knapsacks, and his wool overcoat with the two bullet holes under the arm. Only now did she light her cigarette. She blew smoke up at the ceiling.

Max stood. "You don't trust me. I understand. I'll go."

"Non." Justine stood. She was whispering again. "You wait, okay? Remain here? You must be hungry, yes?"

"I could eat a horse," Max said, recalling this phrase from the POW camp.

Justine frowned, an endearing curl of her mouth that made her look ten years younger. "Another expression, I hope? In any case the horses are gone." She grabbed the Luger off the desk and slid it into the pocket with her cigarettes. "I will procure some food. Relax yourself now. Lay down."

How could Max argue with that? Any food would make his rations last longer. He sat back on the settee and listened to Justine DeTrave's feet pitter-patter down the hallway. Just having her in the room seemed to have warmed it up. He placed his tommy gun on the floor, and his gear. He stretched out. He closed his eyes, but he did not sleep. He imagined himself as he had Zoock with a café owner's daughter. They would feast together. Drink wine. He thought he'd caught a twinkle in Justine's eyes and he hoped it was not simply a reflection of the snow outside. If she demanded his secret in the heat of passion, he would admit that, *yes, he was an American deserter, and she was all he had now* . . . He smoked another Chesterfield. Who cared if they ran out? Women made the worst times bearable.

She was coming back. He sat up. The pitter-patter was faster, louder, more like a rumble. He grabbed his tommy, shoved the knapsacks under the settee and crawled behind the desk, crouching. Slowly, he released the safety.

"Lieutenant? Meester Price," Justine was saying.

Max heard the jingle jangle of gear, and the heavy breathing of men. They were in the doorway. He stayed down.

"Lieutenant, you in here?" said a new voice. It sounded American, but refined. Max lifted the bottom hem of linen and saw the muddied, snow sodden boots of two Americans. A second voice said, "Sir? Can ya come on out? The good lady brought us up." This other voice was twangy, the words leaning up against one another.

"Who goes there?" Max growled. "Password?"

A chuckle. "Shee-it. Sir, know you must be good and rattled, but you're in good hands—"

"Stand up, Lieutenant," said the refined voice. "That's an order."

Max rose, aiming the tommy. At the doorway, two Americans smiled at him. They had their hands up, but only halfway. One was a captain, the other a sergeant. A black pipe hung from the captain's mouth and the sergeant smacked gum.

"All right, then," Max said. What else should he say? Stock phrases swirled in his head.

"Had enough? Happy now?" said the sergeant.

"Boy, am I glad to see you guys," Max said. He set the tommy down.

"Likewise," said the captain.

"Sorry. Just can't tell who's who these days," Max added.

"Ain't that the whole truth?" said the sergeant.

Justine was peaking in from the hallway, rubbing her hands together. The captain smiled for her. "See now, Ms. DeTrave? Everything's fine."

"Yes, yes, I see," Justine said, but her fingers were twitching—trembling with fear. That's why she was rubbing them together. Odd, Max thought. The newly liberated don't tremble. They hug, they sing, they kiss and dance, but they don't tremble. Max was the one who should be trembling, and the very thought made his blood rush.

He put on the biggest grin he had. "No, just can't tell who's who," he repeated as he strode over to the doorway, his arms out wide for handshaking.

Eighteen

"What was that about a password?" the sergeant said as Max, still grinning, shook the sergeant's hand. The hand was cold—the sergeant had come in from outside.

"Nothing, nothing. I was only hoping to trick you off guard. Ha ha." Max stepped over to shake the captain's cold hand. "Name's Price—Julian Price."

The captain looked Max straight in the eyes. "Lost your way, Price?" he said. Max nodded. "Join the club, then. It appears we're only a little less lost than you."

Justine DeTrave had stopped trembling, yet her frown returned. "I come back," she said and marched off down the hallway.

Max stuck his head out to her. "One moment, honey. Where's the chow?—you know, the food?"

Justine held up a hand, her back to him. "Yes. I come back. You will wait in the den room."

Max sighed and threw up his hands. He turned to the two Americans. The grin on his face felt silly, if not grotesque, yet it terrified him to let it fade. In this moment it might be the only thing keeping him American. The captain and sergeant stood shoulder to shoulder, eyeing him. They stopped smiling. "Boy, am I glad to see you guys," Max repeated, and he patted the sergeant on the arm.

The captain shifted his pipe to the other side of his mouth. "Lucky man."

"Yes. That's me." Max yawned, and let the sickly stupid grin fall away. He slapped his hands together. "All right. So what's the latest?"

"Good. Right. We'll trade stories, compare facts," the captain said. The sergeant pulled the linen off the desk to reveal a grand Empire replica. He whistled and felt the shiny, gold-inlaid top, dropped his map case and helmet on it, and sat on a corner.

Max remained standing, in case he had to flee.

"This isn't an inquiry," the captain said.

"Ha! No, of course, not." Max's grin was back.

"So have a seat, let's rest our bones." The captain stretched out on the settee, letting one leg hang off the side. The sergeant brought two wooden chairs from a corner. He and Max sat in the hard chairs, their backs to the desk and the bright window light in their eyes, so that the captain appeared almost in silhouette.

"My name is Slaipe—Aubrey Slaipe," the captain said, sliding his pipe into a trouser pocket. He introduced the sergeant as Smitty. Sergeant Smitty smacked gum and nodded. "What's your unit?" Captain Slaipe asked Max. Max told him, handed over his papers. Captain Slaipe turned to the window and studied the documents, cradling them in both hands as if they held gold dust.

Sergeant Smitty shot Max a half-smile, as if to say, sorry for taking up your time.

They kept to general questions about Max's unit makeup, sector, losses. Max answered as he was trained, sparing no details. He reacted as the theater trained him, drawing from life experience. His unit didn't know what hit them, he said. He saw friends die. They asked about his time lost behind enemy lines. He told of hiding in dark woods and damp barns as roaring, clanking panzers passed. He kept his sentences short. He mispronounced French and German words on purpose. He mumbled the tough American words and lost his train of thought on purpose, blaming it on the shell shock. He kept his overcoat on, his scarf tight.

As they spoke, Captain Slaipe kept Max's papers tucked in his breast pocket. He removed his helmet to reveal the balding, graying head of a middle-aged businessman, although he must have been no more than Max's age. And he was no mere businessman. He spoke with the eloquence of diplomats and professors. His pronunciation of nearby towns revealed he probably knew French. His skin was pink and clean-shaven. Max wondered how he kept it that way. Perhaps he could grow no whiskers, like an albino? His eyes were large with lots of white. Yet the man was also handsome in the same way a mentor or a philosopher was handsome—he exuded wisdom and principle, but also detachment. In an American movie, a dour sort like Fredric March would play him. As for Sergeant Smitty, he was more the All-American type. He had a round face, perfect white teeth, a ready smile. He was younger but certainly no fool, and he showed a dark streak. Max imagined him a crackerjack detective or lawyer in a small town. Captain Slaipe called him his driver and German interpreter. Most likely, Smitty was short for Schmidt or something longer— Schmidtbauer perhaps? Max would have liked to inquire, but the more he talked and reacted, the more they'd ask and the sooner he'd give himself away. Luckily, they seemed little interested in who Julian Price was and what he did back home. These were not average American soldiers. They weren't even hard-boiled. They were too smart for that.

"So. Enough about you," Slaipe said. He told Max the big picture. The Germans had advanced farther west than where they were now. Yet the Americans were counterattacking and the situation was volatile in every front-line sector for fifty miles north and a hundred miles south. This sector, this valley, appeared to be cut off, neither behind German nor American lines. It wasn't even a no-man's land. It was simply ignored. It had no vital bridges, crossings, or depots. From this Max deduced what he could. They probably had a field radio, he thought, since they knew the present situation far better than he. They might even belong to a type of commando team, for he had noticed they didn't wear unit badges on their sleeves. Slaipe finished by scratching his pink forehead and raising eyebrows at Max. "Any questions?"

"Not especially," Max said. "I know your names. What's your unit?"

"Special outfit," Smitty said. "We're doing recon," Slaipe added. They had put their smiles back on. Smitty stretched his arms up behind his head and crossed his legs. He said, "Well. Where you think that woman run off too, anyways?"

"Search me," Max said. How long could he keep this up? They drank from their canteens. They smoked. They talked about the villa and the state of modern architecture, which Max pretended to know nothing about. Slaipe knew his Le Corbusier. Smitty pronounced Walter Gropius like a native. Yet they kept their guns close, Max noticed. Smitty's tommy was slung on his shoulder, while Slaipe's Colt stayed on his hip in a holster.

"You know about the krauts in GI uniforms, I take it," Smitty said.

"What? I heard of it. Sure."

"See any?" Slaipe said.

Max laughed—a little too loud and harsh, he thought. "How would I tell? Do I just ask them, which way to Berlin?"

"Fine. Just asking."

"You have been lost in the woods, haven't you?" Smitty said.

"Maybe. Maybe I have," Max said. "I thought you said this was no interrogation." He grimaced down at his boots in anger and thought of spitting but didn't want to overplay it. Instead, he let his knee bounce in frustration.

"I believe my word was 'inquiry,'" Slaipe added.

Max stood but sat back down, shaking his head. "This is what I deserve? A guy goes through what I have, then he gets a third degree?"

"Okay, pal," Smitty said, "okay. Nobody's roughing you up."

"It's just habit," Slaipe said. "That's all it is. We're curious guys."

The offended bit seemed to be working. The audience was in the moment, and Max milked it. He sighed and paced around the room, glaring out the window. "Maybe I should just push on, find some dogfaces who could use the company."

"All right now. No need for that, Price."

Slaipe was holding out Max's papers. "Sorry. Okay?"

"Okay." Max took the papers. "Who did you say you are? If I didn't know better, I'd say you two are those phony krauts." He added another laugh. "Heck, you don't even have any unit badges on your sleeves."

Slaipe and Smitty shared a glance.

"You've made your point," Slaipe said. "Again, I apologize."

"Fine, sir. Then I too am sorry." Max slumped down on his hard chair.

They sat in silence, staring at their cigarettes. Slaipe emptied out his pipe, banging it against the wall.

Max had to find out more. Knowledge meant survival. He shrugged, exhaled. "I can say one thing, you guys know a great deal. Real up-to-the-minute. I'll bet you even have a field radio."

"I'm not a betting man," Slaipe said. "Yes, we have a radio."

"But, you can't get through."

"Comes and goes," Smitty said.

Slaipe seemed to have lost interest. He'd laid back and closed his eyes.

"The captain said this valley's forgotten," Max said. "How do you know?"

"Scouting party," Smitty said.

Max's sick smile returned. "There more of you guys? That would make me feel better."

Smitty looked to Slaipe. His eyes still closed, Slaipe said, "Had a team of GIs with us. Last time we sent them out, they never came back. It's been hours now."

"Oh. That doesn't make me feel better."

"We said this place is ignored. That doesn't mean it's safe," Smitty said. He shook his head. "Who knows what's out in those woods? Violent deserters? Hungry bear, and none too happy. Wild boar? Fierce SS stragglers bent on killing. Could be krauts left over from World War I, for all we know."

They heard footsteps. Justine DeTrave charged in and, seeing the Empire desk, hurried to recover it. She heaved Smitty's map case and helmet into his lap. "What is the meaning?" she hissed.

Slaipe sat up. "Please Madame, the sergeant meant no harm," he said in excellent French. "He only wished a peek at your fine desk. It helps us feel normal, no? Like something akin to humans?" He added a comically French shrug, and said to Smitty in English, "Smitty here, he really wants to be a desk soldier when he grows up."

Smitty and Slaipe laughed. Max joined in, though he didn't get the joke.

Justine's arms were crossed high on her chest. She had on a frilled apron, which, considering her personality and elegant dress, looked like something she would only wear at gunpoint. She said in French, "When you are finished with my den, I will provide food. Follow me," and she turned and left, her taut ponytail swinging.

Max pretended not to understand. He stared at Smitty, who said, "I didn't get all that—Captain?"

"She's got your chow, Price," Slaipe said to Max. He had his pipe and a bag of tobacco out in his lap. "You go on ahead. We'll be down in a minute. How about it?"

"Starving," Max muttered. He stood, grabbed his chair and set it back in the corner. Then he went to the settee and reached under for his knapsacks. That left only his tommy gun, behind the desk. It wasn't there.

"Looking for this?" Slaipe said. The gun stood below the window, behind the settee. Like magicians, Slaipe and Smitty had somehow managed to move it.

"If you think I should take it," Max said.

"Oh, I would. I don't trust that woman."

"No, I guess you're right." Max slung the tommy upside down on his shoulder and backed out of the room. At the doorway he stopped himself from straightening to attention and saluting. "Well, see you soon," he said and turned out into the hallway.

Justine was waiting for him down around the first corner, her hands on her hips. "Come with me. Never will you find your way through this maze when I don't help you."

You got that right, Max thought in German. "Ain't that the truth," he said in English. They passed through two of the rooms, down short stairs, and then up again.

Max grabbed her by an elbow, pulled her behind a semicircular partition and held her by the shoulders.

"Why didn't you tell me those two were here?" he whispered.

Justine opened her mouth, surprised. "Tell you? But they were not here, not right here in this house," she said. "They were hiding outside, in the guesthouse." She smiled, and it brought lovely dimples to her cheeks. She writhed her shoulders just a little. Max released her, but stood close. She held her chin high, to meet his, and said, softly, "I must confess, Meester Price, I was not sure what I do. I thought it better simply to throw all you men together and comprehend what happens." She was whispering now. She peeked around the partition. "There is something different about those two, do you not think? They are not the average American. But then again, you are not. Somehow. *Mystérieusement.* As you say, one just cannot tell who is the who."

Nineteen

Max followed Justine DeTrave through a bare modern kitchen of chromium counters, Bakelite knobs, and linoleum flooring. She opened a pitted iron door, and they descended a steep stone stairway so old the steps were bowed from use. They emerged in a cellar with an arched ceiling and walls of thick red brick. Max's eyes had to adjust to the dim yellow light. Candles in iron sconces illuminated the rectangular main room. In the middle ran a wooden table. At the far end was a hallway with more rooms (for food and wine storage, Max hoped), and at their end stood a wide, black fireplace stove. The oven doors were closed, but the crackling sound and the warmth on Max's cheeks meant a good fire was roaring inside. Justine could not have made that fire. Her apron was as spotless as ever.

"So. This, below earth, is from the original *maison*," Justine said. "Is comfortable, no? The Germans say '*gemütlich.*' Sit now."

"Cozy, do you mean? It certainly is that." Max sat at the table, unbuttoning his overcoat. The cellar was warm but also damp, and it reeked of soot and mold.

Justine lit the fat candle on the table and shouted in a singsong voice: "*Allo* Annette, *allo*, the first one is here."

An old woman appeared from down the hallway wearing a thick black knitted shawl and white hair pulled back tight like Justine's. She had a purple splotch across her forehead that had to be a birthmark. Max smiled as she shuffled past. She raised a hand and grumbled in French: "Don't tell me—I suppose you're hungry, Monsieur."

Max, pretending not to understand, grinned at Justine. "This is all quite Old World, don't you think? In a fine way, I mean. It's quaint." Medieval was more like it. But he was playing the new world innocent now, and not without irony: Quaint, Old World—how many times had New Yorkers slapped such naive labels on him?

"If you like," Justine said with a shrug. Annette set down battered pewter plates and silverware, a bowl of soup, porcelain pot, a loaf of dark bread, and then she waddled back down the hallway. A door creaked shut. Watching her, Justine said, "How do you say? Annette is domestic staff. She is the only one now. What am I to do? Release her out, into the snow? So go on. You eat."

"It's very kind of you," Max said. He had been dreaming of a meaty Belgian stew with *frites*. He got a soup that tasted like salty milk. Justine said it was supposed to be buttermilk soup with apples—a Belgian specialty, but they had no butter and certainly no apples. In the pot was sweet red cabbage and on a plate poached eggs in aspic with parsley. Not bad there. He tore at the bread with difficulty. The crust had turned tough, but the middle was still soft. He couldn't complain. He wanted to tell her he'd been a baker but wouldn't that be revealing too much of himself?

Justine watched with hands on her hips as if she'd been working hours on the meal.

"It's good chow, thanks," Max muttered as he chewed. A little egg on the bread, then a dip in the soup, followed by a crunch of the cabbage. He was feeling more like Maximilian von Kaspar with every precious gulp. "Truly, it's heavenly," he added.

Justine brought him a bottle of the local monk's ale, popped off the porcelain cap and, after he downed that, produced a sweet black currant beer as dessert.

"Such a fine woman to guide me. You'd make a lovely innkeeper."

Justine's eyes narrowed, and yet she smiled. Only an American would say such a thing to a lady of the manor, he hoped she was thinking—and only an American should get away with it. She mocked a full curtsy, one foot before the other, and snickered: "At your service, my Lord," in French. Then she sauntered up the stairs.

Max pushed his plate away, hunched over the table, the candle flickering. The milk soup had made him tired, and the thought of going back upstairs into that cold, sterile, blue-white world with its linen-clad ghosts for furniture and trickling skylights left him aching. He'd hole up here a couple hours more. The Americans seemed to buy his act, for now. Plus, those woods were no place for him now with the harsh weather and volatile front lines. Out there Germans could mistake him for an *Ami*, and the *Amis* him for a kraut.

Over in the corner was a bedroll. He unrolled it. It was quilted and soft. He crawled onto it. Placed the gentlest bulge of his knapsacks under his head. There. That was better. A little patience never hurt anyone, he decided, while the opposite was equally true. Just ask those black MPs, and Captain Rattner. He unbuttoned his overcoat, just two buttons.

Now, and finally, he believed he could close his eyes and sleep.

At one point Max woke and rolled over to see Slaipe and Smitty up at the table, eating. No harm there. He rolled back over, his limbs and eyelids heavy. Here he could sleep forever. The next time he woke the two Americans were still there, but this time they sat at opposite sides of the table, and the aromas of sweet red cabbage and hearty bread were gone. A rounded bottle and two brandy glasses stood on the table. Max lay back and listened but he couldn't understand them, not fully. Why was it that one could learn a foreign language fluently enough, yet when two natives bantered they seemed to speak a different tongue altogether? He sat up, his back to the bumpy brick.

Slaipe turned from the table, smiling. "Evening, Price. Or night, I should say."

"Night?"

"Without a doubt. It's near midnight."

He'd been asleep for ten hours? His pulse throbbed in his neck and temples. What if they'd searched him? They might have done anything to him, these two. He felt at his American overcoat. Still buttoned the same. He checked under the overcoat and American tunic—his SS uniform was still buried underneath, the closest layer to his underwear. The tommy was still against the wall near him, and his two knapsacks at his head. Near midnight? Soon it would be December 20.

"Dang," he said.

Smitty chuckled.

Max had to urinate; his bladder pressed at his gut like a jagged rock. Next to the tommy was a bedpan—Annette must have left it. He grabbed it and turned to the wall.

"We needed a midnight snack," Smitty said. "And low and behold? Ms. DeTrave came through with dried *Jägerwurst*, if you can believe that."

Max stared.

"That's a stick of jerky—to us Yankees," Slaipe said. "Talked the woman out of her Armagnac, as well. Take a drop? Why don't you? Come up, sit with us."

"Shake those cobwebs off," Smitty said. He lifted his glass to the light so Max could see the copper, Cognac-like hue. "Keep sleeping like y'are, war'll be over."

"Yes, I suppose you're right." Max sat at the end of the table closest to the stairway, his back to the warm oven.

Smitty sat to his left and Slaipe to his right. Between them the candle had become a droopy glob of melting wax.

The jerky was rich with spices and fat, just what Max needed to wake up. He took the glass from Slaipe and washed the jerky down. Splendid.

"Guy could get used to this, heya Price?"

Max nodded, chewing. They smoked. They talked about women. Max had to admit, he could get used to these fellows. Yet the longer he was with them, the sooner they'd find him out. It was up to them. They only had to start asking about his background, get in some trick questions.

Smitty suggested a game of poker. In English the card names were different. If only Max had dared to play in America when he had the chance. "No, no, you guys go ahead," he said. "I'm not in the mood."

He would have liked to play poker with these two. War was a nightmare of lost chances. This thought saddened him, and the intense and aromatic Armagnac didn't help. He drank it anyway. He might as well be back in America—that nightmare of elusive fate, he thought as he swirled his glass. The brandy inspired him, and he wanted to shine like Maximilian von Kaspar. But Kaspar had never really shined, and he certainly would not here, not with this script. He could take no chances with this role. Any striking characteristic could give him away. He was stuck in the role of the vague, American everyman. A man without qualities.

"No poker. Let's leave that for later," Slaipe said, and Smitty, nodding, got up and closed the door to the hallway. He peeked up the stairway. He returned to the table and Slaipe said, in a low monotone voice, "Here's the thing, Price. You should know about Ms. DeTrave and her family. Justine DeTrave is a Rexist."

Max wrinkled his forehead as if stumped.

"French Belgian Nazi," Smitty added.

"A Wallonian fascist," Slaipe said. "Just like her parents. We don't trust her, as if you couldn't tell. You probably felt the ice on her yourself."

Max nodded.

"Old guard like the DeTraves got real chummy with the krauts," Smitty said. "She tell you about a brother gone missing? All bullshit. Truth is he's Wallonian SS. Probably on the Eastern Front if he's lucky—back in Liège they'd be stringing him up by his toenails."

Eastern Front—even in English the words gave Max a twinge in his intestines. He took a sip. "Too bad for him," he said. "And, the parents?"

"Murdered in Liège, by partisans. This Ms. DeTrave survived it. Now she's here."

"Can't fault her for hiding," Smitty said. His face sagged, exaggerated by the shadows, and he drank.

Slaipe cut in. "Oh, she's certainly a good egg, at heart. In her mind they're only defending their monarchy and church from the Reds. But this villa is not the family style, is it?— Probably belonged to one of the many Jews the DeTrave family helped denounce when the Germans came. I would not be surprised."

Max believed them. But why were they telling him? Were they testing him? They wanted to see how he reacted? Slaipe was staring at him.

"Figures. Christ," Max said.

They sat in silence a while, sipping and smoking. They might suspect nothing, Max thought. They might actually trust him. Or, perhaps they'd known all along. They might even have told Justine he was an SS spy, to test her too. He lit another cigarette, and watched it burn.

"How do you know?" he said. "I mean, about Ms. DeTrave?"

"Wasn't hard. We have all the staunch Rexists in our lists."

"Your lists? What are you, the Gestapo?" Max said, chuckling. He was playing with fire, but he had to take chances. No kraut would say anything so stupid. He chuckled loud and deep.

Smitty laughed long and hard, sputtering "that's good, Price, that's a good one." Max laughed with him. Smitty poured more Armagnac all around, but Slaipe put a hand over his glass. He was not smiling. He said:

"More right than you know, Price. Once we make the big push into Germany, the German civilians might well call men like Smitty and me the *Ami* Gestapo. No doubt they will. Because they don't know any better. Sad thing is, the label will probably help us get the job done."

"But, you're not like them at all," Max said. He put down his glass. "Who the hell are you, anyway?"

Smitty and Slaipe shared a glance. Smitty drank. Slaipe said, "No harm in telling you. We're G-2. CIC."

CIC meant Counterintelligence Corps—the expert eyes, ears and brains of the mighty US Army. Max's thoughts raced, and the chances, hopes, and tragedies collided in his head. If he could fool these two, he could fool any American west of the Meuse. Yet he was so far out of his league. He held his glass with both hands and stared into it. "Going into Germany, that's going to be bloody," he said.

"Or, they could cave like old women. If they're smart."

"So, what do we do?" Max said. "About Ms. DeTrave. What can I do?"

"Nothing for now. Just keep an eye," Slaipe said.

Smitty said, "She's not why we're here—stuck here, I should say. We were heading over the border into Germany but got cut off. It's krauts we want. So, I guess it's really up to her. She wants to play cowboy, she'll get the full posse. She toes the line, plays the sympathy card, she might just get off easy."

Max reached for the bottle. Slaipe grabbed his wrist.

"Make no mistake—her day will come. Woman like her can never return to the mess she's made of her allegiances. Once this is all over, we've cleared out, her enemies could well have a field day. Her demons will too, I suspect. Her only hope is to atone for her sins, with open arms, and hope good fate protects her. After all, she didn't personally pull any triggers, did she? She only got caught up in the thing. And, I'd say she does have certain values to offer in the tough days that will come after. Girl like her is still young. She's smart. She could discover a new world and remake herself in it."

Was Slaipe hoping to send him a message, but without provoking him into something stupid and disastrous for all? The captain released his wrist. Max pulled it under the table.

"And her brother?" Smitty said, shaking his head. "Now that one he went too far. Who knows the atrocities he's left in his wake. What sort of tricks he'll go for—might even try to pass himself off as someone else altogether. For that we would not spare the rod, I can assure you of that."

"Sure, right, most definitely," Max muttered.

"And till then? It's a waiting game," Slaipe said. "We hole up, and we observe, and we be ready to jump at a moment's notice. Right now Eisenhower is screwing his head back on. We'll counterattack in full force soon enough, it's just a matter of resupplying, getting new troops from the rear. You understand, this is a war of attrition, Price, time, weather, and materiel are all on our side, and they always will be. You're either with us, or you're on the wrong side no matter where you hide."

"I understand," Max said. He reached for the bottle again. They let him. They watched him drink. "Ms. DeTrave is a looker, in any case," he said. "Have you seen it when she smiles? A different lady altogether."

"Certainly. It's no lost cause."

"She could inherit much," Smitty said, "she plays her cards right."

"No need to rush it. No need to accuse her," Max said.

"No, no. Locking her up here wouldn't do any good. Create undue tension."

"She's not going anywhere," Max added.

"That's the hustle," Smitty said. "She's on ice and we're on ice. So we might as well enjoy it while the fronts firm up. The big counters might not come till Christmas Day."

That was four days off. How could Max make it that long? He choked down more Armagnac. "A white Christmas," he mumbled.

"Damn straight," Smitty said. "Even thinking of cutting me down a *Weihnachtsbaum*."

"Say again?" Max said, forcing a smile.

"A Christmas tree. You know. Wouldn't have to go far looking either—there's good ones right here at the edge of the woods. So whenever you're itching to help me out with that, Price, well, you just say the word."

Twenty

December 21—Max's second day at the DeTrave villa. He'd let a couple hours become days. And why not? He was alive, and warm, and fed. He, Captain Slaipe, and Sergeant Smitty each did solo watch shifts up in the villa's tower. When not on watch, he volunteered to move the last of the coal to the cellar and, since the stash was dwindling, cut down some small trees in the classical gardens (with a reclining statue of Neptune as his sawhorse). Meanwhile, Slaipe and Smitty wrote reports, studied their maps and files, and deliberated in hushed and sometimes heated voices. The two slept in short stints and random spots about the villa with their weapons close at hand. Once Smitty made a short trek into the woods where, Max suspected, they had a jeep stashed. The heap was probably out of gas. And Max didn't want to know about it. He'd had enough jeeps for three lifetimes.

Late in the evening, as Max descended into the cellar, chilled and tired from his second watch, Justine met him at the bottom of the stairs.

"I brought you a blanket, for your bedroll," she said.

"Hi. Oh, thank you. Very kind."

"There is nothing to thank. It is *nécessaire*. The fire is out just now, and coal we have not much to remain. You may become cold, yes? If you wish, we will sleep together. Side to side. It is for the warmth of the body."

She'd said it businesslike, as if she was telling him they were out of Limburger but she could offer Gouda. Max cracked a nervous smile. Stalling, he slid the tommy off his shoulder and set it against the wall. Perhaps she had true physiological reasons for her proposal, since she slept upstairs with a tricky 300-year-old Dutch tiled heating stove that Annette struggled to keep lit. Or, she was simply making her first play for the new conquerors, commencing that crucial change Slaipe spoke of. An American would feel awkward yet inspired by her move. Max was less roused. In a flash he saw millions of young, hungry, and bored German woman making the same play once the Allies took Germany. He didn't feel jealousy, but rather a hot tinge of cynicism. In their sorry place, he'd be doing the same thing.

"I tell you something," he said, his English wobbly after hours of wintry silence. "If you become too chilled, you come to me. How's that? *D'Accord?*"

"*D'Accord*, Meester Price," Justine said, as if he'd said he'd make do with Gouda. Then she lit him a couple candles and headed upstairs.

Justine never came to Max that night, although it turned as chilly as she predicted. He had to sleep in his overcoat and gloves, and curled up for warmth. Still, he was relieved she hadn't come. This was what he told himself. This girl was playing a sick trick on him and she could hardly know it. She was reminding him too much of his Liselotte—a colder, harder, even opposite version of his Liselotte, and yet the damn die had been caste.

As Max huddled there in the cellar, too cold to sleep, how could he not think about the good warm days? His return to Germany in 1939 had been almost as big of a shock as his arrival in America eight years earlier. When he left, the average German was still struggling, troubled, and wary. No more. The reformed economy and higher living wages had created in many a childlike loyalty to Hitler. After all, wasn't Germany's rebirth the Führer's doing? (Providence, they were calling it.) Never mind the Nazi's persecution and their blather about revenging past defeats and betrayals. Faced with such optimism, such conviction, Max saw it was

senseless to argue. All he had to do was look around him—
the streets of Hamburg revealed a city, a country, a nation
transformed. It seemed all the buildings in this once grim
port had been scrubbed and repainted, their windows clear
as camera lenses—from the most trivial factory to the
holiest cathedral. Even the cracks between the cobblestones
were spotless, and the old red bricks seemed to sparkle. And
so many new roads! So many automobiles! So many bright,
alert faces! Every day people dressed as if going to church or
an afternoon party, with their shoes gleaming and shirts
white as snow, and the strangers greeted each other as if
longtime neighbors. How ironic, Max had thought then—in
those first few days back he'd believed he experienced more
hopefulness than all his time in that idealist's El Dorado,
Amerika.

This was hardly the mood of a people bent on war. On the
ocean liner, certain British and French in the know had
assured Max that another war was imminent. Just in the past
year, Hitler had seized Austria and Czechoslovakia, and the
man was far from finished—the appetite of that Bavarian
Corporal was insatiable. Max nodded along and let them buy
him drinks, but after he was in Hamburg a few days he saw it
differently. He wished he could buy his British and French
traveler friends one more drink and tell them his fellow
Germans were too happy for war. They had gained too much.
Why would they want to bring all this down again? Hitler
might not know when to stop, but surely the people knew,
and that would be enough.

In the theater world Max's American credentials
impressed (despite the lack of meaty roles), and his first
week back he signed with a prestigious talent agency,
Agentur Unger. Max's agent, *Herr* Kunz, got him two
supporting roles first thing—one in a film and another on
stage. In celebration, Max splurged on a spacious apartment

with a view of Hamburg's bustling harbor. The endless auditions and parties kept him hustling, his contacts swelled, and he had to hire a part-time assistant just to answer the phone while he worked on his lines.

At one of the parties he met Liselotte Auermann, an opera singer on the rise. She was a tiny thing, but she put her curves to full use with splendid dresses and the highest heels, like some exotic bird that fluffed itself up. Her eyes were so wide and shimmering blue. Yet she was also delicate beneath the diva fluff. When Max first met her, she was out on a balcony alone, feeding caviar to a stray cat.

She was everything that he had hoped for in New York. Her apartment had a salon and a ten-person auditorium like a tiny chapel. She drank champagne daily, but never to excess. She kept life in perspective. The New Germany was like the surprise success of a provincial show, she told him. Relish the run—and the attention—while it lasts, but don't let it destroy you when it falters. There will always be another show.

September 1939. Germany invaded Poland—after being "attacked" by Polish border troops— went the official line. But most Germans did not cheer and shout in the streets as they had in 1914. They gathered around newspaper kiosks and spoke in hushed tones as if gossiping about a deceased relative. Max, for one, woke from his naps with deep worries. His acting aspirations had always seemed like a race against time. Would they now become a sprint to outrun death?

"This silliness will end," his Liselotte assured him. "Germany is only rejoining its place among the civilized nations. The chaos of the last war will not return. My father assures me of it." Her father was an influential staff general, from a long line of officer corps standouts.

If only his *Mutti und Vati* Manfred and Elise could see him —before it was too late. He wondered how much young

Harry had grown. Max had to laugh. Suddenly he was sentimental? He told himself he would write them when he had really made it, but when would that be? It was happening so fast. He and his *Liselottchen* shared apartments in Berlin, Munich, Vienna. She held certain thoughts on the direction of his career. Here his stage name of von Kaspar would not work. The "von" modifier would have to go, since he wasn't true nobility.

The agent Kunz loved her ideas for Max. "Germany is changing, and we must change with it," he said. By the spring of 1940, Kunz was getting Max roles for a year in advance, and the actor now known as Maximilian Kaspar was becoming a moderate hit among directors, producers, reviewers, and informed theatergoers. His was a face you could trust for the role, they said.

At the same time, Max was no fool. Perhaps he was only an actor but his head was not that far in the sand. He saw how the Nazis were exploiting Germany, how they had been for a long time. The buoyancy and bustle masked scowls and perverse cravings. Take his agent, *Herr* Kunz. Kunz was the former assistant of Agentur Unger's namesake, the legendary Julius Unger. An elderly Jew, Unger had been forced to leave Germany in the mid-1930s, first to Paris and then Switzerland. He left the business with Kunz under the gentleman's agreement (in Germany Jews had lost their civil rights) that its name would never be changed. Yet in the spring of 1940, with times good and the business booming, Kunz changed the name to Agentur Kunz and transferred all remaining disputed royalty commissions to himself. And, not being one who simply danced to a tune when he could sing along too, Kunz joined the Nazi Party that same week.

Fall 1940. Germany had conquered France, and Great Britain was sure to be next. Max played Berlin's Prussian State Theater for the first time—a small role, but it was still a boyhood dream come true, while Liselotte sang in Paris to rapt German and French audiences. Max tried to be sensible. He wasn't the only actor for whom the goose-stepping and bully swagger were a solid bore. Still, a gig was a gig, and a well-paying one offered an income most could only dream of. Besides, where else was a German actor going to act in his own language? Certainly not in New York. As long as one was not "racially undesirable" or did not act "subversively," the brownshirts left a man alone. Of course, it was sad what happened to their Jewish friends, the Socialists. Naturally it was humiliating for those dandies, salon contrarians, and anyone else who'd livened up their days and nights. One muted one's shrill tone or one disappeared.

The more coveted the role, the darker Max's mood grew. Success brings not alleviation, only new pains—hadn't the old hands always said that? They were making deals with devils, every day, everywhere one looked.

At least he had had his Liselotte. She too was playing her share of kitsch. She let the thug SS officers and crass party bosses kiss her hand, escort her to dinner and functions. Yet she always came home to Max. To fall asleep she always snuggled his back, spooning him, her toes nestled into the bend of his leg.

Twenty-One

December 22, late afternoon. As the sun set, Max and Captain Slaipe kept watch up in the villa's tower. The gray sky turned a pale violet, the treetops were skeletal silhouettes, and the snow fell in light flurries. Up here the captain looked fiercer than the intellectual warrior Max knew down in the cellar. He wore bulky tank goggles and a thick black scarf and carried German Army binoculars. Instead of his pipe he smoked unfiltered Camels. His mood had dimmed, too, and Max hoped it was only the cold.

They had their backs to each other, scanning the dark surrounding woods with their binoculars. "Buzz bomb," Slaipe grunted as a V-2 rocket droned high overhead. The distant clatter of war had returned—thuds of artillery, cracks of tank battles, the snaps and burps of small arms— and now and then Slaipe called out the faraway weapons' types.

"Wonder where it's heading," Max mumbled, unsure how to answer. This was the first time Slaipe had joined Max on watch. Max was used to being alone up here. He could keep his mouth shut. He had his thoughts to himself. Sometimes he hummed and sang, in a whisper. A couple times he'd watched Smitty or Slaipe trudge through the snow below, making the short trek to the villa guesthouse that stood off to one side of the classical gardens, within a ring of trees. Max had been in there. He'd expected to find their field radio but only saw old pine furniture, a stone fireplace, maps and briefcases, and a couple US Army bedrolls.

"I have some bitter news," Slaipe said.

"Oh?"

"You've heard of Malmedy? The town? Your unit probably passed through it."

"Of course. It's not too far from here." Max pointed out, westward.

"You haven't heard what's happened there. No, of course, you couldn't know."

"What? What's happened?"

"I don't know if 'happened' is the word for it," Slaipe said. He groaned a long, slow sigh. "About fifty of our boys were withdrawing down a road, but they ran right into Waffen-SS —the First SS Panzer Corps, to be exact. Our boys surrendered, but these SS thugs—these unholy pigfuckers, they didn't keep them prisoner. They herded our GIs into a field and gunned them down. In cold blood. Murdered them." The captain's voice was cracking. He paused, what must have been a full minute, and then he cleared his throat. "Battery B, 285th Field Artillery Observation Battalion, 7th Armored. Only a couple got away, by playing dead. Rest? Frozen corpses, in the snow."

First SS Panzer Corps was the spearhead force Max had ridden with into battle only days before. "Horrible," he said, his chest tightening. "War is war, but . . . who could do such a thing?"

"Any German in SS uniform, it seems. Vicious gangsters basically. First SS Panzer has been on a rampage. Cutting down civilians too, we hear."

It must be true. The offensive was to move fast and instill terror, and far more soldiers than Felix Menning and Captain Rattner would have discovered a passion for butchery. Better men. Scared men. Max shook his head. "It's mad. There are no words for this."

"Yes, well, there might be a silver lining. The word on Malmedy's traveling faster than small-town gossip along our lines, from the far rear to the front foxholes. Calling it the 'Malmedy Massacre.' Our boys are mad as hell now, which is exactly what we'll need for the counterattack." Slaipe's voice lightened, and he said, "Wouldn't be surprised if we're taking less prisoners ourselves. War being war."

"Still, it's no excuse. There can be no justifying it."

Max squeezed at his binoculars and tried to concentrate on his watch, but the woods were blurring in the dim light. They heard the muffled screeches of missile launchers. "*Nebelwerfer*," Slaipe said. A couple minutes passed.

Slaipe said, "Remember those Germans posing as Americans? Smitty asked you about it."

"Yes. I didn't run into any as far as I know."

"No, but others have, and some are seeing a connection between the Malmedy Massacre and the Germans posing as GIs. Think about it. Both appear to be SS ops. And the fake GIs we've tagged so far? They were wearing SS uniforms underneath. Some even ran with the First SS Panzer, we're hearing." Slaipe lit a cigarette. "I can tell you, Price, we needed a big wake-up call and now we got it. Security is the new priority all along the line. Every platoon's using passwords. No one's above suspicion. Real GIs with accents have even been shot, on accident." Slaipe gave a sad chuckle. "Some say a select few Germans in GI uniform want to assassinate our generals, but I say it's bunk. I just don't think they're up to it."

Max chuckled, stalling. Why was Slaipe telling him this? What was his game? Was there even a game? Max lowered his binoculars. It was getting too dark to see even with the naked eye. Yet he kept his back to the captain. Anything but face him.

"And you want to know why?" Slaipe continued. "About two months ago, the German High Command, in its infinite wisdom, sent out a Wehrmacht-wide request for English speakers—and for volunteers at that."

"They what? Idiots. They might as well have sent you—us—a letter."

"Exactly. We intercepted it, of course. And what does that tell you, this request? Germans were desperate for the qualified English speakers. Still, they were lucky if they found enough to fill a few jeeps, I'm guessing. I know I wouldn't volunteer, but that's beside the point . . . They probably got few true soldiers. Ended up with English teachers, writers, artists, most likely. Few of whom are capable of assassinating a general, let alone a fly."

Max had trouble breathing, and he started to wheeze and shake. "I'm sure it's true," he muttered. "They're hopeless. Has-beens. Washed-up. Yet I wonder, Captain . . ." He started to ask what happened to the fake GIs who were caught, but his stomach burned and swelled in waves. He steadied himself on the rampart's edge.

"Price?"

Max couldn't swallow or feel his throat, a cold sweat smeared his lower lip and forehead and a hot flow gushed up and out his mouth, right over the edge.

"All right, get it all out, all right," Slaipe was saying, a hand on Max's shoulder.

Max hugged the rampart and heaved again, the steam rising, and again, not even bothering to wipe his mouth.

"Sorry to shake you up," Slaipe said when Max had finished. "Go on downstairs. I'll take over."

"All right. Yes. Thank you . . ."

Max scrambled down the ladder and stumbled through the house. Down in the cellar he stripped to his SS tunic, tore the thing off and threw it into the oven's fire and slammed the doors shut. He was alone here. No one could challenge him. He only hoped the foul wool didn't pollute the chimney's smoke—how sick and horrid it probably reeked, if one had the nose for it.

December 23. The next day. In the morning Max overheard Smitty reporting to Slaipe that the clouds above the Ardennes were starting to break. In their secluded valley, however, the same dim gray weather persisted, a stubborn pocket of snow flurries and chilling wind. Max stood outside and could hear American airplanes beyond the clouds, spotting the reckless German advances and seeking new targets. The American counterattacks would soon be launched just as Slaipe predicted. Max went back down to the cellar and sipped his coffee. He could not flee, not yet. Timing was everything now. It was true he had shed his SS tunic, but if he fled and was caught in an American uniform —amid the fury of an American counter—he was certain to be found a spy to be shot on site. And if he stayed? His only hope was that one big break. He'd certainly paid his dues.

In the afternoon, as he was pulling on his gloves and overcoat to relieve Smitty from watch, he heard yelling and stomping upstairs. He grabbed his tommy, threw on his helmet, and rushed up the stone steps.

In the foyer stood a small old man. A half-conscious German soldier leaned on his shoulder. Slaipe and Smitty had tommy guns on the two, but the old man was more concerned about getting the soldier off his shoulder. He yelled and they yelled, a clash of languages. Justine was there, shouting for Annette.

"Everyone—calm yourselves," Max shouted and helped the German soldier off the old man. The soldier was heavy, so Max set him down on a linen-covered sofa in the next room, which made Justine swear in French and throw up her arms. The soldier was regular army, not Waffen-SS, and so young he could have been Hitler Youth. He was wet and muddy, and bleeding from a chest wound that was dressed with ragged scarves.

Slaipe and Smitty searched the old man in the foyer, and Justine hurried off to find Annette. Max had Armagnac in his canteen. He let the soldier smell it and his eyes fluttered open, glaring wide as they focused on Max's American uniform. "I am surrendered, okay? No problem," he said in thickly accented English, and wheezed and coughed with a horrid screech that smelled even worse. He continued in rapid German: "*Komme aus Freiburg . . . In der Ecke, nahe der Schweiz . . . Mein Name ist Widmer—Martin Widmer . . .*"

He was from Freiburg, he'd said, from down in the corner of Germany near Switzerland. His name was Martin Widmer. Max shrugged as if he didn't understand. "You surrender. I accept. No problem," he said in English, pointing and gesturing.

Yet young Martin wouldn't quit with the life story. He had wanted to go into seminary, he said, but the war came. Then he'd wanted a French girl, but they shipped him out too soon.

If only Max could speak to him in German—he'd tell him to shut his trap. "It's okay, okay, it's okay," he said, chanting it, and finally Martin passed out.

Annette rushed past Max. Max followed her to the foyer. She squealed something in French dialect and lunged at the small old man, hugging him with so much force he stumbled back. He wore a worn tweed cap that was too big for him and a fur-lined overcoat that reached his ankles, reminding Max of an overage paperboy. Justine, smiling now, told Slaipe the story: This was Annette's husband, *Alter Heini*—Old Henry. He was from the borderlands between Belgium and Germany, just east of here, and belonged to the ten percent of Belgians who spoke German.

"More German? Jesus, we're surrounded," Smitty blurted to Slaipe, who could only grimace. The surprise arrival had shaken them. They kept their tommys raised and, despite Annette's protests, led old Henry into the kitchen and had him sit up on the counter, like a child. Max stood just beyond the doorway, listening and peeking in as Smitty interrogated and translated and Slaipe paced back and forth. Old Henry stammered with fear but told them what he could. He'd walked straight from Waimes, the nearest village to the east, where he'd been working for another family. He'd passed no recognizable front lines on the way, only a few Germans and a few *Amis*—all of them lost, hungry, in shock. He found the wounded German in the forest and couldn't let him die. He didn't mean any harm.

"Please, please," he said in clanging Belgian German, clasping his hands together. "I only wanted to see my dear wife for Christmas, you understand?"

"Understand," Slaipe said in rough German.

Max stood in the doorway, showing himself.

"In der Patsche sitz' ich nun. Sie sprechen Deutsch, oder?" Old Henry said to Max, rubbing at his little hands—"I'm in the soup here. Don't you speak German?"

"Uh-uh," Max said, shaking his head.

Smitty glared at Max, aiming his tommy. "What are you doing here? Huh? What?"

"I, I thought I could help—" Max remembered he was a lieutenant. He straightened. "Sergeant, remember whom you're speaking to. I don't care if you're CIC or, or . . . Ike's son—you respect the rank."

Smitty lowered his tommy. "Sorry, Lieutenant, sir. It's the nerves." He gave a half-salute.

Max's presence seemed to have the reverse effect on Slaipe. He stopped pacing, and he set his tommy on a counter. "Point well taken, Price. But I think what the sergeant meant was, one of us should be up on watch. Who knows who might have followed. So, why don't you go up in the tower? All right? One of us will relieve you."

Smitty relieved Max hours later, well after dark, and took great and humble care to apologize once more. Down in the cellar they'd put Martin, the wounded German, on Max's bedroll. The young soldier was sleeping, on his back. Slaipe sat at the table.

"Evening," Max said. Slaipe nodded. As Max pulled off gear and set down his tommy, Slaipe poured him an Armagnac. Max sat opposite the captain. They drank, saying nothing.

Slaipe set down his glass. "Annette and Old Henry are down the hall in their room. Reunited. I'm happy for them."

"Me too. And Ms. DeTrave?"

"Up in her room. Sleeping, I hope." Slaipe shook his head at Martin. The young soldier's peach fuzz glowed in the candlelight. "Poor kid, keeps muttering German. It's a decent language I've always thought, German. Solid, Latin-style rules. Logical. No room for ambiguity. Not like English at all." Slaipe lifted his glass in an imaginary toast. His eyes were glazed over. He might be drunk, Max realized. "Wish I could say something to that kid," he added.

"It seems you know a lot about languages," Max said, lifting his glass.

"Even when I don't know them?" Slaipe chuckled. "Maybe we could teach the kid English, me and you. God knows he's going to need it if he survives this. They're all going to need it."

"You don't think he'd try something? Become desperate?"

"And what then? Where would he go? No, kid's going nowhere—couldn't if he wanted to. I gave him what I had left of an ampule."

Ampule—Max had never heard such an English word. He nodded.

"Tough wound," Slaipe said. "Near the lungs. And no medic in sight." He drank.

Max drank. Annette had left jerky sticks and bread on the table, but for the first time in days—weeks—he didn't feel hunger. Slaipe refilled Max's glass, even though it was still half-full. Then the captain crouched over before the oven and began to build a fire, clumsily, rocking back and forth.

"Annette would not approve of a fire so late," Max said, and they shared a mischievous smile.

Slaipe got a good fire going. It cracked and popped behind the oven doors, and Slaipe sat back down. He gazed at Martin, sleeping down on the bedroll.

The Armagnac had loosened Max up. Feeling the warmth, he unbuttoned his overcoat. "You're not so tough, CIC," he said to Slaipe. "You made that fire for the kid Martin over there. That kraut."

Slaipe slapped at his chest. "Got me. I'm really just a soft touch. Then again, it's not as if the kid's Waffen-SS, is he?"

Max smiled. They stared at the oven, as if they could see the fire. Slaipe nodded toward Martin. "They're forcing my hand, you know—Old Henry and his soldier boy. Yours too."

Forcing one's hand—Max guessed it was a poker term. He chuckled, and he shook his head. "Sure, sure," he mumbled.

"You don't know what I'm talking about," Slaipe said.

"Come again?"

"Come again? Don't you think you're overplaying it a bit? I mean, really."

Max opened his mouth, but nothing came out. "How's that?" he said finally.

"The whole mediocre Yank act. You're no more a Babbitt than I am."

Max didn't know Babbitt either. He stared. He raised his eyebrows. He drank.

"That first day here, you didn't even salute me. Taking it a little far, don't you think? Even for an *Ami*."

Dread and shock were working its way up Max's chest and neck, a rolling shudder that sent him into a shrill giggle. "A what? What? Hey, I was just happy to see you guys."

Slaipe was frowning, his lower lip jutting out. He had one arm down low, under the table. Max was sure Slaipe had his Colt aimed on him.

"That wasn't the only thing that tipped me off," Slaipe said. "That first day, you referred to our 'insignia badges.' It's called 'unit insignia' in American English. In this man's army."

"What? No, I've heard lots of Joes say badge—"

"And, how could you have heard—only heard—about krauts in American uniform, if you hadn't been behind American lines yet? If you hadn't seen any. You couldn't have known."

Max hardened his jaw. "Look. Captain. This is silly, and quite frankly it's beginning to insult me. You've had too much to drink. Perhaps—dare I say, you've been out in the field too long."

"Oh, of that, you can be sure." Slaipe stared, into Max's eyes. Max let him. He didn't blink. Finally, Slaipe said, "You were thinking of the word '*Abzeichen*,' weren't you? Did I pronounce it right? The German word for insignia, Smitty tells me, but it's most often translated as 'badge.' I've noticed about five other examples, not to mention the variations in accent. I used to teach linguistics, you see, in another age. Another life."

"Thus the interest," Max said. He placed his hands flat on the table so the captain could see them. Slowly, he reached for the bottle of Armagnac.

"An ampule is a vial of morphine, by the way. You've done a fine job, don't get me wrong. I especially like the way you handled Smitty in the kitchen earlier. For a while you even had me, let's say, misdirected. I knew there was something funny about you. But I thought maybe you were only light in your loafers."

Max wanted to laugh at that—Felix would have loved it. He could only grimace. "I'm not that way," he said.

"Of course not. Ms. DeTrave can see that. And so I see it."

They sat still a while, saying nothing. Thinking. Max had nothing more to offer. No line. No gesture or prop. Nothing. He shrugged once. Slaipe sighed.

"I'm an actor, you see," Max said.

"I figured it was something like that."

"You don't need that pistol."

"I didn't think I would. You showed me that up in the tower yesterday. Retching like that—such disgust—is no acting job. That's why I'm letting Smitty stay up there now. Still, I had to be sure you'd react like a wise man, which you are."

"I'm not going to fight this, captain. Lock me in a room if you want, but you don't have to worry about me."

"No. We'll keep the ammo away from you. You can keep your empty tommy for pride—a provisional souvenir. How's that?" Slaipe attached a sad smile.

"Smitty won't like it."

"Tough. I'm his superior, and I believe in constructive punishment. You know what he wanted to do when I first suspected you might be a German? Strip you naked and send you out into the woods."

"He must be ashamed of Germans. Of being one."

"I suppose so. Your wars keep wrecking it for them back in the states. In our eyes you used to be something special. A little too literal and formal, but a classy folk. Now you're looking far worse. You're either Prussian Nazis or these poor refugees stripped of all dignity . . ." As Slaipe spoke he stood, the Colt in one hand, and moved around the table to Max.

Max stood with hands up and Slaipe frisked him, slowly and thoroughly.

"So I've discovered," Max said.

"This isn't a stalemate, mind you. You're done. I just don't see any point in playing jail warden." Slaipe emptied Max's tommy clip and ammo bag and rummaged through Max's knapsacks.

Max was still standing, though Slaipe had let him lower his hands. "How do you know I don't have a weapon stashed somewhere?" Max said.

"Because you just mentioned it. There's that and the fact that you could have tried it earlier and didn't. Plus, I can tell you're not stupid. It would get you nowhere."

Perhaps there was another way to get to America, Max thought. He could provide intelligence to the Americans. Other captured Germans were doing it. He didn't know much, but he had fought the Russians, who the Americans were sure to face someday. It didn't have to be so bad. A few days of interrogation and then a modest sentence back in America. "You're not stupid either, Captain Slaipe," he said.

"Thanks. Now, why don't you take a seat?" Max sat. Slaipe sat across from him and topped off their glasses. "So. A few questions, if you don't mind. You mentioned being in America. About discovering things."

Max told Slaipe everything. He told him his real name, Max Kaspar. He revealed his stage name of Maximilian von Kaspar and he and the captain shared a laugh over that. Max told the American more than he'd probably told even Felix Menning. America chewed him up, he admitted, because he didn't adapt. He'd been too rigid. You have to be a chameleon to make it, but he wouldn't turn the right color. He couldn't get the roles because of that. Worst of all, he'd made a grave mistake by leaving America in '39. If he could only have a second chance, knowing what he did now, then he would make it right. That was why he went on the mission. It wasn't to defeat Americans. It certainly wasn't to kill American generals. Odd as it sounded, it was for freedom. To make a new start.

Captain Slaipe said he believed Max. He had worked with émigré artists' relief organizations in New York State. They might have even run into each other before the war, he said. So he understood Max's plight. Max had not been a persecuted German, that was his problem. He hadn't fit in. Wrong place at the wrong time.

"Yes, yes, that's it exactly," Max said. "You understand it better than my agent." He had dropped the casual American bit—the carefree speech, the ready smiles and the hanging of his arms and legs off every ledge in sight. He even let his accent slip. "And then to think that such a crude and silly secret mission would help me come back to America? This was my little plan, *Herr Kapitän*—cross over the Meuse. And how close I was. But what a fool I am, too."

Slaipe was frowning. He didn't seem to enjoy the real Max. "Well, here's a bitter pill for you," he said. "You can't go back. You can't because that part of your life is already gone and you can't bring it back. Even if there wasn't a war on. You're a different person now. We all are. The Meuse is more than just a river, Kaspar. No, the main thing now is, to make this right. For what you have done. All of you. And that's not about place. It's about deeds."

Deeds? Max didn't want to hear it. All his life he'd been preached to about proper deeds, conduct, performances. He was tired. He just needed to think.

"Yes, I understand, captain," he muttered.

Annette had left out a second bedroll, in the corner across from young Martin. Justine's blanket sat on top, neatly folded. Max heaved himself up, shuffled over, and unrolled his new roost. "Now, if you don't mind, I think I'd like to retire. And then I will think about what you say."

"Of course, of course. But first I'm afraid I have more details to go over."

Max nodded, wearily, and sat up, his back to the rough old bricks. Slaipe had a notebook out on the table, and a fine Parker pen. Max knew what Slaipe needed now—intelligence, the nuts and bolts. He told the captain about his jeep team and about Felix Menning, and even Zoock. Still, he left out Rattner and the incident with the MPs.

"All right. What about Malmedy?" Slaipe said.

"What about it? We were never there. You think I could do something like that?"

"They'll think you were involved. You're SS, officially."

"I discarded my tunic. I was never in the SS. They made me wear it. Said we wouldn't be shot as spies if we wore them underneath."

Slaipe nodded along. He probably knew all this. "Doesn't matter. It's in your sector," he said. He scribbled notes and stared at them, for what seemed like minutes. "So, let's go over this. This sailor, Zoock. If he's as clever—and harmless—as you say, and his American English that good, he might be the only one who could make it. Not a problem there. Now, I've heard of your comrade Menning, I have to tell you. *Hauptgefreiter* Felix Menning, right?—a.k.a. Corporal Herb Fellowes. He's to be shot. Firing squad. Today or tomorrow. As soon as they're done questioning him."

It was a bluff. The captain was trying to spook him. Menning would never let himself be caught. "How do you know this?" Max blurted.

"I have a radio, remember? We do get through now and then. They caught Menning near Spa, trying to infiltrate First Division HQ. You're all being shot. There's a farmhouse, just north of Spa. It has a good and tall stone wall for it . . ."

"The little devil," Max grunted in German, "that skinny goddamn juggler." He jumped up and marched around the room, his neck and head hot, his hands balled into fists. He kicked at the table bench. "Why are you telling me this? I might do something stupid now. Isn't that right? I could. Kill you. Kill them. Anyone."

"No. Not you. Listen. Sit down. I saw the first of the firing squads, you know that? On my way here. Four men—from your Jeep Team E, I think it was. Have you seen one of these things? How they do it? A grisly act, to be sure. They stand you up against a post, tie your hands behind your back. Pin a little round white piece of paper to your heart as a target. Offer you a cigarette, if you're not jittering too much to keep the thing in your mouth. A priest asks you, do you have any last words? That was the turning point. All four of those men's heads were high until then. Then, in an instant, three of them cracked. Vomiting, shrieking. Crying for his mother, one of them. And the fourth? Shouted Heil Hitler, of all things. What a sap."

"Please, captain, get to your point."

"My point being, none of them saw it coming—not one of those men had a clue how this game is really played. But then again, they were a bunch of amateurs, weren't they? Chefs, and dancers, and writers . . ."

Max slumped over the table. "Very well, captain. So you want something. What is it you want?"

"That's just the thing. I'm not sure I have any leeway here. They'll want your head just the same." Slaipe tapped his pen at the notebook, and his chin. "But I'm working on it, and I'll be sure to let you know if I find a way."

As Slaipe spoke Max, out of the corner of his eye, spotted Justine DeTrave's immaculate blue loafers planted at the top of the stairs. He stood. "Who's there? We're fine here. Everything's fine," he shouted in his best American English.

Finally, Slaipe left Max alone to sleep. Max left one candle flickering, crawled onto his bedroll, and closed his eyes, taking deep breaths. How could he sleep? He turned on his side and watched the young soldier, Martin. Martin snored a bit, and he groaned at times. His eyelids twittered. His eyes opened. He stared.

"I thought you were an *Ami*," he said in blunt schoolboy German.

"I am," Max said in English.

"Weren't you speaking German?"

"What? No. Forget it. It's the morphine. You're dreaming."

The kid blinked, twice. "You changed sides? Is that it?"

Max sighed. "I never took sides," he said in German. "Not ever. Perhaps that's my problem."

"I never did either. So, how can we change sides then? If we've never taken any?"

"I don't know. You tell me. Now go to sleep. And keep this our secret, clear?"

Martin nodded and turned over.

Some time later, Max woke—to fingers on his lips. Soft, warm, lean fingers. Justine DeTrave was hovering over him.

"Me, I become cold now," she whispered in French. She let loose her hair, and it tickled Max's forehead. Even her hair was warm. Kissing him, caressing him, and murmuring in French she worked her way in, and down, under his borrowed old blanket.

Twenty-Two

After, they slept. Max woke once. He had never been so
warm since being drafted. He lay on his stomach. Justine
DeTrave was snoring, lightly, like a cat purring. She had
curled up behind him, grasping at him, with one leg up
around his waist and the other tucked under him, her toes in
the bend of his leg. Of course, she'd used the same maneuver
as Liselotte. If only this were Liselotte. Together they would
have worked this out. He would come up with a grand
scheme and Liselotte, ever the composed diva, would follow
it through. She'd appeal to Captain Slaipe in language he
understood. How many auditions, roles, and engagements
had they landed each other this way? She was the one who
had made Hitler's New Germany bearable. It had been an
even harder trick to pull off, and yet she'd managed it until
well into 1941.

Spring 1941. April 8. The first dark hours of a rainy Tuesday
in Hamburg. Max, in bed, heard a droning from far above.
He'd heard it many times since the Battle of Britain began—
another wave of German bombers heading for England. He
rolled over, pulled a pillow over his head. Yet the droning
didn't pass. It grew louder, rougher. This wave was roaring
low and coming their way. Above the city, the flak bursts
cracked and popped.

   Max jumped from bed. The windows shook. Dust
fluttered from the ceiling. He yelled for Liselotte. She was
long gone. She'd risen well before sunrise to hit the open-air
markets down by the wharf as she so often did, to connect
with the "real folks," as she called them. Max grabbed his

dressing robe, stumbled down the stairs and out, joining the stream of neighbors into the new air-raid shelter two streets over, asking—shouting—again and again had anyone seen Liselotte Auermann? No one had. They huddled down there as the upper world boomed, rocked, hissed. People slapped their hands over their ears and hugged children they didn't know. Minutes became hours. The air turned stale and hot with the stench of sweat, worry, hungry breath. Max did his part. He'd helped the old folks down, and when the bombing and flak ceased, he sang for the children. His dear *Liselottchen* would have done the same, he was certain of it. She was probably doing it for the fishmongers' *Kinder* down in a shelter by the harbor.

Three hours later Max returned to their building. The apartment was intact. Liselotte had not returned. Out their window, their lovely harbor view was a hell scene. Rampant fires and black pillars of smoke rose into the dim clouds, which reflected red and orange and seemed to churn like hot lava. Ships had strayed about the harbor and the water shined black, slick with oil. The silhouettes of familiar buildings had vanished, replaced by storms of dust; and even with his windows closed a reek of soot, burning rubber, and what smelled like rotting meat had settled into the room. The phone lines were down. He tuned their radio to the BBC, not caring who heard him. London was reporting that almost 300 British bombers had hit Hamburg, the first major air raid on Germany in retaliation for months of major German strikes suffered in the Battle of Britain. Over in Piccadilly and on Trafalgar they sang and danced. In his apartment, Max sat on the floor and waited. After two hours he left a note and headed for the harbor wearing only an overcoat over his robe and boots he borrowed from the concierge.

On the way he checked with friends and acquaintances, their restaurants and bars. No one had seen Liselotte. He headed toward the smoking harbor district with his silk handkerchief pressed to his mouth, tiptoeing around the wild flowing streams of sewer water and oily mud. The closer he got to the harbor, the more horrific the scenes. Firefighters had laid out rows of corpses. He sidestepped them, looking away. When he pressed on, climbing over rubble when he had to, he saw the corpses were everywhere, half-buried some of them, roasted brown and purple and black. Tiny blue flames flashed from them, and puddles of their own melted fat began to firm up like jelly. Deep under the rubble people screamed and moaned, their genders unintelligible. Then Max heard gurgling sounds. Boilers had burst, leaving steaming bubbling pools in which flesh and bone cooked, bobbing at the surface like noodles and dumplings. Was he really seeing this? This was the war the party fat cats wanted? Goebbels would later proclaim this madness "Total War"? Apartments fire-bombed, the children boiled in their own bath water? And the Allies, they called it "Strategic Bombing"?

The harbor district was off-limits. It was far too dangerous, the guards told Max. The British bombers had hit everything—the open-air markets, rows of apartments, even two bomb shelters. Max hurried on, the handkerchief now tied over his mouth. At the nearest hospitals they could tell him nothing. They were sorry but he would just have to wait. He returned to the apartment after midnight. The phones were still down, but the electricity worked. Yet he didn't bother to switch on a lamp. He sat in the dark, on the bed, and waited for first light. The clouds reflected red and orange well into the next day. The carnage created a stench that smoldered and shifted with the wind. Down at the harbor Max joined the "rubble gangs" who cleared debris and bodies. He worked there for days, from dawn until dusk. He extracted many bodies. They never found hers.

For months after, a stupor blurred Max's days. Unable to concentrate on his lines, he left his current role to a greenhorn understudy. Moments of clarity came and went— he thought he heard Liselotte's voice on the street or he saw her stepping onto a streetcar, the soft lines of her neck glowing with sunlight. For a time he got wild ideas. What if she was living a secret double life resisting the regime and had to get out? She wouldn't have been the first German to live as an impostor. Emboldened, he inquired with Liselotte's family lawyers about the possibility (they suggested he take a long cure) and became a kind of roving detective, checking ship's manifests and questioning railway conductors who staffed the international routes. Months of this passed.

In the fall, as the harbor excavations turned to rebuilding and the first snows threatened, the harbor morgue was able to identify the remains of Liselotte Auermann.

1942. America the sleeping giant had declared war on Germany, and Great Britain looked to be saved. In North Africa, every German victory was followed by a costly defeat. Hitler had invaded the Soviet Union the year before, yet the advances were volatile and Moscow held out. Then came the bitterest loss, at Stalingrad—147,000 Germans dead and 91,000 taken prisoner.

The films and plays waxed patriotic, and the roles were trite. Once, Max had vowed never to play a hackneyed character. In America he'd avoided doing the monocled Prussian and the sinister Nazi. Now he was playing the dashing lord and the brave lieutenant in period melodramas. The scripts were all the same—Teutonic Knights tales, Alpine Singspiels, Frederick the Great epics. One was filmed on a grand Louis the Fourteenth studio set while, just beyond the soundstage walls, heaps of smoldering rubble loomed and children wandered the crooked paths, calling out for parents.

The depression set in Max, a black rolling wave of it, blacker than any he had suffered alone in New York City. Why would a people want to sell itself out, and destroy itself? It was happening to him, too, wasn't it? Was not the theater world a microcosm of Germany's affliction? The producers, directors, and Kunz's were like the party leaders, generals, and ministers while the actors, dancers, and musicians were the poor foot soldiers. He was going along with a cruel scam; he was a cog in a machine engineered to self-destruct; he would end up no better than his father, the common baker who aspired to something he could never be.

1943. Total defeat in North Africa. Hitler's exalted Latin ally Mussolini fled for his life, leaving only the north of Italy in German hands. The air raids hit German cities night and day—the Brits by dark, the *Amis* by sunlight—and the lost Liselottes could never be counted. Men were drafted, young and old. Shows closed, the roles dwindled. Max lost his apartment and moved in with the assistant who once answered his phone. Max was one of the lucky ones. His agent, Kunz, was taken away by the Gestapo, and for what Max never learned. All were suspect now.

Max carried around a flask of *Korn* in his breast pocket like some smalltime speculator, a little in his *Kaffee* to kill the pain. And why not? His favorite café was rubble, his corner store squashed along with its owners, a kind old couple who called him *Herr* Maxi. He had let America chew him up, and now he was letting his own land blacken him on the insides. Did he have so little understanding of the world, and his part in it? He truly was the classic self-centered actor. And that's what the New Yorkers had seemed like to him—self-centered? He did not drink alone though. Not this time. Many of his friends had turned to the bottle, dope, and vice. Some clichés were true—the funny thing about being on the losing side was, you really did celebrate as if every day was your last. Max woke up with Liselotte look-a-likes, Lucy Cage doubles, dancehall girls and wannabe actresses fresh from the League of German Maidens.

He purposely played his roles badly. No one seemed to notice. He stopped looking for roles. Theater officials from the party called him in to discuss what they called his "questionable behaviors." If he wasn't interested in landing the patriotic roles they could send him into the *Truppenbetreuung*—the Troops Entertainment Section. How would he like that? Performing near the front, with wooden stages on mud, a cold barn to sleep in. "If you think that's how I may best serve the Fatherland, then I welcome the opportunity," Max told them, adding a bow. He only wanted to hurry this up, since he had a date with a general's daughter in a half hour. This girl, Hedwig (no stunner but a bold wit), was fast becoming his prime contact in his moonlighting gig as black market operator. Like many with contacts up high and roots down low, Max began playing intermediary between those who controlled scarce foods and liquors and those who craved them. Along the way he often came into possession of rationed bulk goods, such as meats and wheels of cheese, milk and coffee, baby formula. These he practically gave away, letting those at the top believe he was charging exorbitant prices when it was the needy who were getting the deal.

Spring 1944. The Russians pushed west on multiple fronts, and the invasion of German-held France was sure to come within the year. Max was detained for questioning over his black market activities, yet he kept at it. War rationing had grown harsher by the day, and he was practically giving away whatever bulk goods he could get his hands on. Families with more than four children got the milk and meat free. All he had to do was charge the fat cats more for the finer items. His deeds warmed him at night and kept him singing in the dim air-raid shelters.

Before the spring rains ceased, he was arrested twice and warned to watch whom he was gouging. He shrugged it off with a smile. Why be sensible now, Max?

Summer 1944. Max was drafted. He saw it coming. Film production was stalling, and fewer than ten theaters and operas were left performing. By the end of June he was on the Eastern Front in the uniform of an army private.

By the fall of '44, it was the horrid darkness of Eastern Front. Cold so severe it slowed your heart. Roadside blazes so hot they singed eyebrows. Scorched, shrunken corpses. The dead toddlers. An enemy so maddened, so dogged, that Germany was sure to pay dearly for the pain it wreaked. Huddled in dark foxholes, shaking, Max had made the wildest secret vows. He was never going back to the Germany he knew—the Germany that had betrayed him.

Twenty-Three

Under his bedroll blanket Max was cold and his joints stiff, even though he could hear a new fire crackling in the cellar oven. It was the next morning. Justine DeTrave was up and gone. Max sat, pulling the blanket up with him. Young Martin was still sleeping in the next corner, and Max watched to make sure the young soldier's chest was still rising and falling. Martin turned to Max and blinked. Max smiled.

"So then, what are you going to do?" Martin wheezed in German.

"I don't know . . . what you're talking about," Max said in English.

Martin kept staring, and blinking as if unsure of their previous conversation (perhaps it had been a dream?). Max heaved himself over to the table, where Annette had left a pot of coffee. It was empty. He shook his head at it and sighed. Today was December 24, 1944. Christmas Eve. Back on the Eastern Front, he had doubted he'd live to see it. And now after all he'd been through these last weeks? It was a wonder.

He pulled on his overcoat and, leaving his unloaded tommy gun in the far corner, slogged up the stairs and walked about the villa. He called out names but no one answered. Captain Slaipe would be up in the tower, he figured, and Sergeant Smitty was probably on their radio again. He reached the den. His thigh muscles ached so he sat on the settee, pulled the linen over him, and stared out the window at the gray sky like some invalid in an *Altenheim*. How could he not be weary? He had no idea what was next for him. Not even Captain Slaipe could know, it seemed.

"What's the matter?" Justine DeTrave rushed into the den and closed the door behind her. She stayed at the doorway, staring at him.

"Nothing's the matter. I'm just tired. Morning. I missed you, waking up."

"Never mind that," she whispered in French. "I know everything."

Max showed her a puzzled look. Lieutenant Julian Price didn't know French. "How are you? Come on over and sit by me. Come on."

A broad smile stretched across Justine's face, and her head cocked to one side. "*Ich weiss alles von Dir,*" she whispered in rough German—I know all about you, she'd said.

Max stared.

"Yes, I heard it last night." She pranced over to him. She sat on the settee and pushed hair off her ears. The strands shimmered gold in the white light. She grinned. She chirped in French: "And you know, I think I knew it all along, my dearest."

Max glared, out the window. He had to nip this bud. He said in rusty French, "All right then, but for God's sake use one language."

Her eyes bulged. "Yes, yes. Good," she said in English. "It's best they do not know what I know. Is that not the way?" She put a hand over her mouth, holding back another grin. "Oh, this is—how do they say?—Providence."

Max pushed off the linen and held her shoulders. "No, it's not that. It's simply what they call 'dumb luck.' It's unintended. Coincidence. An accident, you understand?"

Justine wagged her index finger. She placed the finger on his thigh, and then all her fingers. "*Mein Schatz*, you must not play the role with me. I know that you plan things. The American *capitaine*, he thinks you give up, yes? But we can fix this now. You see there are five of us, and only two of them."

The way she said *Schatz*, as if singing it, forced a twinge in Max's gut. Certainly she'd said it many times, to her German lovers—staff officers, most likely.

She scampered over to the doorway, peered down the hallway, and then hurried back. "And do you know? I know where their radio is."

Max moved closer to her and placed her hands in his. "Look, *ma chère*, you must listen to me. Forget the radio. Forget about the five versus two. It's over for you, and for me. Germany, as you know it, will soon cease to exist. As I know it. It's the Americans' show now. So let's be sensible." He repeated the last sentence in French.

Justine's smile faded. She shook her head. She yanked her hands away. "You're tired. It's food you need, that's all," she said and stood, brushing her hands on her spotless apron. "I'll find Annette, get you a pot of coffee. Where is she? Her man is here, that's the problem, and she's really lost all sense of the propriety . . ." Her words trailed off. She bent to kiss Max but stopped, inches from his lips. It was all he could do not to pull her down to him.

She pecked him on the forehead and rushed out.

Back down in the cellar Annette and her husband, Old Henry, treated Max as the same barely tolerated guest he had always been. They knew nothing. In front of Max they spoke between each other as they never would had they known Max understood their French and German. In this respect Captain Slaipe had kept his word—exposing him and locking him up would only create confusion and fear.

Sergeant Smitty was another matter. He came downstairs pulling a small Christmas tree that trickled with melting snow. Max was at the table playing solitaire. He moved to help but the sergeant waved him away and stood the tree in the same corner as Max's unloaded tommy.

The "cat had been let out of the bag," as the Americans said. Or was it "the chickens coming home to roost"? Max forced a chuckle. "So, I see it's no presents for the tree this year, eh Sergeant?"

Smitty said nothing. He passed the table and checked on Young Martin, who was still sleeping, and then he warmed his hands at the stove with his back to Max. His tommy was still on his shoulder.

Max slapped down a few more cards. "Good morning?" he said finally.

"Don't be so sure," Smitty spat in German.

Only openness would do now. Max played a few more cards and said in High German, using the formal address, "*Herr* Sergeant, please understand that you shouldn't have to worry about me. I intend to behave just as the captain wishes. Keep your weapon close if you like, but it's my hope you don't view me as a threat."

Smitty kept his German gruff. "Aren't you? Think that's pretty clear."

"I understand your meaning. You mean Malmedy, yes? And all the rest. All the horrible tales to be revealed after Germany is defeated. You are certainly correct. But I myself pose no threat. We're 'done for,' as you say. I've known it for years. Hopefully the captain told you my story—"

"You want to do penance, fine. But you didn't surrender right away, did you? To me, that's shifty."

What would a man like Smitty have done in his shoes? "In any case," Max said. "I had looked forward to helping you with the Christmas tree."

Smitty, staring, slid a Camel in his mouth. Max offered his lighter, but the sergeant only stared at that, too. "I'd like to think there's a few krauts with common sense," he said, now in English. "Maybe you're one of them. Maybe because you were in the states. Or, maybe you're just a chameleon, being an actor and all. Truth is, I don't know and I don't care. So just watch your step, every fucking step. *Alles klar?*" He mocked a stiff Prussian bow and stomped out, up the stairs.

Max stayed in the cellar until his turn at watch, playing more solitaire, watching over Martin, and helping Annette and Old Henry attend to the young soldier. Martin's face had grown sallow and sunken, and he broke out in sweats. In his sleep he mumbled, promising his mother he'd return from the war, unlike his father and his brother. It made Annette glower with bloodshot eyes and Old Henry swear and punch at his chest. And their distress made Max think of Felix Menning, caged in, facing a firing squad at a cold, stone wall. He had expected Felix to gulp down his poison lighter before any interrogation. What if the sly little juggler had confessed about killing the those MPs? In American eyes Max would be no less guilty than Felix, or Rattner. Yet Max could still make up for it. He only had to choose. Wasn't that what Captain Slaipe was really telling him?

Time for watch. Max climbed to the top of the tower—still without his tommy. Cold air bit at his eyes and cheeks. Some clouds had broken at the horizon and the sun was setting, twinkling behind the treetops. Captain Slaipe smiled at him, his cheeks red. "You made it. Still here. That's a good start, Kaspar. Sleep well? How's our young soldier doing down there?"

Seeing Slaipe filled Max with a rush of emotions he hadn't expected. This captain was the only thing that stood between him and a firing squad, and the man was smiling. Caring. Max stammered: "Young Martin? Not so well, but, Frau Annette and her *Alter Heini*, they do what they can for him. Captain, I, just want to thank you. If I may. You might have tied me to a tree and let me rot in the cold, and no one could have blamed you. I think you are a human man." He did a little bow at the waist.

"Aren't we all? I'd like to think so." Slaipe sighed. He took a long last look out and said, "I'm thinking we won't keep you up here too long. It is Christmas Eve after all."

The sun went down. More clouds broke now and then, revealing black gaps in which Max saw stars for the first time in what seemed like weeks. He heard no airplanes now. All battles seemed to have ceased for the holiday, and the quiet was a joy. He daydreamed of what might have been on a Christmas without war. *He and Liselotte up in the Alps, engrossed by winter scenes much like these, holed up in a warm cabin . . .*

A couple hours later Old Henry came clattering up the ladder waving his cap. His cheeks were red like Slaipe's and he chirped in broken English: "Now you go under, Joe, yes? With us in cellar. It's the festively time."

Captain Slaipe had called off watch for the rest of Christmas Eve. Max thought this foolish but the captain knew better than he did. Everyone was down in the cellar. Annette had decorated the Christmas tree with whatever she could find—strips of torn linen, a couple sticks of jerky, matchboxes, rotting turnip and carrot stubs, empty cigarette packs, a headless doll for the top, and, at Young Martin's urging, photos of the young soldier's family. She'd also baked what she called her "*Noël patisserie*" and Old Henry a "*Weihnachtsstollen*." It was a Christmas bread unlike any Max had ever seen, a dark brown oval blob instead of a loaf or log, and it lacked a proper dusting of powdered sugar. For spices she had only cinnamon, and she'd apparently used it in bulk, for when she cut a few thick slices Max caught an aroma that could only compare to burnt bacon fat. Lodged in the slices were a few small hard raisins and chunks of apple, some of which Annette had dyed red and green to resemble more varieties of fruit (where she got the dye, Max didn't want to know). Annette explained she was doing what she could with the few goods she had, and who was he to tell her how to bake?

They praised Annette's efforts, lit all the candles, and sat at the table except for Young Martin, who they propped against the wall in the corner. The Christmas bread and candles seemed to perk Martin up, which wasn't necessarily a good thing. Too much talking or laughing caused fits of coughs and blood to his handkerchief. Next to Max sat Justine, now as withdrawn as when they first met. Slaipe and Smitty faced them, Slaipe cheery but Smitty just as grumpy. Old Henry and Annette each took an end of the table as if they were the parents. They ate the bread, drank their ersatz coffee, and played cards, conversing politely in a mix of languages, each doing their best to stay clear of politics, history, war, and their sorry fates that weighed on this cellar like a thousand of these villas. Slaipe smoked his pipe. Smitty averted Max's gaze. Max felt silly acting like an American now. If he could only be himself—he'd certainly translate better than Smitty, who'd interpreted *Stollen* as "fruitcake," or Justine who, in her apathy, called the American Santa Claus "*Monseigneur Noël*."

Even Justine could see the party was stalling, so she called for Annette to break out the family stash of fruit beer. The fine beer helped the mood. For it Old Henry proclaimed Justine a "*heilige Jungfrau*"—a virgin saint, and Slaipe, amused, called the peach brew a splendid substitute for champagne. Justine then called for the Armagnac, and Old Henry proclaimed her an angel from heaven. Yet Justine hardly smiled. She refused to engage Slaipe in conversation, and Smitty glared as if this was Max's fault.

Max only smiled back. He was glad the talk had not turned to back home, where one was from, whom they loved. They were living in the moment, and he was through with the lies. Didn't the Armagnac follow the fruit beer quite nicely? And he was feeling lighthearted. He was still alive, despite it all. He toasted to this, under the bland ruse of "Here's to our continued good health—and to surviving this goddamned war." All hoisted their glasses, even Martin, whose glass was a metal canteen cap of the blood and spit he kept coughing up.

By now Annette and Old Henry had joined up at one end of the table, thick Annette perched on the little man's lap, and they smooched, laughing and flirting in their peculiar pidgin of French and German. Admiring them, Justine moved closer to Max. Soon she was practically nuzzling up to him, her skin hot. As Slaipe watched her, his smile faded. He and Smitty shared a sobering glance. Max spread out, arms on the table, to give himself some room. This only brought Justine closer. She caressed Max's leg under the table and began to whisper in his ear, in French.

"I want to sing," Max blurted to the group. "Wouldn't that be nice on Christmas?"

Justine pouted, folding her arms high on her chest, but Old Henry stomped his feet, saying, "Yes, yes, we sing. Who wants to sing?" and Martin banged his metal cup against the cellar stone.

Smitty barked: "Sure, Price, let's have a song." Was he challenging Max? Just then, Max realized he didn't know any Christmas songs in English. Luckily, Old Henry pushed Annette off him, stood on his chair, stretched out his arms and began a shaky rendition of *In dulci jubilo*—"Now Sing We, Now Rejoice." He halted, began in again, but had to stop. Drunk now, he'd forgotten lyrics he'd probably known since boyhood.

"Come now, come back down, *Heinchen*," Annette said, her eyes glazed with sadness, and Henry slumped back in his chair, muttering.

Silence. Max drank and stared into his glass. They all drank. Slaipe watched Max. Smitty watched Slaipe. Justine glared, at all of them.

"Now, I like that you sing," someone said. It was Young Martin.

"Sorry kid, I'm not such a good singer," Max said, eyeing Slaipe and Smitty. "Anyone else?"

Martin opened his mouth to protest, but a horrid screeching cough hit him. It echoed in the cellar and left him shaking, sweating.

Slaipe focused on the young soldier, his eyes glazed like Annette's. "Go on," he said to Max. "For the kid."

Singing could give Max away. Already Justine knew. Martin suspected him, and Annette and Old Henry had to have their suspicions. Yet if they all grasped, openly, that he was a German in disguise, then the balance was thrown completely. It would be just like Justine had wanted it— Slaipe and Smitty against the four of them (five, including Martin). Yet Slaipe was going to take his chances with Max? Max could not let him down.

Justine was caressing Max's knee again, keeping him still. He removed her hand, rose, and walked around the table. All watched. He stood near to Martin. He unbuttoned his tunic, took a deep breath, and began, in baritone:

Stille Nacht, heilige Nacht
Alles schläft, einsam wacht . . .

"Silent Night," in German. As Max sung, Annette and Old Henry's eyes opened wider, and their faces lost color. Without background music it was clear Max was a native German. Max sung on, the third verse now. Old Henry looked to Smitty and mouthed, "Is it true?" Smitty nodded, grimly. Meanwhile, Justine's eyes narrowed and her face went red— she had recognized Old Henry's loyalty to the Americans.

Down on the floor Young Martin was beaming, calm and unshakeable now, his shoulders squared high up against the brick wall. Max's chest filled with warmth as he returned to the first verse, his voice rising.

". . . Slee-eep in heavenly peace," Slaipe began, singing in English. Annette and Old Henry joined in, with French and German. Smitty was swaying to the melody; he took a big gulp of brandy and began in English. Then even Justine sang, in French. Young Martin grinned and mouthed along to the words. Smitty sang the German, and tears ran down his cheeks that he rubbed with his thick fingers.

Third verse again. Max ended, and the chorus died out. More silence. Eyes met around the room. "You'll want an explanation," Max said in German. "All of you. I've been found out, you see. Yes, I am a German. I was sent out undercover. But my mission is over. And make no mistake—I'm not sad. I think this might be the best thing that ever happened to me." As Smitty interpreted for Slaipe, Max lifted his glass from the table and held it high, as in toast.

Slaipe nodded a thank you and lifted his glass. Old Henry and Annette hoisted theirs and clapped and hooted and Young Martin banged his cup.

"Never mind all that—how about another song?" Old Henry roared, and Max could only oblige. He did some classics in German—"The Faithful Hussar," "Lili Marleen," of course, "Mack the Knife" even, and he busted out the American standards. Smitty of all people requested "Mairzy Dotes" and Max let him lead. Then, Max took a chance. He did his old Hitler impersonation just as he'd done on the Eastern Front. He pranced around and shook his fists and played up the Austrian dialect. He spat and stomped and sweated. Annette and Old Henry, Slaipe and Young Martin loved it. Smitty laughed out loud. "Not bad," he said, clapping. "Chaplin's is better, but I gotta say it's *nicht schlecht.*"

Justine DeTrave sat in shock, her face taut. She stood and marched up the stairs, mechanically, her arms stiff at her sides.

After Midnight. It was Christmas Day now. Annette and Old Henry had retired to their cellar room down the hall, and Young Martin slept. Smitty had taken the tower watch, where he'd sleep off the beer and Armagnac. Justine had not returned. Only Max and Slaipe sat at the cellar table. Slaipe, weary yet content, had been asking Max about the German lines to "Stille Nacht," comparing the English to the German, Latin and French versions, but now they sat in quiet, with a couple candles left flickering. Max said:

"I'm not fooling myself. I understand that your trust—however much I appreciate it—does not simply come from your heart. It comes from the mind, also."

"That's right, Kaspar. I'm making an investment."

"Certainly. And, you have something in mind for me."

Slaipe placed both elbows on the table. He reached for the empty Armagnac bottle, and set it among the empty bottles of beer and uneaten pieces of Annette's horrid Christmas cake. "You could go back," he said.

"Back. Back?"

"Across the Rhine. Back into Germany. Your homeland. Return. This time, it's for us. You'd be working for us. Contact underground resistance if there is any. Then, after, who knows? All the doors might reopen for you. Your crimes forgotten."

Max hadn't considered this. He forced out a chuckle.

"I can't promise it, of course," Slaipe added.

It was the last thing Max wanted. America was supposed to be all that was left to him. Slaipe knew it. "Captain, this is quite a surprise. I did have hopes for providing intelligence to you, but not in this manner . . ."

As Max spoke, Slaipe rearranged the bottles like pieces on a chessboard. He popped a chunk of the cake in his mouth, chewing slowly. He swallowed and said, "The main problem with that is, we already have scores of VIPs—Nazis far more important than you—who are ready to talk. And when Germany surrenders? Our lists are just too long for a small fry like you. No offense. You just don't have much to offer there. And you owe us a great deal."

"I see. No, no offense taken. Though I'm not a Nazi."

"Of course not. Just a figure of speech."

"Fine. So there's that. There's also the fact that I'm an actor."

"Exactly. You can pull it off. You've proved it to us here—passed your first audition, so to speak. Others would buckle. Or they sell us out."

"I wouldn't sell you out."

"Good. I thought so."

"Nowhere else to go," Max muttered. He stared into the table's knotty planks, stalling, the wood so worn it shined.

"It has to be done. It's your only hope. I'm not even sure I can pull it off, as I said. Have to clear it with higher brass. They might want you at that firing squad. I'll do what I can. In any case, you won't have much leeway. You're ours now. Though we always welcome suggestions." Slaipe added a tired smile. He reached for another piece of cake and offered it to Max.

Max shook his head.

"I don't blame you," Slaipe said. "Awful, isn't it? All her grand intentions aside."

Twenty-Four

The middle of the night. Slaipe had gone upstairs for a short few hours of sleep. Max waited up for Justine, but she never returned to the cellar. He lay awake, on his bedroll, agonizing over his dwindling prospects. He would have to concede yet again, it seemed. Slaipe had made that clear enough. And yet his whole point in getting west—to America—was to cut no more deals, make no more compromises. His worst sins began when he'd returned to Germany. He'd done deals with devils, and he'd paid by losing Liselotte. He was too genial and too obliging, that was his problem. Letting Justine DeTrave under his blanket was certainly proof of that. He rolled on his side, facing the wall, and pulled the blanket tight to his neck.

Hours later. He lay awake again. At the top of the stairs, white lines of light showed at the edges of the old iron door. The sun had come up on Christmas Day, 1944. He turned and faced Young Martin, a dark mass in the corner opposite. The kid had not wheezed or coughed for hours, and Max told himself it was a good sign.

"You awake, *Junge?*" Max said in German. "You had it right the whole time, didn't you? I'm a German, just like you. And now I can tell you, from my heart, Merry Christmas."

Martin had not moved. "Hey, Kid," Max said. He shouted it. He scrambled across the stone floor and pulled at Martin's shoulder, flopping the kid onto his back.

Martin's chest was still. A smile had set on his face, and his eyes remained half-open. Max touched a cheek. It was cold and hard.

"Of course you are," Max muttered, recalling the strange, rough gurgling noise he'd heard in the night. He thought Martin was clearing his throat. It was his death rattle.

Max drew Martin's blanket over Martin's head. He felt around in Martin's pockets, as cold as the stones beneath them. He found fine leather gloves, which he pocketed, and the kid's letters. All had the return address of a Frau Widmer in Freiburg. Taking only one—the rest could go with Martin, he went over to the Christmas tree in the corner and snatched the photos of Martin's family from the branches. He would write to Frau Widmer and send back these photos. Her boy lived his last days as a caring lad who'd rather hear more songs than sleep a wink. This was the truth and Frau Widmer was going to get it.

He turned to put on his overcoat—and stopped. Something wasn't right. He pushed the tree aside.

His tommy gun was gone. He searched the room, went down the hall, into Annette's room, and found nothing, no one.

He sat at the table and took a deep breath. Think, Max. Slaipe or Smitty must have taken the gun. That was all. Besides, the thing wasn't even loaded. He only had to check upstairs and everything would be okay.

What if it wasn't them? How could he tell them the silly gun was missing? Would they believe it? Would Slaipe believe him?

He stood, he sat back down. Wait. If it wasn't the Americans, it had to be Justine. She probably had no clue the thing wasn't loaded. The first thing to do, before anything, was get to Justine. He could set her straight before it was too late, put the gun right back where it was. If that didn't work, the best thing was to be honest, Max told himself as he pulled on his boots. And he trudged up the stairs.

Up in the kitchen, the clatter of footsteps and gear clanging. Max stopped to listen. They were coming his way. "Show yourself, Kaspar," Slaipe shouted as he and Smitty charged into the room wearing helmets and full battle gear. Smitty aimed his tommy gun, Slaipe his Colt pistol.

Max's hands went up. "What? What is it?"

"Keep 'em up," Smitty barked and kept coming. He kicked Max's legs out wide and frisked him, panting, the sweat steaming and rolling down his face, and Max smelled Armagnac and Christmas cake. Annette and Old Henry followed them in, waddling and hunched with humility, their faces ashen. They had coats and hats on. All four had snow on their heads, shoulders.

Smitty pulled out Martin's letter and tossed it. He pushed Max backward, into the counter. "Now where is it? Huh? Where?" He pushed at Max's chest.

"Where is what? Please." Max looked to Annette and Old Henry. They stood back, squeezed together in the doorway. He looked to Slaipe. "What?"

Slaipe stared, his jaw set hard. "The radio. Our field set."

"Your radio? It's missing?" Max had lapsed into German.

Smitty jabbed his tommy barrel into Max's gut. "Don't give me that. How'd you know it was missing?"

Max sputtered a laugh. "How? The captain, he just asked where it was—"

"Shut up." Smitty turned for the cellar. Slaipe cocked his Colt.

"No," Max shouted. "Young Martin, he couldn't have done it. Not . . . anymore."

"Why not?" Slaipe snapped and in the same moment must have read the answer on Max's face. He bowed his head, lowering his tommy gun. Annette buried her face in Henry's chest, and the old man squeezed his eyes shut. Smitty leaned against the counter. "Aw, hell," he said.

"In his sleep," Max muttered. He couldn't give up Justine just yet. Even if she had both the radio and his machine gun, she was still only a naive, spoiled aristocrat. She probably had no clue she could be shot for this. He glanced at Slaipe.

The captain holstered his Colt and lapsed into thought, staring at the linoleum floor. "Well, that leaves only our host," he said, in a monotone. "This could be a misunderstanding. God knows there's enough of those going around."

"One too many, I say." Smitty gnashed his teeth, clenching his gun.

"If I may," Max said, lowering his hands. "Perhaps something spooked her. You mentioned a brother, Captain. She may even be helping us. Has anyone even seen her?" He repeated this in French.

"She has not been in her room all morning," Annette said from the doorway.

Smitty was scowling at Max. "And what about last night? Eh, Kaspar? Or the night before?"

Max said nothing. What could he say? She was only keeping warm?

Slaipe glared at Max, his eyes pinched. "Sergeant," he said to Smitty, "seems we should've been playing by the book all along." He heaved the tommy gun off his shoulder. "You, and you," he said to Annette and Old Henry, "get over with the prisoner," meaning Max, and the couple huddled around Max with their arms up. "Now get going. Move."

Slaipe and Smitty marched Max, Annette and Old Henry through the villa at gunpoint. "Gentlemen, look," Max said, "if we only locate Ms. DeTrave, I'm sure there's an explanation—"

"Shut it," Smitty said.

They reached the foyer. Slaipe cocked his tommy and said to Old Henry, "Only one option left, *Mein Herr*. We're pulling out. *Wir gehen. Verstehen?* Break out if we have to, and we'll release you two just as soon as we're in the clear." Smitty translated, careful to emphasize the "you two," and Old Henry nodded along.

"Merry Goddamn Christmas," Smitty added for Max.

As Smitty opened the front doors the wind yanked them free and they banged against the walls. Wind and snow whirled in and struck their faces like sawdust. A blizzard had found their valley. Yet the light was golden, as if the sunshine could break through.

"Captain, perhaps you'll allow me to fetch my greatcoat," Max said, but Slaipe nudged him on with his gun barrel.

The front steps were recessed in an alcove. The five squinted and shuffled down the slippery steps, stooping as if navigating an Alpine precipice. Smitty shut the doors behind them.

Max's missing tommy gun lay about fifty feet out. Footsteps spread out from the gun, so new the snow hadn't covered them. Max tugged at Slaipe's sleeve. "Captain, look there—"

Smitty saw it. "Get down," he shouted and he and Slaipe crouched about five feet apart, using the alcove's corners as cover. Max dropped to the steps between them and Annette and Old Henry ducked back, cowering near the shut front doors.

The wind shrieked. The snow swirled, dusting Max's tommy.

"What d'you got?" Slaipe shouted at Smitty. "Anything?"

"Nothing here. Nothing but white."

"Back inside," Slaipe shouted.

The wind shifted, sucking snow into the alcove.

The front doors swung open. Justine knelt in the open doorway aiming a machine gun. Annette and Old Henry lay prostrate before her.

Smitty and Slaipe had their backs to her, their guns aimed in the opposite direction.

"Free him! Let him go," Justine shouted.

"Me? Free me? No," Max shouted, and to Slaipe: "Captain, I'm no part of this. She's acting on her own."

Slaipe nodded, slowly. Smitty was still, his eyes locked on Justine.

Her gun was the deadly accurate new StG 44—the "thousand-hole punch," they'd called it in the East. Justine shouted in French: "Now! Give him your guns."

Smitty turned to fire. He got off one burst. Justine shot and sprayed the alcove. Smitty tumbled back, down the steps. Slaipe slumped.

Max jumped up. "Idiot, stop, what are you doing?"

The recoil had knocked Justine back and she sat with her legs spread out, squinting through the driving flakes. Holes riddled the alcove, plaster everywhere. Smitty lay out in the snow, on his back. Slaipe, heaving breaths, raised his arms.

"No, no," Max muttered.

Justine stood. "Back inside, all of you! Grab the guns," she shouted to Max.

Smitty's tommy lay on the bottom stair and Slaipe's loose at his feet. Blood ran from Slaipe's upper arm. He stared up at Max. He kicked his tommy over to Max's feet.

"Hurry," Justine shouted.

"Captain, it's probably best I take your pistol, but slowly," Max said. Had he said this? Was this happening? It sounded like a line from a script.

With his good arm Slaipe opened his holster, and Max pulled out the Colt.

Out in the snow, Smitty's chest had stopped moving. Steam rose from rips in his tunic but none from his mouth. Red surged out from his back, seeping into the snow.

"By the book," Slaipe groaned, and turned to head back up the steps.

Annette and Old Henry helped each other up. They screamed at Justine in rapid French and German. Annette spat.

"Go then! On your own. To hell with you! I don't care," Justine screamed back, her voice breaking now, and Annette and Old Henry ran out into the blizzard holding hands.

Back down in the cellar. Justine kept the StG 44 on Slaipe, who sat at the table, patiently, his hands in his lap. His wound was a graze, from a ricochet, and he'd torn off strips of blanket and wrapped his arm. Max pulled on his warmest gear—overcoat, scarf, wool beanie, helmet, and Martin's leather gloves on his trembling hands. He kept Slaipe's tommy aimed at the floor.

Justine's eyes filled with tears. Rather than lower her gun to wipe her eyes, she let the tears roll down her face. They twinkled in the candlelight.

"Where did you get that weapon?" Slaipe said to her, in French.

Justine looked to Max. Max nodded. "Jean-Marie," she said. "He left it for me. He said he would be back. He hasn't come back."

"And that's your brother?" Max said. Justine nodded. "Where is he?"

"*Légion Wallonie*—the Walloon SS." Justine sniffled.

It was like talking to a child. Max had made love to this child. She was ridiculous. He was pathetic. "Go on," he said, his voice rising.

"Eastern Front. 'Somewhere in the north'—that's all Jean-Marie said."

A bitter taste rose in Max's throat, like hot mustard. "Then he won't be coming back, will he?" he blurted, grimacing. He knew it was cruel. He meant it to be. For the first time in his life, he'd wanted to be. "He's dead already," he added.

Justine gaped. Her chin quivered.

"And the radio?" Slaipe said. "Where is that now?"

Justine scowled at Slaipe. Her tears had stopped, and she grinned. "What do you think, you fool *capitaine*? I shot it full of holes, didn't I? That damned thing."

"That's unfortunate," Slaipe said.

Only a ridiculous child would do such a thing. Max closed his eyes to it, and felt his fingers, chest, and whole body hardening up, like the metal of Slaipe's tommy gun tight in his hands. "Are you that stupid?" he shouted at her.

Justine gasped, a shocked laugh. "Stop that nonsense, lover, *mon dieu*, screw your head back on why don't you?"

Max moved closer, a crazy grin spreading on his face. He couldn't stop it. It was like water, or an oily ooze. Oil in a machine. It went where it wanted.

Justine stepped back, raising her gun. "Lover? Dearest, what are you doing—"

Max's right arm thrust up. The butt of the tommy struck her jaw. She let out a squeak as she dropped, and the StG 44 clattered away and clanged against the wall. She lay flat on her back, her lips bulging with blood. She was out. Maybe she was dead. He did not care. He turned to Slaipe:

"Captain. I have one request—give me a few minutes head start, will you?"

Slaipe stared, thinking. Slowly, he reached in a pocket and pulled out his pipe, which he placed on the table. "All right. That's all you'll have now, I'm afraid."

"It's all I've ever had, it seems." Max was backing away. He set Slaipe's Colt out on the floor. "Thank you, Mister Slaipe," he stuttered, "I, you know, I was hoping we could have met in Manhattan one day, say, a drink at the Plaza, perhaps, or the 21 Club would have been swell . . ."

Slaipe was nodding now, but not smiling. Max was backing up the steps. He set down the tommy, carefully, as if the thing was blown of glass, and he sprinted up and out.

Twenty-Five

Max ran out the front doors and down the steps. The snow had stopped. The last of the flurries shrouded Sergeant Smitty's corpse. Only his clenched hand and the toes of his boots poked out of the freezing white. Max trudged across the villa grounds through waist-high drifts of powder, focusing on his escape and trying not to think at all. One thought plagued him—he'd forgotten Young Martin Widmer's letter. Smitty had tossed it on the floor of the kitchen. How could he write to the kid's mother now?

He entered the woods, kept going. His boots crunched at icy snow and underbrush and he hopped over fallen trees and trickling streams. What a fool I am, he thought. How could someone who can memorize lines and sing songs and sway audiences, someone with an uncanny gift for American accent, prove so stupid? He shouldn't have entered the villa. He never should have auditioned for Special Unit Pielau, but then again it was never his choice. He was better off on the Russian Front. The forest grew thicker, darker. He headed downhill, ducking for the low hanging branches, and a jagged trail sent him into a tight rocky ravine, the stones slathered with wet moss. He only hoped Annette and Old Henry made it. The last thing he wanted was to find them frozen, hugging each other. That he could not take. And what was Slaipe doing? Still sitting there, smoking his pipe? Making his way back? Burying Smitty? Or Justine? Max had saved the captain's life, possibly. Yet how much did it count? It was only one life saved, from so many lost.

Level land again. Melting snow fell from branches in wet slaps. Sunlight shot through the trees, white like stage light.

Max tilted his head back and saw, up through the intertwined limbs, a crisp and wide blue sky. The weather really was clearing, just as Slaipe had promised. He heard the drone of Allied bombers up high, their white exhaust trails streaking across the blue sky.

He pressed on, his hunger gnawing, an aching hole. He checked his watch. Two o'clock in the afternoon. In two or three hours it would be dark. He needed more light. The forest edged a road. He headed out into the open lane, squinting and blinking at the sun. A grinding roar rattled his bones—a plane was passing above. He dropped to the road and peered up. The plane was an American spotter, a recon plane, flying so low its shadow blocked the sun. On the horizon it pulled up to come back around. Stumbling to his feet, Max sprinted back into the trees and dropped behind a wet trunk, straining to catch his breath.

With the weather clearing, who knew who was watching him? He sat still and could hear the battles raging again, far away. The Americans would be counterattacking in all sectors, Slaipe had said. This very sector might have been retaken. He could be spotted, stopped by anyone. He stood and his knees shook, weakening from hunger.

Keeping to the edge of the forest, Max followed the road. He reached a junction. He sat within the trees, waiting and watching. American jeeps and trucks passed through heading one way, then the other. Then it was the Germans' turn—a few ragtag units on the run. Sometimes a vehicle would stop and soldiers got out, shared a cigarette, threw up their hands and slogged onward. Max could have—should have?—gone out to any of them. He would rather wait for darkness. For anonymity.

Across the junction stood an inn. Bullet holes riddled a wall, and fire had scorched a window. Beyond the inn stood a couple houses and barns. As dusk fell, the traffic stopped.

The inn's lights never came on, nor did those of the houses and barns. Darkness came. The air carried a hard chill, from the clear sky and the stars out shining. Crouching low, Max made his way across the junction, went into the inn and found the place deserted. All was in German here though he was still on the Belgian side of the border. A sign read: *"Zimmer Frei"*—Vacancy. An ad for a local ale promised *"Die Erfrischung!"*—Refreshment! He passed into the kitchen and used his field flashlight sparingly, clicking it on and off to take stock. On the floor, in a bucket, he found chunks of bread. In a cupboard, a sack with two sausages, and two tall bottles of homemade cider. Was he lucky? There was a day when he would have thought so.

He carried his meager plunder on to the barn at the farthest edge of this dead village. Inside he found a patch of dry ground, where he sat. The bread had mold, he could smell it in the dark, but he easily picked it off. The sausages were cooked but slimy so he wiped them good with his sleeve. He kept the cider bottles between his legs—to take the chill off them. He popped the porcelain cap off a bottle, drank. The cider had chunks of apple and a thick sweetness that coated his throat.

Moonlight shined through the windows, through the breaks in the old roof, and his eyes adjusted to the darkness. Hanging on one wall, he saw, were a farmer's clothes— floppy brimmed hat, peasant shirt, overalls, long denim jacket. A thick pullover. He crawled over to gather this up. A large carpetbag lay there too, so he stuffed the clothes in it and dragged the bag back to his spot. He sat there like a caveman in his cave, his legs crossed, hugging his carpetbag.

He drank more of the cider. It warmed him and numbed him and, to his amazement, like a man who suffered a terrible accident and lived to tell about it, he began to see how fortunate he still was. He was still in one piece. He could still sing. He could still act. Love a woman. Couldn't he? Speak in three languages. Walk and run and dance. What was so horrible about a genial man? He wasn't a caveman here. He was a monk and a pilgrim, who'd wandered far and wide and was finally seeing the light. A holy man. It wasn't that he'd taken things too far. He'd not taken them far enough.

He drank, lay back, and closed his eyes, and he dreamed of singing for a dance hall full of beautiful young women. The most remarkable part was that he dreamed it was after the war.

Footsteps. Voices? Hushed American voices. Max sat up, silently, and watched two men enter the dark barn. The moonlight glistened blue on their skin—they were black American soldiers. One was large and thick—big-boned, the Americans called it, the kind who could serve in the infantry for three years and never lose the heft while the other was small and wiry, like the horse jockey who could eat pie all day and gain no pounds. Like Max they had bags and satchels strung over their shoulders. Their rifles hung upside down on their backs, worn and ignored, as if they were field shovels the two hoped they'd never have to use.

Max cleared his throat. "Evening," he said in English. "Or is it morning?"

The two started, but they didn't run. They faced the darkness, from where Max's voice had come, and let their eyes adjust. Like Max, these two had learned somewhere that patience was an old friend.

"Mind we shine a light?" the small one said, in a tinny voice.

"I don't mind."

The light flashed on, off, maybe two seconds. The small one sighed, and they trudged over and sat facing Max—not close to him, but near enough to speak softly. They pulled off their bags and satchels. Max could smell the road on them. This was what he must smell like—all sweat and grease, dirt and smoke.

He held out his bottle. "Care for some apple juice? It's the hard variety."

The small one grinned shiny white teeth. He took the bottle and handed it to the big one, who drank from it with both massive hands. They studied Max as best as they could, the moonlight glinting in their eyes.

"You lost?" the small one said.

Max shook his head.

"You quit this scene?" the small one said.

"He done gone over the hill," added the big one, his voice all slops and clicks, as if he were chewing. "That right, mister?"

"Do you mean, have I gone AWOL? Yes, I have. After a fashion."

The two shared a glance. "Us too," said the small one. "It can't hurt to tell."

"Never going back neither," added the big one. "Copacetic? What's there for us? So we hang our hats in Paris. We can play and they like us playing."

Smiling, the small one shoved at the big one.

"You play music. That's swell. Horns, is it?"

The big one nodded. "Skins, that's me," added the small one.

"Skins—that's drums, I take it." Max could have gone on like this for hours. They had no idea. His English was that perfect now. He might have fooled them all the way to Paris. The sad irony of this made him chuckle. "Funny thing, fellas —I'm a singer. Mostly done acting though. Gave it a shot in New York. Tough there, a rat race. Still, I got some gigs."

"Don't say? We could use a singer. Couldn't we?" The small one chuckled and the big one joined in. "Small problem though—you aren't no brother." They laughed together, snorting and shaking their heads.

"No, I'm not. I'm a kraut."

The small one scrambled to his feet. The big one fumbled for his rifle.

Max waved a hand. "Please, please. I'm not that kind of kraut. Look at me."

Their field light flashed on, off. "You're not an American?"

"Nope."

"Not in the army?"

"Not in your army, I'm afraid."

"But, that uniform?"

"It's all I have to wear." Max shrugged. "Listen. Please. You, sit, and you—why don't you let that carbine down? OK? Have some cider, and I'll tell you about it."

The big one held up a hand. "How come you speak so good English? American-style, too. You're one of them krauts was raised in America, goes back to fight for Hitler? Man, that's a jiveass move."

Max laughed. "Something like that." The two nodded, and crossed their legs, and Max passed around the bottle. He pulled out his pack of Chesterfields and passed those around. He kept his story simple. Once the Ardennes offensive started, he'd gone AWOL. Soon he scored some GI fatigues. He'd only wanted to get back to America, to make a new way for himself. No matter what he tried, he told them, a black cloud had followed him. The DeTrave Villa was supposed to be the start of his big break, but it proved to be just another knockdown. This would not stop him. He knew there was something—someone—out there for him. He had a hand on his heart, and the bottle in his other hand. As they listened the two black soldiers nodded, slowly. He told them about Liselotte, and the big one squeezed his eyes shut, in pain. Still, Max didn't tell them about the mission. I helped kill one of your brothers, he might have confessed. Lynched him. He had already realized something: Somewhere, right now, wasn't someone doing the very same to one of his innocent kin? On the Eastern Front, surely. No, that part of his life would vanish, he had decided, and the only one who could bring it back was Captain Aubrey Slaipe. He'd been thinking this for hours. He had realized he would be singing the same old sorry tune if he made it back to America, or even to Paris. There would only be more sellouts, more compromises. It wasn't the direction he had been running— it was the running itself.

The small one scooted closer. The big one followed. "Here's the thing, Jack. We're going to start over, you know? Just like you probably want to. Remake ourselves. And in a whole new place. Won't matter if we're Negro, not as much anyways."

"Paris is worth it," Max said. "For the right guy, it is."

"Bet you know Paris, by the looks of you. You got that chauncey look. Chasing the ladies."

"Well, yes, I have chased a skirt or two. I had."

He kicked off his GI boots and his GI trousers, and separated out the farmer's clothes from his carpetbag.

"What, it's not for you?" said the big one.

"I'm afraid not," Max said.

The two stared. "You're not going where I think you're going?" said the small one.

Max nodded. "I am."

"You one brave mother," blurted the big one.

"Oh, I'm hardly that." Max tossed off his tunic and pulled on the peasant shirt.

"Crazy, more like." The small one's forehead wrinkled up. He lifted the bottle to drink. He put it back down. "We were in Aachen. We know. Where you're heading? It's crazy. Hopeless. Won't be nothing left. Cities are piles, just smoking. Folks starving. All those poor children. You all going to get the whip. Sure won't be much singing to be had."

The big one slapped at his knee. "Don't agree." He leaned toward Max. "Sure it's no good, at first. But then? All told? Just the thing for a kraut knows American. Long as you didn't run with Hitler, you'll be okay. You just have to have the hope."

"I'm afraid you both may be right," Max muttered. He pulled out his cigarettes. He only had a couple left. They shared one. The big one hummed as he smoked. Max didn't know the tune. He choked back some more cider. It had been so easy to talk in the dark. Now the sun was coming up, painting the horizon pink and filling the barn with a strange, gray-orange light. Max saw their faces much better. The big one had drooping, sleepy eyes and a silver tooth. The small one, a pointy chin and hooked nose. Both had beard growth. Any alert MP would spot them for what they were, and it would only get tougher the farther west they ventured.

"Listen, I know of a hideout," Max said. "It's on your way west. In a remote valley, not far from here. The very villa I told you of. I'm sure the American intelligence men are long gone. I can mark it on my map."

"You need your map."

"Not anymore. Not where I'm going. Just be careful, all right? Make sure everyone's gone. Take the cellar. There's a working oven down there. A friend of mine died there. You might have to bury him." Max folded his GI gear in a pile and placed it before the two. "Now. Here. Take what you like. There's a compass in there. The map."

"Much obliged," the small one said, "much obliged."

The big one nodded along, with difficulty, as if trying to swallow.

Max pulled on the denim jacket. It smelled like grimy chicken feathers, and chicken shit.

Max swore that if he survived this, he'd never take a nature hike as long as he lived. He trudged along another forest road lined with snow banks and stayed in the open, always out on the roads, alone. Let everyone see him. No soldier on the run or undercover would try such a stunt, only a sad and confused farmer. Soldiers hidden in foxholes and machine gun nests were probably watching him the whole way.

An American armored car sat to one side of the road, firing into the woods at random. GIs stood around the armored car, laughing and passing a canteen. Max kept to the middle of the road, in full view, slogging through the mud that disguised his GI-issue boots, the only American item left on him. A couple GIs glanced his way. He kept his head down.

"Hey straggler," one of them said.

Max cracked a submissive smile, threw up his hands. "I no Engleesch, Joe," he babbled in his thickest Hollywood-German accent. He shuffled past and they let him.

The distant thunder of battle—of the fierce American counterattacks—roared on as it had for hours. The trees were behind Max and he hit open plain, snowy white with bulges that were wrecked tanks, jeeps, bodies. He passed through one last small Belgian town and reached an American checkpoint, at a river. Young GIs in new gear were manning a temporary pontoon bridge. Beyond loomed the open frontier, still void of trees. Rising billows of black smoke lined the farthest horizon, rising up like so many clawed fingers and intertwining high in the sky to create one dense, heavy cloud of blackness. A city. It might be Cologne, Max thought.

He approached with his shoulders sagging, a sick frown on his face. A man in a black overcoat stood with the GIs—a town official, Max guessed. "Kind sir, might you please let me pass?" he said, imitating Old Henry's Belgian German. "Look at me. All I have is gone. Destroyed. I hope to find my kin. They're that way, across that very river, far to the east."

The town official matched Max's frown. The man smelled sweet, like a cheap hair tonic. He translated in Queen's English for the lead GI, a pale corporal chewing gum. The official added:

"He wants to go into Germany. He's mad, I say."

"Poor SOB wants to head straight into hell, fine with me," the GI said. He patted Max down, showed him a smile, and pushed him out onto the wobbly floating bridge.

Author's Note

The false flag special mission depicted in *The Losing Role* is based on an actual operation Hitler devised for his surprise Ardennes Offensive of late 1944 that launched the Battle of the Bulge. Under the code name *Greif*, German soldiers who could speak English were trained and equipped to impersonate American units behind the enemy lines, where they would wreak havoc and secure depots and bridges in support of the main offensive. The German offensive caught American troops resting in Belgium's forested Ardennes region completely off guard, and in the bloody chaos the rumor spread that the American impersonators were crack enemy terrorists out to kidnap or kill US General Eisenhower, commander of the Allied Forces. The lore of German agents impersonating American soldiers reemerged in films, fiction, and even history books as a frightening and deadly ploy carried out with skill and cunning. The commander, SS Lieutenant Colonel Otto Skorzeny (who has a brief cameo in *The Losing Role*), already had a daredevil's reputation that didn't temper the legend.

The reality was altogether different. The Germans hastily put together units of English-speaking soldiers using whatever troops and materiel they could gather. The men came from all branches of the German military and possibly included civilians. The ones who spoke English best had lived in America or Britain, but these numbered very few. Many of the English speakers had been sailors and naive students before conscription and were far from ideal soldiers let alone crack terrorists. One, Otto Struller, had been a professional ballet dancer, and it can be supposed

that some had occupations such as waiter or writer. Some
appear to have been misled about the mission and couldn't
back out. At least one was shot for a breach of secrecy. The
planning and training were slapdash, the mission desperate,
its chances slim.

As part of Operation *Greif,* Skorzeny and his officers
placed the better English speakers into a special commando
unit, *Einheit Stielau.* They were sent out in captured
American jeeps to infiltrate the American lines, and
managed to confuse (already bewildered) American troops
by switching signs, passing along bogus information and
committing sabotage. The Americans captured some of the
Stielau men and promptly shot them by firing squad,
including Struller. As the main German offensive sputtered,
Skorzeny called off Operation *Greif* and the false flag
infiltrators fell back to join regular units. If anything, the
commando mission helped the Americans, since the wild
rumors about cutthroat Germans in GI uniform gunning for
Eisenhower only served to keep American counterintelligence
alert and strengthen the troops' rattled resolve.

In 1947, the Allies' Dachau Trials were to make an
example of the infamous Skorzeny and his officers for
running a villainous ruse that ran counter to the so-called
rules of war, but the defense brought in Allied officers who
had to admit they'd been running similar special missions all
along. Skorzeny and all defendants were acquitted.

My research included solid sources in English and
German, but I left details about military strategy, top leaders'
decisions and so forth to historians. My version of this story
remains true to overall events, though I changed or invented
some aspects for fiction's sake. Max Kaspar is a fictitious
character, after all, part of a fictional commando team that
infiltrated American lines in a US jeep disguised as American
soldiers. Whether in fiction or reality, surely not all the false
flag infiltrators like Max were accounted for. One imagines a

good smart one or two disappeared into the night and got as far away from war and tyranny as they dared. I attempted, with respect for the history and with some dark humor, to tell the story of one of these inspired and probably doomed dreamers.

—Steve Anderson, September 2011 (revised)

Suggested Reading

Those looking to find out more about the actual events fictionalized in *The Losing Role* will find a scarce but insightful mix of personal and historical accounts.

Heinz Rohde, a young Luftwaffe sergeant in 1944, was given the identity of US Army Sergeant Morris Woodahl and sent over the front lines as an Operation *Greif* commando. Soon after the war he dared speak about his experiences in the German news magazine *Der Spiegel* ("Mit Shakespeare-Englisch," January 10, 1951). The article is in German but parts of it later appear translated in English-language histories, including those of Schadewitz and Pallud below.

In 1950, Otto Skorzeny wrote about leading Operation *Greif* in *Skorzeny's Secret Missions*. Other memoirs followed. Writers of history have found Skorzeny's accounts useful for their first-hand view, while recognizing cases where he attempts to aggrandize or displace blame.

Greif commando Fritz Christ infiltrated the American lines as US First Lieutenant Charlie Smith, but a German fighter plane soon strafed his commando team's American vehicle and he barely escaped. He finally spoke about it sixty years later in *Stern* magazine ("Operation Eisenhower," April 20, 2004). The *Stern* article is also in German, but a condensed English version in *The Daily Telegraph* ("Revealed: Farce of Plot to Kidnap Eisenhower," May 2, 2004) captures the absurdity.

Among the history books, the most in-depth account remains Michael Schadewitz's *The Meuse First and Then Antwerp: Some Aspects of Hitler's Offensive in the Ardennes* (1999). Originally published in German and expanded for the English version, it includes interviews from intelligence reports and other sources, including Heinz Rohde. Schadewitz's effort easily eclipses others in its thoroughness.

Jean-Paul Pallud's *Battle of the Bulge: Then and Now* (1999) includes substantial description of Operation *Greif* and *Einheit Stielau* and has photographs comparing wartime photos with those of their current-day locations. Heinz Rohde also appears here.

Many overall histories of the Battle of the Bulge include brief mention of Operation *Greif*. Two that explore the details are Charles Whiting's *The Ghost Front* (2002), and Gerald Astor's *A Blood-Dimmed Tide* (1993).

I also tell this fragmented true story in the brief Kindle Single e-book, *Sitting Ducks* (2011).